FORGOTTEN
NO MORE

USA TODAY Bestselling Author

Christina McKnight

BOOKS BY CHRISTINA MCKNIGHT

A Lady Forsaken Series
Shunned No More
Forgotten No More
Scorned Ever More
Christmas Ever More
Hidden No More

The Undaunted Debutantes Series
The Disappearance of Lady Edith
The Misfortune of Lady Lucianna
The Misadventures of Lady Ophelia
The Season of Lady Chastity
The Desires of Lady Prudence

Lady Archer's Creed Series
Written with Amanda Mariel
Theodora
Georgina
Adeline
Josephine

Craven House Series
The Thief Steals Her Earl
The Mistress Enchants Her Marquis
The Madame Catches Her Duke
The Gambler Wagers Her Baron

Standalone Titles
A Kiss at Christmastide
For the Love of a Widow
The Earl of St. Seville
The Lady Loves a Scandal
Bedded Under the Christmastide Moon
Bound by the Christmastide Moon
Fated for the Duke

DEDICATION

To Marc

*My very own Harold. You are always there to rescue
me...even if it's only from myself!*

ACKNOWLEDGMENTS

I'd like to thank all the people who believed in me and my writing journey. You never gave up on me, even when I lost sight of my own dreams! Especially Marc McGuire, Lauren Stewart, Jennifer Vella, Brandi Johnson, and Latisha Kahn. You have all been very patient and wonderfully supportive of my eccentric ways.

A very special thank you to my editor, Jen Blood. I look forward to many future endeavors with you. Jen Blood can be contacted by email at jen@jenblood.com.

Proofreading done by Anja at Hour Glass Editing.

Cover art and wraparound cover design credit to Teresa Spreckelmeyer at the Midnight Muse Designs.

Finally, thank you for supporting indie authors.

PROLOGUE

Hyde Park
7 April 1783

NOT A FIBER of my being knows why I seek to put this terrible moment to paper, to commit the wrongs against me to a tangible surface. Part of me believes— no, hopes—if I do not acknowledge these foul sins I have made against my family, then all can be forgotten. Alas, I can no more hide from my misdeeds than one can hide from the plague. It consumes me, inhabits my every waking thought, devours me in my dreams...

Verily, I did not wish to bring this dishonor down upon my husband. I did not go in pursuit of falling— falling so surely I can no longer be whom I have always been. So drastically I have changed...or perhaps not I, but my perception of my world and my place in it.

I was the Honorable Miss Pearl, daughter of an English Baron.

I was, and have been, Mrs. Pearl St. Augustin for

over ten years.

But what I have always sought to be is a mother.

Mayhaps I set my sights too high for what the good Lord planned for my husband and me.

Or possibly He has forgotten me altogether.

I know naught. I ceased caring what the Lord had planned for me the night I met the man who ripped my heart in two, tore my very soul from within, and dashed every dream, every desire for life I had within me. He did this all whilst placing the beating heart of a precious child in its place.

He was to be my salvation and instead he has damned me to an eternity of hiding. Hiding my sins, my love, and his child.

Possibly I write this to remind myself of the evils of seeking what is not meant to be yours—to warn others, including my unborn child, of the malevolence of mankind.

CHAPTER 1

London, England
January 1816

MISS RUBY ST. AUGUSTIN glanced over her shoulder as she ran down the endless dark hall toward the safety of an empty room. Skidding to a halt, she eased the door open and slipped soundlessly inside. She leaned back against the solid door, breathing heavily as the latch clicked into place. She hoped she hadn't been followed, though she couldn't be certain.

She'd only been in town a few days, but was finding it harder and harder to escape the notice of her mother. The woman attended every social engagement from afternoon teas to grand balls.

It quickly grated on Ruby's nerves. She wasn't ready to face the woman. There was still information to gather, emotions to sort out, and a certain man to locate—even though by doing so, she was working in direct opposition to her mother's wishes.

Ruby looked around as her eyes adjusted to the dim glow of the room. The smell of after-dinner cigars engulfed her. It was standard London style: massive desk no gentleman of the *ton* actually used, two straight-back chairs facing said monstrosity of a work area, and an enormous hearth large enough to burn the abundant misuse of wood in the room. Two chairs were cozied up nicely for maximum heat, an assortment of collectables and books scattered about. The only thing that changed from house to house was the color scheme. Lord Trenton, or possibly his esteemed wife, had selected a mix of blood red and gold. Gaudy, yet the height of fashion this season.

Ruby had quickly learned that stealth and efficiency would benefit her greatly if she hoped to find the object she sought without being caught by another guest or—heaven forbid—the lord of the house. A servant she could handle, blaming her presence on being lost looking for the ladies' retiring room, but anyone else's suspicions would be difficult to allay. Moving into action, she went straight for the desk and opened one drawer after another, pushing papers to the side or gently lifting objects, careful to put everything back in its place. Her mother had detailed the thing so specifically, Ruby felt she could sketch it in her sleep.

A handcrafted letter opener, polished metal with inlaid rubies, and the inscription, *The course of true love never did run smooth*. She knew the quote well, even without her mother's reasoning for selecting the line. Penned by William Shakespeare, and performed at the local playhouse the night her real father had laid eyes upon her mother. As her mother had written it, it was true love at first sight, the line coinciding with the moment their eyes had met across the crowd—Pearl ensconced in her dear friend, Lady Darlingivers', box, her father meanwhile consorting with the commoners in the general seating area.

Her mother wrote countless pages of how she'd sold her most prized possessions to have the opener crafted for 'her love,' as she'd called him early on in her journal. Her mother had gushed with pride when she wrote of presenting the gift to her lover: How he'd accepted it with reverence and declared his own love. The words and feelings within the journal were as foreign to Ruby as the people it described. She did not know her mother as a woman who could care about another so much that she'd give up her own funds to make him happy.

Only a few pages later, her mother wrote of her desire to stab her lover with said letter opener when their affair went awry. The words, so wisely inscribed, had proven prophetic for the pair—assuming the man had ever loved her mother at all. She lamented on and on about the injustices of the world, the fickle hearts of men, and the burden of living with one's decisions.

Despite the inadequacy of her methods thus far, Ruby saw no other way to gain what she sought without approaching the only woman with the knowledge to set her mind at ease. Still, a part of her hoped that someone would tell her what she'd found in the attic of their country estate was a ruse, the writings of an imaginative mind, the journaling of a lonely and bored woman of the *ton*.

Unfortunately, Ruby would not—could

not—trust the mother who had ignored her existence for all her adult life, treated her like an inconvenience, and then as soon as she was able, shipped her to the country estate of a friend to become a young lady's paid companion. The irony of the situation was not lost on her: For years her mother sought to avoid her, and now Ruby did everything in *her* power to evade the woman.

Ruby slammed another drawer closed after finding nothing of use. "Where are you?" she muttered. Pulling another open, she moved papers, extra ink, and a sealing kit aside in her search.

She did not, for one, minute regret her years in the country, spent with her nearest and dearest friend, Lady Viola. But Vi was now married and starting a life of her own with Lord Haversham, so she had no need for a paid companion.

How Ruby wished she could go back to that time when she'd been unaware of her mother's deceit. A time when she'd thought her mother, Mrs. Pearl St. Augustin, only a detached woman with limited motherly instincts unhampered by attachments. Was it truly only six months ago? And only a few short weeks since she'd found her mother's journal, detailing her extramarital exploits?

Closing yet another drawer, she turned her attention to the last and the largest of them all. She eyed the keyhole suspiciously, as if it would click locked if she grasped the handle too quickly.

Ruby took a deep breath before trying the final drawer that could hold all the answers to her past, her true heritage. Her lungs expanded;

she held the air inside. She didn't exhale until it burned. With trembling fingers, she reached for the last drawer and pulled.

Her nicely trimmed nails nearly snapped when her grasp on the handle slipped from the force of her tug. The drawer hadn't budged.

Locked!

"Oh, poppy cocks!" she hissed. Moving her hands to the folds of her evening gown, Ruby procured a small pouch tucked neatly into a hidden pocket. Setting it on the desk, she pulled out her array of lock-picking devices, really only hairpins and small wires she'd collected since her first night—and her first failed attempt at breaking into a desk—to help her disengage the drawer.

She had to know what secrets *this* lord held. Would she find an envelope inside labelled 'Abandoned Daughter,' or a report from the Bow Street Runners with details about herself—her hair color, the particular green shade of her eyes, places she'd been, perhaps the details of her activities over the course of her life?

Nothing worth finding was that simply ascertained.

No man, married or not, would leave record of their nefarious past. It was more likely her father had not spared her, or her mother, a second thought after throwing his pregnant mistress from his townhouse in the middle of the night with no coat and no means to get home.

Ruby was anything but a fool, but she found herself continuing to search regardless. She didn't need a signed confession—she just needed that letter opener.

Picks in hand, she knelt before the locked drawer and eyed the keyhole, blowing a wayward strand of hair that had fallen across her face. She'd been unsuccessful more often than not when attempting to open locked drawers. But luck may have been on her side this evening. She'd entered the ball with little fuss, shortly after the host and hostess had quit the receiving line. It was surprising how similar the layout of most London townhouses were. Ruby had navigated the halls of the second floor and found the room she sought fairly quickly, encountering not a soul.

The pins slipped into the lock and her tongue darted out of her mouth to lick her lips as she concentrated on moving them exactly right to click the lock over. She fought to keep her hands steady when sweat broke out across her forehead. She was running out of time.

Ruby applied a bit too much pressure and the pin snapped, falling uselessly into the locked drawer. "Damn you to hell, Mother!" she cursed and sat back, wiping her slick brow.

She'd always viewed herself as a sensible girl, a dutiful daughter, and an honest friend. She could only imagine the horror on Vi's face if she saw her now. A common thief. A midnight prowler. A defiler of privacy.

Although, it could not be helped.

She sought answers and at the moment all she had was an endless list of questions.

Gaining her feet once more, she bundled her kit and slipped it back into her pocket. She turned her attention to the long table against the wall behind the desk. Leaning over, she ran her hand along the underside of the ornately carved piece, feeling for hidden compartments or—if her luck returned—a forgotten folder of papers.

"Sherry, Miss Ruby?" an oddly familiar

voice asked behind her.

HAROLD JAKESTON WATCHED as she stood. Her back straightened and her body tensed.

She slowly turned in his direction, her eyes wide and her mouth gaping.

He wanted to laugh, but feared startling her any more than he already had.

Even though she'd matured, Miss Ruby St. Augustin still resembled the dirty ragamuffin who'd tagged along after Brock and him in their youth. Her eyes had always been filled with mischief and adventure, as they were now. The green of her irises fairly glowed in the low-lit room. Her hair no longer hung limply around her shoulders, but was caught up in a fashionable pile atop her head. She'd always been tall; now she towered close to his six-foot height.

His gaze traveled back to hers. "Can I offer you a sherry?" he asked again, holding his glass out to her as he admired the delicate tilt of her slender neck.

"Mr. Jakeston...I...well."

He relaxed. "It is a simple question." He paused, bringing the glass to his own lips for a sip. "Either you would enjoy a glass of sherry or you would not."

When she only stared without a word, Harold continued, "Do you not know what you want?" He was badgering her. She most definitely was not doing the same as he, hiding from the masses for a few minutes of quiet after an arduous evening. Her cursing and rifling through Lord Yorkton's desk clearly showed she was looking for something—and hadn't located it. But *what* precisely did she seek?

"Pardon my rudeness, Mr. Jakeston. No, I do not wish for a glass, but thank you ever so much for the offer." She rubbed her hands down the front of her evening gown. "You startled me. I thought I was alone." Her glance darted around the room, as if she expected someone else to emerge from the shadows.

Harold chuckled. "I gathered that much. Would you like to join me by the fire?" he asked. Not waiting for her response, he sank into the overstuffed chair he'd vacated moments before. The room was modernly appointed and satisfied Harold's need for space. He'd expected a few minutes to decompress from the many people he'd met throughout the evening, but found he was not opposed to her interruption.

While highly improper of him, he sought to lure her into sitting—and hopefully an explanation about her presence in Lord Yorkton's private study.

Her reluctant footsteps could be heard as she crossed the room, tentatively taking the seat next to him. While the chairs faced the fire, they also angled slightly toward each other. He took in her uplifted chin, perfectly coiffed hair, and the emeralds that hung elegantly around her neck and from her ears. He'd wager a pretty penny they matched the shade of her eyes perfectly— eyes that currently stared intently into the fire as she perched on the edge of her chair.

After several moments of silence, he asked, "Are you enjoying your evening? I was not aware you were in town."

"Why would you know if I were in town?" She never turned away from the fire.

"I suspect that Lady Vi, I mean Lady Haversham—the name is still so new to me—would be bursting at the seams with your arrival."

She finally looked at him. "When have you seen Vi?"

"Every morning, the noon-time repast." He paused to take a large swallow from his glass. "And then on the carriage ride here. I am staying at the Haversham townhouse after all, being a poor vicar-to-be."

Everything about the woman was suspicious, from her muddled search to her anxious attitude. If the light was exactly right, he could most likely see her skin glow with perspiration.

Her back stiffened. "But I have not..." Her words trailed off. "Mr. Jakeston, I can—"

"Please, it's not as if we don't know each other. It's just Harold." He chuckled at her obvious discomfort. "Mr. Jakeston, or rather Vicar Jakeston, is my father—or either of my older brothers."

She nodded but remained silent, her fingers clasped tightly in her lap as she wrung the folds of her gown.

"May I ask you a question, Ruby? It is agreeable that I also drop formalities?"

"Of course."

He eyed her suspiciously. He remembered her as a boisterous child, precocious to the extreme. Their short acquaintance the year before had also shown Ruby to be articulate, jovial, and open. "What were you doing rummaging through Lord Yorkton's desk?"

Her expression remained devoid of all emotion, betraying nothing.

"Do you prefer I guess? I've always prided myself on my reasoning abilities." He tapped his fingers against the glass in his hand. "Let me think... What could a lady of the *ton* possibly be doing ransacking—"

"I most certainly was not ransacking Lord Yorkton's study," she exclaimed.

"Well, well, well, the lady can speak after all," he chuckled. "Allow me to rephrase my comment. What could a lady of the *ton* possibly be doing gently searching—is that better?—through the personal desk of a lord, while acting as a guest in his home?" He smiled and raised a brow in her direction, hoping she'd offer some bit of insight.

True to form, she held her tongue.

"Oh, I have it!" He pointed his finger skyward. "You are strapped for funds and are looking to *borrow* a bit from our kind host. Maybe a bauble or such that not a soul would miss."

"I would never—"

"No? Let me try again. You recently ended a tryst with our generous host and forgot a trinket in his study." Perhaps his outlandish insinuations could pry some truth from her.

"Now, that is just ludicrous!"

"But not as farfetched as most would assume," he said. "But again, I must be wrong. Possibly does it have something to do with your mother?"

Ruby fully turned his way and reached for his hand, a concerned expression upon her face. "Please tell me you aren't acquainted with my mother. She mustn't know what you saw this evening." Clearly believing she'd said too much, she fell back against the brocade chair in silence.

Harold refilled his glass from the bottle on the table next to him. "Are you sure you do not want any?" he asked without looking at her.

Silence greeted his question.

He was curious, yet feared spooking her before he ascertained her true motive for rifling through Lord Yorkton's things. He shuddered at the consequences if she'd been found by anyone other than himself—not only the potential harm she'd have faced, but also the tarnish that would transfer to Lady Haversham due to their friendship.

"Miss Ruby, exactly how are you acquainted with Lord Yorkton?"

Her response was low, barely audible—like the whispering of lovers in the night. "I saw him two evenings ago, and again tonight when I arrived."

"And do you know anything about the man?" he prodded.

"Not overly much."

"He is not a kind, nor a forgiving man."

"I did not plan to further our acquaintance this night."

"This night?" Her answers only piqued his interest and unease. The evening was turning more intriguing by the second, a nice reprieve from the pressures of his own dilemmas.

"I really must be going."

He wanted nothing less than for her to go. But he also knew the dangers of someone stumbling upon them alone together. "That would be wise. May I escort you to the ballroom?"

Ruby stood, smoothing the creases she'd wrung into her dress. "No, thank you. That will raise suspicion, as well." She stared at him as if taking stock. "Can I trust you will not speak a word of this to anyone?"

He was unsure exactly who he was to speak a word to, but at that precise moment he'd promise her anything...and everything, if only she'd stay. "Not a word shall cross my lips."

"Thank you," she said. "...Harold."

Harold adored the sound of his name on her lips.

She stood to leave, her dress rustling as she moved toward the door.

Making her escape.

Her captivating spell over him broke, freeing them both.

"Ruby," he called from his seat.

"Yes?" From her muffled tone he knew she still faced away from him, just as he faced away from her.

"You look absolutely stunning this evening." He'd intended to say so many things: encourage her to think of Lady Haversham when putting herself in less-than-savory positions, or to curb her cursing while about town. Instead, he'd blurted the exact thing he'd been thinking since she entered the room. "Please be careful in your future endeavors."

He heard the door open on well-oiled hinges and the click of it closing.

"Until we meet again, my sweet," he mumbled to the empty room and downed the rest of his drink.

CHAPTER 2

WHAT HAD SHE been thinking?

She hadn't been thinking. At least, not clearly since she'd found her mother's journal. She'd only sought to find answers—but hadn't thought about the cost.

And by the night's end, the cost may well outweigh the reward.

The crackle of the fire in the room she'd fled was the only sound in the abandoned hall, seeping under the door and echoing around her. Satin-covered feet glided toward the grand staircase as she made her way back to the crowded ballroom below. As she descended, the laughter and music from the festivities below greeted her.

She needed to be more careful in her search, more vigilant in her movements, and more alert to her surroundings.

What if she'd been found by the lord of the house or one of his servants? She could have claimed she'd been lost or feigned confusion and made her way hastily downstairs. Or would she have the nerve to ask Lord Yorkton the question that tore at her?

Had he fathered a child, out of wedlock, with Mrs. Pearl St. Augustin?

The question sounded absurd. She could only imagine how insane the words would be spoken aloud; not only to Lord Yorkton, but to every man on her growing list of potential fathers.

Father—the term clawed at her. All of her preconceived notions about the word were null and void. She'd called a most loving, nurturing man 'father' for her whole thirty-two years. He'd attended her play tea parties as a toddler, bought her fetching muslin dresses as a child, and taught her to ride a horse in her youth. The day they'd put him in the ground had been surreal. She remembered the long walk to the family burial plot at the back of their property, following the carriage, her father's casket inside. No young girl, still in the schoolroom, should have to experience the loss of a parent.

She'd reached out numerous times that day for her mother's hand—she did not know if she sought to receive comfort or to give it—but her mother always walked just out of her reach. Her mind's eye saw her mother so clearly as she'd appeared that day, and the many days that followed. She hadn't shed a single tear. Ruby never heard her cry herself to sleep as she herself had done for weeks after his death; she'd never had that faraway look most had when they tried to relive fond memories.

Her mother's lack of grief hadn't alarmed her then. Pearl St. Augustin had always been distant and aloof. It was only now that Ruby realized her mother had been in a perpetual state of grief since before Ruby had been born.

Had her father known of her mother's deception? If so, he'd sought to make up for her mother's coldness with his ever-present attention and love. He was a man above all men, not seeking to punish the child for the sins of her mother. Part of Ruby yearned to also forgive Pearl, to erase the years of hurt and loneliness and face the future united together, whatever the outcome.

She wiped away the wayward tear that fled down her face. Now wasn't the time—truly, she wasn't sure the time to grieve the loss of the man who'd raised her, for a second time, would ever come.

"Damnation, Mother!" Ruby cursed under her breath as she moved through the milling people toward the veranda, avoiding eye contact. Now was not the time, she scolded herself. She'd let Lady Haversham's coachman know she'd only be thirty minutes and to keep the carriage in the drive. With the time it had taken her to slip into the house and then upstairs unnoticed, an hour had passed more quickly than she'd thought possible.

As she moved through the crowd, nodding to the few people who'd made her acquaintance in her short time about town, she heard the ramblings of guests.

Her tall stature afforded her a view of the crowd, enabling her to avoid any contact with her mother or her close circle. She could only imagine the dressing down she'd receive if she were caught in London, directly disobeying her mother's wish that she remain in the country due to their limited funds.

It had been advantageous for her that her nearest and dearest friend, Lady Viola Haversham, happened to be departing for London the very same day Ruby had arrived at her estate, a dark secret on the tip of her tongue. She'd been ready to confess all to Vi, but held back when she saw the staff hurriedly packing to depart for London. Ruby had only contemplated her next move for a moment. She needed to be in London if she hoped to gain answers.

Ruby was thankful for Vi's generosity, even though her friend made it very clear that she had her own selfish reasons for wanting Ruby close. She was carrying her first child, and was frightened of being alone. While Ruby knew nothing of babies and childbirth, she looked forward to sharing this special time with her best friend.

With Vi's increasing condition, Ruby's excuse to accompany her to London—against her mother's wishes—meant the opportunity to start the search for her true father as well. She hadn't had much to go on when she first arrived, with only a luggage trunk and her mother's old, faded journal. She'd obtained a copy of *Peers of the Realm* from a shop on Bond Street, while Vi shopped for a new pocket square for her husband. Ruby had worked quickly, making her list of all the unmarried lords of a certain age. After eliminating those who had not been in London during the time in question, and adding to those the homes she had already searched, she found her list had dwindled to a mere six names.

At least Ruby's mother's motivations for keeping her isolated and out of the public eye now made sense. Mrs. St. Augustin could not take the chance of her daughter—and therefore herself—being linked to a man who was not her late husband.

Looking around, Ruby saw one gentleman whose stature mirrored her own willowy form; another with her exact shade of green eyes; yet another whose hair color and complexion matched her own dark features.

For what seemed like the millionth time, doubt, uncertainty, and hopelessness filled her. Doubt that she'd never learn who she truly was, where she belonged, where her place in this world lay. Uncertainty whether or not she even wanted to know the truth; if the man who'd fathered her wanted anything to do with her; if she would like where her search led her. And hopelessness that she was in any way qualified to be searching at all.

"Ruby?"

She stopped several feet from the open veranda doors—and her freedom from the crowded house.

Pasting a smile on her face that she hoped would reach her eyes, she turned. "Vi," she said. "I had no idea you would be in attendance tonight, or I would have accompanied you and Lord Haversham."

Vi eyed her skeptically. "I am sure I mentioned it earlier today during my dress fitting."

It hadn't been that many months ago that Ruby had eyed Vi in much the same suspicious manner. "I don't believe so, but I'm glad to see at least one person I know." Ruby grasped Vi in a tight hug to smother the questions her friend was dying to ask. Questions for which she had no answers.

After a moment, Vi returned her hug and then held Ruby at arm's length. Her friend's crystal blue eyes took her in from head to toe and back again. "You look splendid this evening. Did Sarah fix your hair?"

Ruby smiled. She knew she looked exquisite in the satin dress, her hair swept high atop her head. "No. I decided at the last second to come out tonight." Ruby still grasped Vi's hands. "I did not seek to inconvenience Sarah or the other household staff."

"Nonsense, you are our guest."

Tears welled once more, but this time for a completely different reason. After her father passed, Ruby hadn't known the love of a family until she went to live with Vi as her paid companion, which turned into a friendship many envied. They'd been inseparable for years, spending every holiday as sisters would. Lord Oberbrook, Vi's father, had even purchased Ruby a superb new wardrobe for the ill-fated week she and Vi had spent in town last season.

Currently, she wore a fine puce evening gown she hadn't worn before. Some may pinpoint the fashion as last season, but Ruby had never felt so elegant. The dress transformed her thin frame into the willowy, lithe body of a sophisticated woman of the *ton*.

"It is only that I do not wish to trouble anyone," Ruby responded. "You and your family have already done so much for me." She glanced over Vi's shoulder. Thankfully, her mother was nowhere to be seen. Ruby needed to make her swift escape before it was too late.

Vi released Ruby's hands and stepped back. "Enough of all this. Shall I find you a dance partner?"

"No, please. I fear I am a bit overheated. I was making my way to the veranda for some fresh air when you spotted me." Ruby nodded to the French doors not far from them. "I will take you up on your offer after I have cooled down a bit."

"I'll join you —"

"No need for that," Ruby cut in. "I see Brock making his way toward us now. I do suppose he longs for your company. I will join you in a moment." With another quick hug and a peck on the cheek, Ruby moved toward the open doors.

"Hello, my love," Ruby heard Brock greet Vi as she moved out the door, away from the prying eyes of the *ton* and far from her mother's clutches.

The cool night caressed her heated skin, but quickly turned cold. She wished she hadn't left her shawl in the carriage, but she'd had no choice. The servants at the front door would have looked suspiciously upon her for not leaving the item with them upon her arrival, and she simply could not afford another if she had to leave it behind. Arriving *sans* shawl had been a necessity, and the walk around the house to the drive wouldn't be very long.

She wrapped her bare arms around herself to ward off the chilly breeze and moved to the steps leading to the garden, careful to keep her head down. While she didn't know many people in town, she couldn't risk someone recognizing her before she was ready. That would be sure to start a round of gossip that would only interfere and complicate her search. The veranda was sparsely attended and she was able to make her way down the steps and toward the gate along the well-lit garden path.

Reaching the gate, Ruby took one more glance over her shoulder to make sure no one followed. What greeted her stopped Ruby in her tracks, her hand poised to push the gate open.

Harold stood at the edge of the veranda, his sherry flute raised in salute to her.

The man presented a striking, elegant figure; one Ruby was hard pressed to take her eyes from with the glow from the open ballroom doors illuminating him. The cut of his shirt may appear last season, but broad shoulders never went out of fashion. She'd found it difficult to keep her eyes trained on the fire before her earlier, wanting to take in the sight of him, yet fearing her eyes would give away the absolute terror she'd felt at being caught. She found him alluring and distracting, though that was the last thing she should be focused on at the moment.

She tried to look away before he noticed her stare, but he nodded in her direction and took a sip from his glass.

If she wasn't mistaken, his laugh echoed through the garden as she turned away.

CHAPTER 3

HAROLD LAUGHED AS she slipped through the gate and moved toward the front drive of the estate, no one but him the wiser. Her wide-eyed look of shock when he'd acknowledged her had been worth his mad dash through the house in pursuit of her retreating form.

It had been to make sure she arrived back safely to the ballroom, he'd told himself. She had departed in such a hurry, he'd worried she would trip on the stairs or be accosted in one of the dark hallways by a drunken party guest.

One could never be too cautious. The fact that the first sight of Ruby St. Augustin had piqued his interest in a way few had since he'd arrived in London, he assured himself, had nothing to do with his concern for her well-being.

The woman wasn't only captivating in her beauty, but held an air of mystery thanks to her rushed search and hasty departure. As far as

Harold was aware, Miss Ruby hadn't attended a London season nor had any connections in town besides the new Lady Haversham and, of course, her own mother. He could not fathom her purpose for sneaking into Lord Yorkton's study in the middle of a ball to rifle through his personal effects. A man's study was his personal domain; many kept their most prized possessions or hidden secrets within this private sanctuary, knowing that none dared cross the threshold without invitation.

He couldn't disregard the nagging suspicion that she'd gotten herself involved in something and was in trouble, and therefore needed his assistance.

"Harold, is that you?" Lady Haversham called behind him.

She stood a few feet outside the ballroom door. Her smile dazzled him, as it always had. Harold could not have selected a more suitable bride and life partner for his best friend, Brock. "It is I, your ladyship." He bowed in her direction. "How are you feeling this eve?"

"I am a bit tired, but thankfully Brock is making sure I have plenty of rest between dances." Her smile brightened further. The spark reached her clear blue eyes and brought a new light to the darkened terrace. "How many times must I tell you to call me Vi?"

"At least once more," Harold countered. "My lady."

Lady Haversham glanced around the terrace.

"Can I help you with something?" he asked.

"I am uncertain," She scanned the garden before continuing. "Did you happen to see Ruby come out this way a few moments ago?"

Harold debated his options for answering. If he told Vi he hadn't seen Ruby, then she would worry. If he told her he'd seen her leave through the far garden gate, that would also cause her to fret about her friend. But what other alternative did he have that would keep Lady Haversham from harrying off after Ruby, involving yet another person in the situation afoot?

"Well?" Vi's brow shot up in question.

"I did encounter Miss Ruby only moments ago. She came outside for a spot of fresh air. She said she was not feeling well, so I accompanied her to her carriage. My apologies for not locating you or Brock sooner with the news." He regretted the need to lie, but didn't hesitate to think of the consequences.

Lying to his best friend's wife to cover the nefarious deeds of a woman he barely knew was something he'd never foreseen.

Vi sighed and the tension left her body. "Oh, no worries. I hadn't expected to see her this evening at all. I will check on her when we return home."

"When you return home..." Harold let his words trail off in question.

"Why, yes. Ruby has been staying at the Haversham townhouse since I arrived. Have you not seen her?"

The bloody hell she had been! He'd seen neither hide nor hair of the woman. Nor had Ruby told him of her accommodations while in the study. She was truly up to something, and chances were Brock and his wife hadn't the faintest idea. It appeared Ruby sneaking about hadn't only escaped his notice, but also theirs. He'd played billiards with Brock two evenings prior, eaten with the couple that very morning, and ridden to tonight's ball in their coach. And her name hadn't been uttered once, not a glimpse of her emerald eyes seen, nor the sound of her melodic voice drifting down a corridor.

"I was unaware until this evening, my lady."

Vi laid her hand on Harold's sleeve and leaned close, as if imparting a confidence. "Do not feel left out. She does not seek her presence here in London to be known."

He lowered his voice in hopes of gaining more information. "That is very interesting considering she only just left a ball attended by close to three hundred of London's most affluent."

"Truly it is only one person she wishes to avoid." A light chuckle accompanied her words.

His ears perked in interest. "And who shall *we* be avoiding during our stay?"

"What have you said to bring such a laugh from my wife?"

Harold turned at the same moment Lady Haversham did the same. Brock—Harold's childhood friend and Vi's husband—stood framed in the candlelight slipping out the open doors. His friend, recently retired from active duty to the King, struck a daunting figure.

"I jest." Brock moved onto the terrace and joined the pair. "Don't look so frightened or I will have no other choice but to assume you seek to steal my wife."

"If I thought I stood a chance at winning her hand I would have made my move last season while you were still removing your head from places unknown."

Lady Haversham released her light hold on Harold's arm and moved to her husband's side. "I thought you had retired to the card room, my love."

"I fear no games caught my interest this evening, and I wanted to see that you are feeling well. What were you two so deep in conversation about?"

"After we danced, I came to check on Ruby," Vi said. "I had not seen her return to the ballroom and I became concerned."

Harold agreed Lady Haversham should be concerned, but about something entirely different. "I was explaining that Miss Ruby was not feeling well, and I escorted her to your carriage."

Brock's brow pulled in concern. "I hadn't even realized she was attending this evening. Should we return home to check on her? I can call for a physician, if needed."

"No, no, that is not necessary," Harold cut in. He had no idea if she was indeed headed back to the townhouse. "She said she was going to rest for the evening and see you both at morning meal. I believe it is only a headache that ails her."

He saw little need to worry either Brock or Lady Haversham until he knew more. He sensed that something larger was going on, but with little evidence beyond the discovery of Ruby rummaging through Yorkton's desk, he could not in good conscience sound the alarm. She could very well turn the tables on him and ask his purpose for lurking about the same room.

"Ah, well, that is settled. If you are not overly fatigued, may I have the next dance, my darling?" Brock asked.

"I fear my dancing skills are a bit rusty," Harold said.

Brock and Vi laughed as they joined arms and moved back toward the ballroom as the strings of a waltz floated through the open doors.

"Do not wait up for me," Harold called to the retreating pair.

"We wouldn't dream of it," Brock said over his shoulder.

Harold longed to call Lady Haversham back to finish their conversation. To find out who Ruby was avoiding and if she was in trouble—or somehow the cause of trouble. She'd certainly appeared anxious in Lord Yorkton's study and downright frazzled when, he assumed, she hadn't found what she'd been searching for.

For the second time that evening, Harold was happy for the reprieve from his own worries and problems. He hadn't had a spare second to dwell on his much-needed return to his father's home or his dull future as a country vicar. His brothers, the lucky bastards, had escaped the family home and forged their own way in the world. Unfortunately, as the youngest son Harold would not be afforded the same luxury—and his father was running out of patience.

He sighed. His days about town, and his freedom, were coming to an end all too quickly. Responsibility knocked louder and more forceful each day.

His life was a mess—did he have the right to get involved in someone else's? Part of him doubted his ability to weigh in on Ruby's actions when he lacked the fortitude to deal with his own situation.

Time was fleeting and Harold would spend the remaining weeks—or possibly days—doing what made him happy before settling on what satisfied his father.

In his hand, his glass stood empty. He set it on a small table and went in search of his own dance partner.

CHAPTER 4

27 November 1783

My time is near, and while I should be ever grateful for the kindness shown to me by Sir St. Augustin, I fear I am a wretched wife and soon to be horrid mother. For you see, dear journal, I want naught to do with this child. Whether it be a male with his eyes and penchant for romance, or a girl with my dark hair and formidable stature, I worry I cannot love it. How can I be made to live every day with the reminder of his child about the estate?

It is with sadness that I write this, what is to be my last correspondence within these pages. It is time I find another outlet for my grief and anguish, as my obsession with these words cannot improve my countenance.

Life is full of hardships, and I have suffered more than most women must. I trust that one day I too can be happy...though I fear my happiness will never come to be with my husband and child. Perhaps one day I will be strong enough to escape it all and find my true destiny.

Ruby closed the journal and laid her hand flat upon its cover. She'd held the book, pored over the words within it so many times the binding was wearing more with each passing day. The image of her mother scribbling frantically or holding the journal close was always in her mind.

She closed her eyes tight, suppressing her emotions and focusing on her anger. Her resentment. Her need for validation.

Every day, she swore she would never open the cursed book again, but time after time she found herself needing the reminder of why she was doing what she was doing—risking all she was in search of the truth. And to achieve this, it was imperative she not allow her emotions to get the best of her, to ruin her concentration and motivation.

She pored over the pages written in her mother's neat handwriting, looking for clues to her father's identity. With every reading, she found no mention of a name. Not a single morsel of information as to who this mysterious cad might have been.

She was disheartened, but continued to push forward.

The want to burn the book, turn it to ashes, was overwhelming. It would be so easy to return to her room and toss the damning tome into her own fireplace, watch the flames lick up its bound sides and the pages catch blaze, all of her mother's deceptions vanishing before her eyes. Not a soul could prove what she knew—all she'd read.

Instead, she slipped the journal into the pocket of her apron, not trusting it to sit in open sight for any and all to see.

Ruby's list was dwindling—and quickly. She crossed off yet another name. Lord Yorkton's study hadn't held anything of use to her. There was not a love note, a ruby-encrusted letter opener, or treasured playbill to be found. It had been the same in each home she'd searched. There was no evidence that proved any of the men she'd thus far crossed off wasn't her father, except the few that had not been in London at the time. Now, with little else to go on, she needed to focus on a person who did possess some indication that they might be linked to her.

Her mother had written incessantly about the daily notes she'd sent her lover and how she'd poured her heart and soul into each one. Truly, it was foolish for Ruby to think the notes or the handcrafted letter opener had meant anything to the man. He may have discarded them just as he'd discarded her mother.

The heartless cod.

But, no. Ruby would not feel sorry for her mother. Every time those pesky, bothersome emotions crept up on her, she pushed them down and locked them up tight. She would not pity her mother's loss; she could not condone her actions, and every consequence sat clearly on her mother's shoulders.

Life was about choices.

Every day, every minute, a person was forced to make a choice. There were small choices that barely affected a person's life, like selecting the blue muslin walking dress or the peach silk. Life was full of these inconsequential decisions—and they were made rashly more times than naught.

But life was also chock full of major life choices. It was these decisions that defined the person, guided every future life choice.

Ruby retrieved a fresh sheet of stationery from her desk drawer and scribbled the major life choices her mother had made, each in direct conflict to what Ruby wanted for herself. She'd often listed these transgressions to help keep her focused—and as a reminder of how easily her mother had fallen.

1. *Unfaithfulness*
2. *Disloyalty*
3. *Dishonesty*
4. *Unloving, uncompassionate, and uncaring*

Pearl St. Augustin had chosen, wholeheartedly and continuously, to drag her life and her family through the mud. Ruby hadn't noticed the stain and stench on herself until recently, and could not rid herself of the dishonor forced upon her very existence by the person who should love her—cherish her—unconditionally.

"Damnation, Mother!" Ruby cursed.

"Tsk, tsk. Most of the words I have heard you utter curse your lineage."

Ruby's back straightened and she moved a book to cover her lists. She hadn't heard the door open. The thrill that coursed through her at the sound of his voice astounded her. Against her better judgment and much to her own dismay, thoughts of Harold Jakeston had crept into her mind more than once since the previous eve.

"It is bad form to insult one's mother, is it not?"

"You have no clue of what you speak." Ruby did not bother turning—it had been too hard to get the man from her mind the night before, she saw no point in tormenting herself any further. She kept picturing him as he'd appeared before the fire, or saluting her from the terrace as she'd rushed from the garden.

Mr. Jakeston chuckled, a deep, masculine sound. "Cat does not have your tongue today, I see."

Ruby set down her pencil and faced the infuriating man. His lips turned up in an alluring smile. "What has or has not got me is none of your concern."

He stood close. "It could be my concern," he countered.

"Why do you care?"

"I am an honorable man, Miss Ruby. And you are the damsel in distress—"

"Whatever makes you think I am in distress? And a man who proclaims himself honorable is rarely thus," she continued without allowing him time to answer.

"Touché." He smirked. "Do you feel that?"

"Feel what?" The house was silent and still. No breeze entered the open parlor window.

"The sizzle in the air. It is fairly exhilarating."

The man was more than infuriating; he was incorrigible, high-handed, and possibly slightly slow in the mind. Though she did feel it, and much more, she reminded herself sternly that it was in her best interest to keep that to herself. "Again, Mr. Jakest—"

"Harold, if you please," he cut in. "We did agree to drop the unneeded formalities last evening, did we not?"

"Very well, Harold." Ruby would placate him—for now. "I was going to say that you must be a bit daft, pardon my bluntness."

"I only seek to be blunt myself, one quality I find most society members lack in spades." He moved to the chaise lounge, a few feet from her, and sat.

Ruby stared. "Whatever are you doing?"

"Sitting," he answered in an even tone. "And whatever are you doing?"

His phrasing and pitch mimicked her own, further maddening her.

"I did not invite you to stay." She wanted to shout, stomp her foot at the man for taking such liberties, but refrained. She wasn't one for such childish displays, though they surely were tempting. "It is not proper for a man and woman of a certain age, unmarried, to be alone."

He laughed. The sound echoed through the large room and out to the hallway beyond. Maybe Ruby's speculation about his mental stability was not too farfetched. Thankfully, a servant would no doubt arrive shortly to intervene thanks to the excessive noise he made.

"What is so comical?" Ruby asked.

"Why would I need to be invited to stay?" he asked.

"Do not answer my question with another question. It is very rude."

"Would you like to know what I find rude?"

She pondered answering his clearly rhetorical question, but kept quiet instead. Ruby glanced toward the door, which stood open as society deemed acceptable for an unmarried woman in the presence of a man without the proper chaperone. She shouldn't care what society thought of her or her actions since she barely hung on the fringes of the *ton*, never making her grand coming out to society.

When she turned back to him, he only stared at her quizzically. In his stare were all the questions he wanted to ask but was too much the gentleman to do so.

He lifted his arm and pointed to the seat across from him. "Do have a seat, Miss Ruby."

Leery of his return to formalities, she again looked to the door, hoping for someone to rescue her.

"I do not bite," he said with a wink. "Unless you want me to, but I fear our acquaintance has not progressed to that point as yet."

Ruby didn't remember the man being so candid. In her mind's eye she remembered the lanky young boy who'd explored the land between her estate and Lord Haversham's. He'd rarely said a word, and she was having trouble assimilating the man before her with the boy she thought she had known in her childhood.

"That is a highly inappropriate thing to say to a lady," Ruby scolded as traitorous thoughts of Harold nibbling her neck floated into her mind. The reprimand sounded petty, but she was at a lack for any other words. "What do you find rude?" She tried to soften the sting of her last comment.

"Ah! Now, that is far more appropriate a topic than biting." He smirked and again motioned to the seat close to his own. "It's very rude that you didn't inform me last night where you were staying in London."

Ruby gave in and sat. "Maybe I preferred not to further our acquaintance." She sounded callous, but she was in London for a reason, a very specific reason—and it did not include renewing outdated friendships nor a dalliance with any man, no matter how tempting. She'd seen how that had paid off for her mother. Harold Jakeston had no place in her life, and she could have no place in his. "I hope you didn't work overly hard to learn my location."

"Oh, it was hardly any trouble at all."

Ruby had been certain to keep a low profile, but had known the inevitability of her and Harold crossing paths while residing in the same townhouse. Now, she only hoped he didn't go about town telling all and sundry of her presence. "If you will excuse me, I have many correspondences to write." When he continued to watch her intently, she rose. "It was nice to see you again."

She meant the words to be polite, yet dismissive. When he continued to look relaxed, her thoughts again settled on his lack of a sound mind. She'd been told that men of the *ton* could be thick headed, but did he not know a dismissal when he heard one?

But Harold was not a man of the *ton*, she reminded herself, any more than she was a lady of the *ton*.

Perhaps she should blame his lack of manners on his many years in the country.

She cleared her throat to gain his attention. "If you do not mind—"

"I do not mind at all, please carry on with your correspondence," he said, settling further into the lounge. "I will not disturb you. Shall I ring for tea?"

She could only gawk as he gazed back at her. There was a polite smile on his serene face, yet his eyes sparkled with mischief.

"That will not be necessary. I think I shall

retire to my room to ready for my midday meal," she said, barely managing the words through clenched teeth. No doubt he was a pretty face, but the man was maddening—and possibly mad. She gathered her things in a rush, more determined than ever that no man, least of all Harold Jakeston, would drive her off course.

SHE FLED THE room as if the devil himself were on her tail. If he needed any convincing that the woman was up to something, then her demeanor proved it beyond a doubt. While he had little experience with women and their fickle actions, he was sure he hadn't offended her so greatly that she'd seek to quit every room he entered.

She made no sense, but what woman did? He was wont to meet one who didn't speak in guarded words, half-truths, or outright lies.

Then again, men were no different. Certainly, he'd been guilty of being less than completely honest with the young women he'd met while in town. Brock insisted Harold insinuate he lived on the property adjoining the Haversham estate, when in truth his father's home resided *on* Haversham property and his family had proudly served three generations of Havershams.

He was discouraged to realize he'd thought Ruby different—above other women of her class. Alas, her words were guarded and at best half-truths, if not outright lies. He wondered what she had to gain by keeping her actions hidden.

Harold was not only loyal to the Haversham family as a whole, but he was indebted to Brock. If Ruby was involved with someone or something that would ultimately shed a bad light on Lord and Lady Haversham, he had a duty— no, a responsibility—to find out what it was and right the situation. Lady Haversham had been hurt by so many in her short life, and Harold would do anything in his power to make sure the one person she trusted more than her husband did not destroy that trust.

Standing, he moved to Ruby's desk. The normal womanly items littered its surface: fancy stationery, a quill and three ink pots, fashion plates, a book, and a wax seal kit. He picked up the book, which sat in the middle of the desk. *Peers of the Realm*. The volume, dated by society standards, was heavy and smelled of years of use.

He thumbed through the book noting several notations within, but the words and the families they were written next to meant nothing to him. Setting it aside, he looked at the papers scattered on the desk. He'd be crossing the line and invading her privacy if he read any of the neatly scribbled words on the loose pages.

He entertained the thought only briefly before he gathered them and moved back to his seat on the chaise. She would not have exited the room, leaving the papers, if they truly were of a sensitive nature. Perhaps her correspondence included simple letters to an elderly aunt or instructions for the headmistress at Foldger's Foundling House, the orphanage that Harold knew Ruby helped Lady Haversham oversee.

But he feared he'd find a letter from someone special, possibly a man awaiting her return in the country. The feeling was ludicrous, utterly foreign to him—and now was not the time to waste contemplating his own inner workings. What he felt for Ruby—if he felt anything at all—would be misplaced and unwanted based on the woman's attitude thus far.

He merely sought to confirm her true nature and the possibility of her less-than-honest actions.

Still, he took in her classic, crisp handwriting, not focusing on the words but on the movement across the paper, so unlike her haphazard movements from the previous night. She'd been hurried, nervous, and consumed by whatever it was she sought. He hoped she'd found what she'd been looking for and would not put herself in danger again.

The door, still firmly closed, could be thrown wide at any moment and the papers—his only means of insight—could be snatched from his hands as easily as that, and this opportunity to know her better would be gone.

He focused on the words before him.

Both sheets held lists—one of titled gentlemen and the location of their homes within London, and the other a list of unsavory qualities.

Time being of the essence, Harold grabbed a blank sheet of paper and scribbled down as many of the names as he could. He recognized a few as either business associates or acquaintances of Brock's. Still, most he'd had no previous knowledge of. The list was comprised of men from every level of society, from a baron to three dukes. They were in no particular order on the sheet. Many were crossed off for no apparent reason, as no notes accompanied the names.

He again studied her odd list of

transgressions. He wondered if they applied to the men on her list or possibly herself. It seemed that every time he ran across the woman, she was up to something.

Hopefully, he would be able to figure out what she was doing before he returned to the country. If not, he'd need to enlighten Brock to his suspicions and any findings.

CHAPTER 5

THE ALCOVE RUBY sat in afforded her privacy while allowing her a direct view of the door to the sitting room. She'd been so perturbed by Harold's intrusion that she'd left the room with only half her things, completely neglecting to gather her papers.

Now she had no other choice but to wait for him to leave—and pray he didn't look through her writing desk in the meantime.

The hallway, windows shuttered against the late morning sun, was clouded in shadows.

"Whatever are you doing?"

Ruby slunk a bit more into the darkened alcove at Vi's question, hoping her friend hadn't spotted her, and instead was addressing a passing servant. The tapping of her shoe against the polished floor erased any hope Ruby had of staying undetected.

She stood from her seat on the shallow sill of the window, stepping into the light of the hall.

"Oh, Vi," she said, adding a note of shock to her voice. "I must have been daydreaming and lost track of time."

Her friend knew the words were a mistruth, just as Ruby feared. "About?"

Ruby had so much on her mind, she failed to quickly come up with anything she could convincingly be daydreaming about.

"Come now," Vi continued. "You've acted oddly since we arrived in London, and you and I both know you're as likely to daydream as to spontaneously begin speaking Italian. Are you under the weather?"

"Under the weather?" Ruby asked, confused. "I feel fine—"

"Mr. Jakeston informed Lord Haversham and myself that you were not feeling well last evening, and he was kind enough to escort you to our carriage. I would have gratefully accompanied you since I was fatigued as well, if you'd only come to me."

Ruby must remember to thank him when next they met, though she was uncomfortable with the untruth. She was grateful for his quick thinking, but she did not need Harold to lie for her.

Vi touched Ruby's forehead. She stepped back, startled by Vi's movement.

"Well, you have no fever." Viola crossed her arms dubiously. "Does your head ache?"

"No."

"I only want to know why you're acting so peculiar," Vi huffed.

Ruby debated whether to confide in her friend—truly, the only friend she'd ever had. But to tell anyone about her mother's disloyalty would tarnish the memory of her father, the man who'd raised her. No matter what her mother had or had not done, Ruby owed her father more respect and devotion than to parade their family's dirty laundry about town. Besides which, while she trusted Vi completely, she could not risk exposing her to any stress at this early point in her pregnancy.

"I'm overly tired, that's all. I just need to acclimate to the hectic pace of life in town."

"I suspect you will adjust with time. Please, do not fret." Her friend smiled in understanding. "I do understand. The change from country life to town life has been exhausting for me, as well."

A door closed quietly behind them and they both turned.

"Good day, ladies," Harold mumbled, bowing slightly in their direction. Without another word, he turned on his heel and walked back toward the main staircase.

"Everyone is acting peculiar," Vi sighed. "Maybe there is something going around."

Ruby was at a loss. There was undoubtedly something going on, if not around as well. Deceiving Vi wasn't what she'd set out to do. If she could only keep her secret for a while longer and discover who her true father was, then she could return to her family estate with no one the wiser. Then she would have ample time to decide her next move—or to forget everything she'd learned, if that was what she chose. She would write Vi from the safety of the country and explain everything.

"I am sure Mr. Jakeston is a busy man." Harold had covered for her the previous evening; the least she could do was extend the same courtesy, even though it irked her to do so. "I must be on my way. I have many letters to write. The children at the Foundling House have taken to corresponding quite regularly since you arranged for their letters to be brought to us weekly."

Vi smiled, as she often did at the mention of *her* children. "I do so appreciate you writing them. I know they love when the morning post arrives and there are letters for each of them."

Ruby comforted herself with the knowledge that she did plan to write a few of the children that day—just not right that moment. "I know you wish we could be with them more often. The least I can do is write, make sure they are keeping up with their studies and not giving Mrs. Hutton a difficult time."

"Brock promised me a trip to the country as soon as he can tear himself away for a few days. If I am well enough to travel, of course." Vi's face lit up at the mention of her new husband. "I do so hope you will come with us."

"There is no place I'd rather be." Another promise she hoped not to break. "I will see you shortly."

Ruby gave Vi a reassuring smile, although it was meant more to convince herself that things would be fine. No one would find her true reason for being in London; no chance meeting would transpire between her and her mother; she would find her true father and, regardless of the outcome of their meeting, she'd retire once more to the country.

"Ruby?"

"Oh, did you say something?"

"I asked if you still plan to accompany Brock and me this evening."

"This evening?" For the life of her, Ruby couldn't remember what gathering she'd agreed to attend this evening. How society members kept up with all the social gatherings during the season was beyond her.

"The ball at Lord Spires's home, you ninny."

How could she have forgotten? But a better question, how had she neglected to call off? "Of course, I would not miss it." And by 'not miss it,' Ruby meant she'd be searching all afternoon for a reason not to attend. She had limited evening gowns and Lord Spires was not on her list of possible fathers.

Time was of the essence and she hadn't any to spare on an evening out.

"Wonderful," Vi said. "I'm off to write a few letters of my own."

Ruby turned toward the room Harold had vacated, hoping her notes hadn't been disturbed.

"Oh, and Ruby," her friend called before she was able to escape. "Would you mind checking up on Alex at the Marquis of Drake's? I worry about him."

The name—the Marquis of Drake—was familiar, mainly because it was amongst the few that remained on her list. "Yes, I will go round and check on him shortly."

"No reason to go out of your way. Perhaps you can write a note and have one of the servants run it round to the marquis' stable."

She'd agree to anything to be done with their conversation and back at her writing desk. "I most certainly will."

But only after she determined whether Harold had looked through her personal pages— and what he might have found. Thankfully, she had at least slipped her mother's journal into her apron before he'd entered the room. It was small comfort, but she would take what she could get.

CHAPTER 6

HAROLD ANXIOUSLY PACED the length of the stable. He had no clue what was taking so long to prepare the coach. There was limited time before it would need to be returned and readied for this evening's entertainment, and he had a pressing engagement about which he was experiencing considerable anxiety.

Finally, he sat on a crate against the stable wall to wait...and think.

The note that had arrived shortly after Harold's arrival in London couldn't be ignored forever. His older brother William requested to meet with him. It being the first contact they'd had in over five years, Harold should have jumped at the chance—if nothing else, only to see how William was getting on, no longer under the thumb of their father.

Instead, he found himself concerned. Was it not possible that Vicar Jakeston had written one of his older sons, complaining about the waywardness of his youngest? If his father had enlisted the help of Harold's brothers to convince Harold to return home, he was unsure what he'd do.

Ruby and her mischievousness had distracted him for a time. He told himself his interest had nothing to do with her tempting grace and kissable lips, and all to do with her suspicious activities. His attraction to her was of no consequence. His involvement extended only so far as verifying that her actions were not putting Lady Haversham's reputation and feelings in jeopardy. And if he repeated that to himself enough, he thought dryly, perhaps he would eventually believe it.

As if he'd conjured her out of thin air, Ruby herself entered the stables dressed in a brocade walking dress of the palest orange. The color would be utterly frightening on any other female, but Ruby's dark hair and green eyes worked well with the shade.

She held her head high as she moved through the stables and toward the lane beyond.

"And where might you be off to?" he asked.

She let out a squeal and jumped in panic. "Harold! Do you seek to try the nerves of every person in your acquaintance?" Her hand lay flat against her chest, as if to calm her racing heart.

"I beg your pardon, but I did not seek you out. It is you who have stumbled upon me awaiting the Haversham carriage."

When she only stared, he continued. "Are you going somewhere? I would be happy to escort you." Harold knew he didn't have time to deliver her to her destination, possibly be called upon to wait, and deliver her back home without missing his meeting.

"I *am* going somewhere," she said hesitantly. "...but I am in no need of a chaperone."

"Do you plan to ride?"

"No. It is only a short walk."

"Would you like company on your short walk?"

"Again, that is not necessary. Lady Haversham is sending me on an errand for her, and I do not expect to be long."

"Mr. Jakeston," a stable hand called. "Your carriage is ready."

He was torn between following Miss Ruby or jumping into the carriage and being on his way. He was already running late.

"Why are you awaiting a carriage here and not having it brought round to the front?" she asked.

He preferred being the one to ask the questions, and this one resonated a bit too closely. "Uh—I'm in a hurry, and the street in front is very crowded this time of day."

"Oh, I see," she said. "Well, I must be going—and I know you're also in a rush. I hope to see you again soon."

From her curt dismissal, he knew she wanted nothing less than to see him again soon, which suited him well. He was in possession of her list, and intended to find out her motives without her help.

"Have a wonderful afternoon, Miss Ruby."

RUBY GLANCED OVER her shoulder several times as she walked down the lane. Harold's carriage had taken him in the opposite direction, but she still worried the man would depart his conveyance and follow her.

Thankfully, he seemed in a hurry and not prone to lagging about for her sake. She hadn't paid much attention to his comings and goings since her arrival in town, but she did wonder what he was up to. Not that it mattered as long as he was occupied with matters other than her. He hadn't mentioned anything about their time in the salon earlier in the day, or their chance meeting at Lord Yorkton's function. It was possible he'd already lay the incident to rest.

Determinedly, she put the matter of Mr. Jakeston out of her mind. She hoped to solve the mystery of her father soon. Then...she had no idea.

Would she approach the man, or would she simply remove herself to the country knowing who he was—even if he was unaware of her?

Time would tell. She feared her emotions would dictate her next actions.

But, at the moment, she was no closer to finding the man than she'd been when she first arrived in London.

With her list tucked securely in her pocket, she went to check on Alex, one of Vi's previous charges. Alex had moved to London the previous year in hopes of working in a fine stable. That Vi had found him employment with the Marquis of Drake—who happened to be on Ruby's list—was a coincidence Ruby saw no point in questioning.

She arrived at the Drake stables with nary a hitch. After she'd convinced herself that Harold hadn't followed her, she entered the busy area.

"Can I help ye, Miss?" an elderly man dressed in Drake black and red asked.

She turned her most brilliant smile on the man. "I do believe you can." Ruby had learned that the surest way to acquire what you desire from a person is to make them feel invaluable to your cause or quest. "I am here to see Alex, one of your stable hands."

"What ye be needing with the cripple boy?" She could see that the man's words were not meant to belittle Alex and his disability, only to show he knew of whom she spoke.

"I was sent by Lady Haversham to check on his well-being." The statement was true...to a point. "He is her ward, and sent me to check that there is nothing he needs."

The man eyed her suspiciously. "The marquis takes good care of his servants, miss."

"Oh, I do not doubt that, but Lady Haversham is like a mother to the boy." She shook her head, as if not understanding the relationship the pair shared.

"Well, I be James, the stable master here," he finally conceded. "Lady Haversham raised some fine stock in her day. We are happy to have the boy around. You be finding him over in the tack room, detailing the bridles and such."

Ruby curtseyed to the man, figuring it couldn't hurt—she may very well need his assistance in the future. "Thank you for your help, James. I will only keep him for a moment."

"See that you do. Lots of work to be done round here and never enough hands." James continued on into the main stable house as Ruby went in search of the tack room.

She was not short on experience in stables. The years she'd helped Vi at Foldger's Foals were some of the best of her life, since her father had passed away.

The room she found Alex in was dimly lit but well-kept. Bridles and ropes hung upon the walls, organized and polished to perfection. Drake ran a tight ship in his stables, but that was to be expected of a marquis of such wealth. Alex faced away from her, hanging a freshly cleaned set of reins. The boy had mastered his deformity so completely that one had to look closely to see that one side moved a bit differently than the other. Involved in a carriage accident only a year into his life, Alex had spent much time concealing his injured arm which, due to limited resources at the time, had not been set correctly. As a result, his left arm was considerably weaker than the other. With much physical exertion, Alex's leg—which had also sustained damage— had acquired an adequate amount of muscle to disguise his slightly unbalanced walk. Many people would have written off children with such severe injuries, but not Viola. No, she funded a home—a sanctuary—for them. A place where they were loved and educated; a place where they were given a chance for a future.

"Alex." Ruby didn't want to startle the boy.

She was the one who was startled, for when he turned around, she was no longer looking at a boy, but a man. Alex had easily added a stone of muscle to his lanky frame. No longer did he resemble the boy with the limp arm who could calm any horse. Now, he appeared the man ready to take on the world and carve his own path in it.

"Miss Ruby?" He moved to her side immediately, taking her hand and bringing it to his lips. "It is so good to see you. I apologize for my appearance."

"Never mind your appearance." She took in his look: sturdy pants, untucked cream shirt, and boots that gleamed. His light brown hair, recently trimmed, was a bit tousled from exertion. He cut a dashing figure, without a doubt. It would not be long before he caught the eye of a very lucky young miss. "I'm only stopping by to see how you fare here."

"The marquis is a fair man, if not a bit eccentric and of a foul mood more often than not," Alex said. While the words settled Ruby's fears, they brought more questions to mind.

"Is he a kind man?"

"Does that matter over much?" he asked. "He is not in the habit of whipping his staff and mainly keeps to himself."

"Lady Haversham will be happy to hear that. Are you allowed any night off of work?"

"I am new here, Miss Ruby, and quite lucky to have employment at all. Maybe one day I will have a day off per week, but not yet." He looked down, a faint blush touching his cheeks. "Besides which, I fear I have no one to visit."

"Lady Haversham would love you to come by her townhouse," Ruby said. "When you have a free afternoon, that is."

"I will do my best to come round."

"I will tell her to expect you one afternoon." They looked at each other for a moment. Ruby knew it was time to take her leave, but she had so many more questions she needed answered if she was to either cross Drake off her list or, alternatively, learn that he was worth further investigation.

"Does the marquis entertain often?"

"Ummm, well, not since I have been here," Alex said, clearly puzzled at the question. "He seems to keep to himself mostly. Not many visitors either, now that I think on it. Why?"

"I only ask because Lord and Lady

Haversham have yet to receive an invitation to the marquis' residence."

Ruby cursed herself inwardly; she would need to improve her questioning tactics if she ever hoped to obtain useful information from anyone.

"Please let them know not to take offense," Alex said. "I have heard that Drake has not invited guests into his home for over sixteen years."

So, reclusive as well as a bit eccentric. "Does he ever leave his home?"

"Only for his weekly evening at White's." Alex grabbed a bridle from a nearby wooden box, signaling his need to return to his duties. "Please assure Vi—I mean Lady Haversham—that all is well here, and that Drake is a fair employer."

Ruby said her goodbyes and started back toward the Haversham townhouse, stopping to thank James on her way out of the stables.

She hadn't gained much information about the marquis from her brief conversation with Alex. Being a fair, eccentric, and reclusive man was not enough to cross him off her list. While she expected to find a cruel, uncaring rakehell, people often changed over time. No, she could not rule out the Marquis of Drake as a potential father just yet. Neither could she focus solely on him, though—there were other names on her list, and she meant to investigate each one.

CHAPTER 7

HAROLD TOOK IN his surroundings as he neared the building where he was to meet William. Situated firmly in Cheapside, not far from the docks, it was a likely place for a blacksmith's shop. It had nagged at him over the years that he hadn't made a point to visit his brother in London, but until recently he had not had business in the city to justify the trip. His sojourn in town the previous season had been so brief and filled with scandal, he hadn't had a moment to think about his family situation.

Admitting his envy at both his brothers' freedom was useless and energy misspent. He shouldn't dwell on the adventurous life of his eldest brother, Edward, who'd been given the funds to buy a commission into the King's navy. Or William's departure for London at the age of sixteen to apprentice with a blacksmith, eventually taking over the shop when the man died several years ago.

They'd both left him; at the time, he'd seen it as good fortune for the pair. No longer did they have to endure their father's wrath or swift-changing moods. At least they were far enough away to create a new life, even if that did not include him.

But his generosity of spirit evaporated around the time his father began his pedantic lectures on the life expected of a man of the cloth. It was then that Harold realized the enormity of his own circumstances. He did not blame his brothers for abandoning him to their father's whims and wiles, yet he'd held out hope that one day they would return for him.

Years older, and hopefully wiser, it would be beneficial for both him and William to set their childhood behind them and create a bond of brotherhood, similar to the relationship Harold shared with Brock. It was easy to cast the fault of their weakened bond on the vicar, but they were both men now—grown adults—with the choice to further their connection without their father's interference.

Increasing his pace, Harold turned a corner. The shop shouldn't lie much further ahead. In the late morning light, a figure leaned against the front of a building. Instinctively, Harold withdrew his hands from his pockets, ready for any altercation that might arise. Brock had warned him about traveling to this part of London alone, but Harold wanted his meeting with his brother to be as informal as possible. He had no idea why his brother was attempting to contact him now, but involving Brock in a family situation was not wise.

"Brother." William pushed away from the wall.

Harold was shocked to see his middle brother, dressed in filthy rags and his hair grown long past what their father would deem acceptable. Standing before him, the man was nearly unrecognizable. Without a thought, Harold drew him in for a hug. "William. I have missed you."

Further adding to Harold's dismay was the feel of bones beneath William's oversized clothes.

When William pulled back, Harold studied his face—thin with dark circles under his eyes, as if he hadn't slept since he'd left home.

"Is all satisfactory?" Harold asked, looking over his shoulder and further down the street. "Where is your shop? I'm sure you won't want to leave it unattended for long."

"I fear nothing is as it should be." William's shoulders fell.

Nothing had ever been but perfect for his elder brothers. "I don't understand."

"Please, come with me and you will shortly."

Harold followed his brother without a second thought. "Lead the way."

"'Tis not far."

True to his word, William stopped only three buildings down. They faced a boarded, half-burned building. Wood boards had been secured in place over open doorways and windows, preventing anyone from entering. The roof was caved in, most likely exposing what was left of the interior to the sun or rain, depending on the weather.

"Where are we?"

"This is what is left of my blacksmith shop," William mumbled. "Someone burned it to the ground shortly after Sir Jenkins died three years ago."

"Three years ago?" Harold was confused. "Why have I not heard of this—what have you been doing since then?"

"I did not have the heart to tell father, but when he sent word that you were traveling to London, I..." William's head hung, "...wanted to see you. I have a way to get back on my feet. Possibly open another blacksmith shop. But..." The last words were spoken so softly Harold was hard pressed to hear. "...I could use your help, brother."

Harold was dumbfounded. Firstly, his brother's meek demeanor was something he'd never witnessed; secondly, he had not a clue what William thought he could help him with. But honor bound him and he would help, if it was in his power. Their years of being pitted against each other in sibling rivalries at the hands of their father were still fresh in his mind. He knew he'd have to put those years behind him and start anew with William. Neither man deserved to be burdened by their past and an upbringing neither could change.

"Where have you been living since the fire?"

"Here and there." William studied the structure before them.

"I won't pretend to know what that means," Harold said. "Do you know who set the blaze?"

"Doesn't matter if I did."

"It matters greatly. There is recourse available; this is not the New World. We have laws. A legal system."

"The legal system does not work for all, and the fire was not aimed at me or mine. You see," William turned as if ready to be done with the empty shell of his previous life. "Sir Jenkins was heavily indebted to others, and they were tired of waiting for their coin."

"But if Jenkins were dead…"

"Then they held the next proprietor of the blacksmith's shop responsible. They wanted their money. When harassing Sir Jenkins' widow produced no return, they set their sights on me. I swear, I had no notion of what Jenkins did when he left the shop for the evenings."

Harold wondered if his brother told the truth—if the debts truly belonged to Jenkins, or to William himself. He shook himself out of that train of thought quickly, ashamed. His dealings with Miss Ruby were leading him to think everyone surrounding him was up to no good, which was no way to think of one's brother.

"What can I do, William?"

"I knew you would help." His words sounded as if they were more to convince himself than any belief in Harold's integrity. "You have always been the intelligent man in the family."

"Thank you."

"No, no. I truly mean that," William said. "And I have a way to pay back Sir Jenkins' debt and put coin in both our pockets."

"The men did not see his debt repaid when they burned his building?" Harold asked.

William shook his head. "I fear not."

"What exactly do you need from me?"

"Well, as they say, it takes coin to make coin."

"And you think I have coin?" No one but Brock knew of the tidy sum he'd made off his and Brock's wager in White's betting book the year before, which allowed him to travel to London, purchase a few new suits, and amble about town with Brock. Not even his father knew of his funds, for he would surely claim it for the vicarage's coffers.

William chuckled. "Oh, I know you haven't a shilling to your name."

Harold didn't know if he should feel relief at his brother's words or unease at what was to come next. "Then how do you propose…"

"I know that you know people who have unlimited funds."

Ah, so there was the hitch. "And who might those *people* be?"

"Why, Lord Haversham, of course. I know you advise him sometimes on his business dealings and transactions."

"That is true, although I have no notion of how you know this."

"Again, that's neither here nor there." William redirected the conversation. "If you could only put in a good word with him about me to a few of his business associates, it would help greatly."

"How can Brock's business contacts help you if you haven't the coin?"

"That was the next matter I wished to discuss with you."

"Well, go on." Harold needed to hear the whole of William's plan before he could talk his brother out of it.

William cleared his throat before continuing. "Brock has more funds than any man knows what to do with. It would not burden him overly if you were to—say—borrow a bit to invest with me. The sum would be trivial to a man such as him."

"Borrow?" Harold was not in the habit of asking Brock for any more than he'd already given—especially not coin. Once a friend became indebted financially to another, the dynamic of that friendship shifted forever. It was a line Harold never intended to cross.

"Yes, borrow, because—" William stood a little straighter, gaining confidence in the conversation. "—we will likely have the money to repay him within a month. And within several months, I will have the funds needed to repay Sir Jenkins' debt and open a new shop."

"I do not see how I benefit in this business transaction."

"Oh, that is quite simple," William said with growing enthusiasm. "You'll continue to manage the business, which would give you the means to continue living in London, unassisted by Lord Haversham."

His brother was playing on Harold's need to escape his family responsibility, giving him the means for an out; the ability to tell Brock to find another family to take over the vicarage at the Haversham estate. It was all he'd ever wanted. Harold suspected his brother hoped he'd jump at the chance.

But with Harold's smarts also came the ability to discern when something was too good to be true—and this moment was reeking of just that. Harold would not ask Brock for financial assistance, but that didn't mean Harold couldn't invest a bit of his own coin in the venture. William didn't need to know the money came straight from Harold's pocket.

"I'm intrigued. What do you need from me?" Harold asked.

"Only a meeting with a man within the shipping trade, preferably someone who manages the incoming and outgoing ships at the dock."

The request was actually quite simple, and much less than he'd expected. He and Brock had traveled to London before the season started to conduct a few business transactions. Brock had recently invested in several ships traveling to the New World with supplies, and had gladly introduced Harold to several men in the trade. Now, Brock stood to gain a hefty sum when the ships returned with goods not available in England.

"Am I correct in assuming this is a shipping venture?"

"Of the sort, yes."

"I will see what I can do," Harold said. "For now, do you have a suitable place to stay?"

"Please, do not let the clothes fool you. I'm not sleeping on the streets just yet."

It wasn't the clothes that led Harold to the conclusion that William was completely without funds, it was his appearance: the gaunt body and sunken cheeks, the dirt encrusted under his fingernails, his long, lank hair. But Harold knew better than to point these things out to William, who would only take offense. William had always been the most resourceful of the Jakeston boys, finding a place for them to stay on nights when their father's temper had taken a particularly nasty turn.

"You know where I am if you have need of anything," Harold said. "How shall I contact you?"

"For now, I have a room at the Carriage and Spirits House a few blocks over. If that changes, I will send word."

They stood side by side, neither fully turning to address the other. It said much about their relationship that Harold didn't have the time or the need to address, but he took the first step to rectify it all when he quickly hugged his brother again, pulling him tight. "It is good to see you, brother. I do hope we do not go long between visits again."

William stood stiff in his embrace, neither wrapping his own arms around Harold nor leaning into him, which was acceptable. Harold did not imagine they could mend all their differences over one talk about a business transaction and the sharing of a single confidence.

"We will be in touch, I have no doubt." William extricated himself. "I'm sure you have pressing matters to attend to, I'll not keep you any longer."

Harold thought the complete opposite. He should return to the townhouse, keep a close eye on Ruby, but instead he found himself inviting William to share a meal with him. When William politely declined, insisting he also had matters to attend to, they parted ways with the pledge to meet again within the fortnight.

CHAPTER 8

THE ROOM WAS stiflingly hot and the stale air settled heavily on her shoulders, making it difficult to breathe. Women dressed in exquisite gowns and overly accessorized hair pieces hung off the arms of every eligible man in attendance. The men appeared positively bored to the core, it being too early to retire to the card room for port and after-dinner cigars.

In true London style, chandeliers hung with glowing candles and fine-cut crystal from every ceiling. Their host had selected the ever-popular cream and blue hues for tonight's festivities, introducing their youngest daughter to the *ton*. Arrangements of cream and baby blue roses adorned every available surface and yards of gossamer cloth draped the walls of the ballroom.

Ruby glanced at her evening gown, happy she'd borrowed Vi's intricately beaded, soft sapphire-colored dress. It paired well with her deep brown hair and green eyes, or so Vi's maid,

Sarah, had insisted when she'd delivered it to Ruby's room earlier. Besides which, Sarah lamented, Vi would be unable to wear the dress for long due to her expanding waistline.

Her mother despised her acceptance of Viola's gifts. Part of Ruby wished she had the means to support herself, as well—but she knew the reason for her friend's generosity, and it wasn't charity or pity. They were both only children, never gifted with a sibling to dote upon. And up until recently, neither expected to marry nor have children, which drew them closer still.

Part of her envied Vi's new life: the chance at a family, a home of her own, security as she grew older. Most of all, she coveted the security a husband would bring. No woman envied living off the generosity of a distant cousin.

The scent of sandalwood cut through her thoughts, and she recognized Harold's presence before he spoke. "May I have this dance?"

The request sent a flood of warmth up her neck. It had been quite a while since she'd been asked to dance—if she'd ever truly been asked. "I fear my skills on the dance floor would embarrass us both, but thank you all the same," she said as she turned.

Her next words stuck in her throat. He was dressed simply in cloth of the richest black, a blue handkerchief the only spot of color. She found it suspect that it matched the shade of her dress perfectly. His hair, short with a slight wave and newly trimmed, fell perfectly above his collar. Her fingers longed to run through his hair to his broad shoulders.

His eyes also traveled the length of her, his smile signaling his appreciation of the view.

"Then perhaps a spot of sherry and a turn about the room?"

She'd planned to find the largest palm in the room and hide until Vi and Brock called her to depart. Currently, the pair swirled around the dance floor, Lord Haversham's smile lighting the room while Vi laughed at something he'd just whispered in her ear. They were still the object of much gossip and odd looks after their public spectacle the season before, but they took the attention in stride.

"Cat got your tongue again?" he asked.

"Mr. Jakes—" she started.

"We agreed on Harold, did we not?"

"Of course," Ruby said. "Harold, as I've said before, our continued acquaintance benefits neither you nor me. You are in search of a wife—"

He raised a brow. "That is presumptuous of you to say."

"—be that as it may, you are in *need* of a wife, and my reasons for being in London could not be further from finding an acceptable mate."

"And what *is* your reason for being in London, precisely?"

"You miss no opportunity to badger me. You are worse than the gossipmongers."

"You wound me, Miss." Harold held his hand over his heart. "If you find it in yourself to confide in me, I would not tell a soul your deepest secrets. You have my word."

Ruby had spent far too much time out in the open. Her continued stay in London depended on her ability to outmaneuver her mother. Standing at the center of the grand ballroom was the epitome of foolishness. She looked about the room. The refreshment table stood in a secluded alcove not far from the terrace doors.

"I believe I would enjoy a cool glass of sherry," she agreed. Then, she could extricate herself from the ballroom and seek refuge in the garden.

Harold, always the gentleman, held out his arm.

She slipped her hand into the crook of his arm and they made their way to the refreshment table. The track, which was the only way to describe it, was slow going as they fought their way through the hordes of people. While she didn't want to admit it, Ruby felt comfortable with him. He led without overtaking her, something she attributed to their shared childhood.

"Lovely evening, is it not?" he asked.

"Undoubtedly so, sir." She longed to question him about that afternoon. Had he read her papers? When she'd finally made it back to the room everything looked as it had when she'd left, but one could never be too certain. "The colors are divine, and Lord Spires' daughter is exquisite."

Harold laughed. "Exquisitely naive? Exquisitely annoying? Or exquisitely dull?"

"Possibly all three." They had no place mocking their hosts' daughter, she scolded herself. The pressure on London's youth was overwhelming, as Ruby herself knew, and she'd never been made the center of attention.

"She's been attached to Lord David most of the evening thus far," Harold said. "If he isn't careful, he'll be forced to make an offer for her hand before midnight."

She'd never understood the strict guidelines of the *ton*. If a woman danced more than twice with a gentleman in one evening they were practically betrothed. And heaven help the young man who danced with the same partner for two sets in a row. A midnight meeting in the girl's father's study would follow.

The advantages of being of a mature age and impoverished did not strike Ruby as such a terrible thing at the moment. No one expected her to dress to the height of fashion. She'd been able to move through the *ton* without anyone taking notice of her—except Harold, but he didn't count. He was likely in the same category as herself. The third son of a country vicar with nary a shilling to his name would not be hounded by the marriage-minded mommas of the *ton*. No girl sought to incite a compromising incident with a non-titled gentleman, no matter how powerfully connected he was. That his dearest friend was an elite member of society meant naught.

She caught a glimpse of him from the corner of her eye, stunned at the noble set of his chin. He was every inch the gentleman, even without the honor of a title.

"Do I have something on my face?" he asked, catching her.

She quickly moved her line of sight to the refreshment table. "Not at all. I was only pondering our similar circumstances." She knew the subject was a touchy one, but was at a loss for another suitable topic that did not include the weather.

"And what, pray tell, is our mutual circumstance?"

Ruby did not want to phrase things indelicately and insult him. "It is only that you and I are much the same. We—"

"…both have sterling personalities?" he cut in.

Startled at this comment, Ruby lost her train of thought. "Well…ummm…of course. I guess that is correct." Perhaps discussing the weather wasn't such a terrible idea after all.

"We both are blessed with understanding and supportive friends."

"Another true statement."

"Let me see, we are both—"

"What I mean is that we are both untitled, on the fringes of society, and with not a shilling to our names. Many must think we leech off of Vi and Brock."

"Most do not give us the time of day to notice we even exist." He laughed. "And how do you know I am without funding?"

His laugh and continued banter put her at ease. It was difficult to find a person she could not only relate to, but with whom she could be completely honest. "You think a woman cannot tell the signs of a less-than-rich man? It is fairly obvious even to someone like myself, who is not searching."

He eyed her as he waited for a servant to hand them refreshments. "Please instruct me on how I can appear more attractive to the fairer sex."

"Your attractiveness is not in question." She wanted to take the words back as soon as they left her mouth; the unintended compliment took their conversation to a new level. A level neither of them wanted, least of all herself. "What I mean to say is your physical attractiveness is not what gives you away."

"Go on." He took two glasses, handed one to Ruby, and steered them toward the terrace doors. "I find this conversation rather stimulating."

"Well, you are wearing last season's fashion."

"All right, yes, I did have this suit jacket tailored to fit last year," he confessed. "But your dress does not appear out of date."

Ruby looked down at her borrowed dress. "Oh, no. Not this dress. You are correct. This one is new, but I fear not mine to claim. This is compliments of Lady Haversham...and possibly her pity."

"Come now," he said. "Lady Haversham in no way pities you, her dearest friend."

"Then explain why her maid appeared at my door one hour before we departed with this dress and matching ribbon?"

"She believed the color would match your complex—"

"Exactly her reasoning, and why I know it is with feelings of pity that she loaned it." She'd told herself all evening this was not true. And she'd almost tricked herself into believing it.

"Be that as it may, you truly do look stunning."

"Thank you." Her face felt flushed at his continued attention. "Also, you arrived in a hired hack this evening."

"Very observant. I dare hope not every member of the *ton* is as watchful as yourself, yet I am flattered that you see fit to keep such a close eye on my comings and goings."

"As you said, most do not acknowledge our existence. That is, until one of their children takes a liking to us. Then they become as sharp-eyed as a hawk looking for his next meal."

"Are you proposing that my pleasing looks

and stellar personality are not enough to distract a fair maiden from the fact that we must walk to a ball because I am unable to afford a conveyance suitable for her—or any conveyance at all?" he asked with an utterly straight face.

Ruby was unsure if he jested, but the image it brought to mind had her smiling.

"What?" he asked with a startled expression. "You would not appreciate the exercise of walking about town? I promise I would carry all your shopping packages—that is, if either of us had the extra coin to purchase something. I fear you would have to cut and sew our clothes before long."

The conversation immediately conjured unwelcome thoughts. She pictured herself living with Harold at the vicarage not far from where she'd grown up. The image surprised her—in it she appeared content and happy. "Oh, but we would be unable to attend city life living so far from town. And I dare say I would be mending the neighboring lord's knickers to put food upon the table."

"No wife of mine will handle the knickers of another man—and especially not for money." He sounded affronted, and again she wanted to laugh at the absurdity of their conversation.

"Then I fear we will both starve, and the children will be off to some dreadful orphanage."

He stopped in his tracks, a few steps from the terrace doors. "Children? I have not asked you properly to marry me and you are already envisioning our children?"

She knew now that he jested, but could not help but sober as they eyed each other.

"Does the notion truly sound so dreadful?" he asked, more softly now.

"It is not that—"

"Then what?"

She broke eye contact and moved toward the doors and blessed fresh air, Harold close behind her. "It's not something I've planned for myself. It has nothing to do with you."

"Oh, what every woman says. 'It isn't you, it is myself.'" His voice rose to mimic the light, whiny voice of a woman.

She stepped outside, the warm night air washing over her. "Is that how I sound? And when has a woman ever told you that?"

Harold again grasped her elbow, angling her toward the steps leading in to the garden and away from the crowd milling the terrace. "There have been too many to name."

His words took her by surprise. What woman would turn him away? If he were pursuing her—and she could accept said wooing—she would count herself lucky.

But he wasn't pursuing her.

And she was not open to being wooed, now or ever.

Therefore, luck had no place in her life. In fact, luck had been working against her since she'd discovered her dubious parentage. It was time she refocused on her search. While she enjoyed Harold's company, it was not something she could fall into the habit of seeking. Their time together did not move her closer to her goal. Harold only put her in danger of discovery, which she could not afford.

"There really have not been that many."

"What?"

The light had decreased the further they moved away from the open doors. "Women who have turned me away."

He winked, telling her he played off her responses. The man was an expert at drawing her in, only to say something shocking, leaving her with the impression he jested but no real confirmation.

She ducked her head to hide her embarrassment at losing their conversation to her own musings. "That's good to hear."

They fell into silence as they descended the steps and continued walking. The night air, infused with the smell of flowers and citrus, washed over her. She could not think of a better feeling. They continued in a companionable quiet, both lost in their own thoughts.

RUBY WAS SILENT as they walked into the garden.

Harold was hesitant to intrude on her thoughts. Her face was at peace, not a hint of nervousness. It also gave him a chance to take her in: the tilt of her chin, her sureness of foot, and the hint of lines about her eyes and mouth. He knew them to be from laughing; how he wished he could see her smile and her eyes brighten at something he said or did.

But she always seemed guarded in his presence.

At present, however, he was content to walk beside her. No bickering, no snide remarks, and no cryptic words. They were only two people, walking amongst the fragrant flowers of an immense garden haven. He searched for something witty to say—anything to draw her attention, vanquish her troubles, and bring a smile to her lips.

As they continued down the path, he watched her touch flowers as she passed them, her fingertips grazing their petals, careful not to disturb them as she admired their silken texture. She stopped alongside a vibrant thicket of blue Canterbury bells, their blooms particularly bright. It was as if they'd spent their life within a hothouse, only to be brought outside for this special evening.

The shade matched Ruby's cream and blue evening gown—and also the pocket square currently nestled in his own jacket pocket. He'd thought the square a gift from Brock, but now knew it was Vi's attempt at subtle matchmaking.

He wondered if Ruby had noticed. He would ask, but feared her anxiousness would return and ruin the moment.

She leaned in ever so slightly to smell the blossoms, then continued down the path.

They rounded a bend and before them stood a clear, placid pond, with nary a ripple on its surface. The moon, high in the night sky, cast a glow upon the water that illuminated a small boat tied loosely to the dock.

Finally, Ruby looked up and when her eyes locked on the sight, she smiled.

"Do you remember the pond at the Haversham estate?" she asked.

"How could I forget," Harold said, keeping his voice low. "Brock and I played pirates every chance we got."

"Yes, I recall." She turned a serious face to him. "I was forbidden to play because I was a girl and you both said women at sea were unlucky and would sink your ship."

He would have laughed if her look was not so stern. "It's true—ask any sailor."

She returned her gaze to the water before them. "You know I watched you boys still."

"I did not."

"Oh, yes. I hid within the shrubs bordering the small lake and watched you and Brock play—sometimes for hours."

Her words shocked him. "Why?"

"What else did I have to do?" Her smile returned. "I would imagine setting sail with you both on an adventure to the New World or India, leave England behind for a life of the unknown." Her voice held a sadness that did not match her smile. If the lighting were better, he wondered if he'd see that her smile did not reach her eyes, either.

Harold looked to the small boat, judging its buoyancy. "It is not too late."

"Whatever do you mean?" she asked.

"Sail with me," he said as he took her hand. "We can leave now, if only for a few short minutes."

"I don't know…"

"Allow yourself to forget the here and now—to be just Ruby, the girl I remember, and Harold—childhood friends."

Her eyes held skepticism when they met his. "I do wish life was that simple."

"It can be. Is it so hard to let go of the things one cannot change?"

"I could ask you the same question." Instead of turning back toward the house as he expected, she took his proffered hand and continued to the dock.

"Maybe it is unfeasible to permanently forget one's life, but…" He smiled as he assisted her into the small boat. "…we can both agree to a short time together, without the questions and concerns of our daily existence. Could we do that?"

He held his breath as he awaited her reply.

"I think that is quite possible."

He stepped in the boat behind her, helping her into the seat at the front of the craft. Then he took his place facing her at the bow of their small vessel. He reached out and untied the line keeping the boat at dock, then took the oars in hand.

"Where to, my lady?"

"Well, my lord," she countered. "I would enjoy a trip to Paris... Perhaps see the latest fashions or visit the Louvre."

"And what if I do not seek a turn about fashionable Paris, but a sojourn in the wilds of Africa?"

"Africa? Who would enjoy the dreadful heat of the desert?" she asked. "I do believe we are not suitably attired for such a journey."

"But we are for Paris?"

She turned a serious look to him. "I do believe you are correct."

With the oar, Harold pushed away from the dock. As he started to row, waves rippled, disturbing the serenity of the water. In the distance he could hear the strains of a waltz and the laughter of the many men and women in attendance, but on the lake, it was only the two of them.

"May I interest you in a peaceful row about a pond in the middle of a garden, just out of sight of a very busy ballroom?"

"That would be lovely, Harold."

She'd dropped the imagined 'my lord,' and that made him happy. He was only Harold, or Mr. Jakeston. A title was not in his future, nor did he envy those who held them.

The quiet of the night was only broken by the gentle slap of the oars as Harold deftly rowed them to the far side of the pond and away from any prying eyes of the *ton* who might also be strolling about the lush garden.

He searched for a safe topic of conversation—one without questions or accusations. He couldn't ask how she was enjoying London, nor if she planned to retire to her parents' home come the Christmas holiday.

"How are you enjoying your work with the Foldger's Foundling House?" There was no more neutral of a subject, and Harold truly wanted to know how Vi's home was doing after all the children had relocated from London to the country.

A spark lit her eyes. "Oh, the children are adapting splendidly. They're learning to ride. The girls to sit a proper side saddle and the boys to hunt. The kitchen is fairly large, so Mrs. Hutton has taken to giving lessons to all who are interested in the art of meal preparation."

"Do you and Lady Haversham plan to travel there anytime soon?" He hoped his question was subtle. He found he was very interested in her future plan, and hoped they included her continued presence in London.

"Most definitely before the winter weather becomes too harsh," Ruby replied. "We must outfit all the children with suitable clothes for the cold season."

"Ah, so you enjoy your responsibilities there?"

"Very much so, yes."

"I have heard Brock has many plans for renovating the house, as well."

"Vi would like to help not only children with maladies, but also unwanted street children. To do that, Lord Haversham has commissioned the addition of a dormitory building that will enable Mrs. Hutton to care for another thirty children." As she spoke, Ruby let the passing water caress her fingertips, much as she'd lightly touched the flowers.

He tore his eyes from the sight and refocused on their conversation. "Mrs. Hutton is truly a saint."

"That she is. I cannot think of a more worthy calling for a woman of her stature."

"And you?"

"And me, what?" She sat a bit straighter at the question.

"What is your calling?" Harold was unsure if talk of their future was also unacceptable for this time 'at sea.'

A pensive look crossed her face and he wondered—not for the first time—what secrets she held; what troubled her so.

"I fear I am much like our little boat here."

"How so?" He paused his paddling to better hear every word.

"I am adrift, with little direction, dependent on those around me. Much like our direction can be altered by a simple breeze, so can my course be changed by a few words."

It was more insight into her life then she'd thus far shared, yet the words only confused him. Her life, compared to his own, seemed trouble-free and without responsibilities or commitments. She could live wherever she deemed agreeable, attend social functions with no reservations, and commit herself to any cause she found fulfilling. He sensed there was more to her world than he was privy to, but he was at a loss as to how he might show her he could be trusted with her struggles.

"I am here to talk if you need someone to confide in."

"That is very kind of you." She looked to the far shore they'd paddled from. With the gesture, he knew their moment was gone and the real world had invaded once again.

"Shall we return, my captain?"

She laughed, and the light mood returned. "I believe we have no other choice. The evening grows late and I expect Vi and Lord Haversham will notice our disappearance before long."

Harold didn't relish relinquishing her to the crowded ballroom. As he maneuvered them back across the water to the dock, he watched her faraway expression return and tried once more to pull her from her own troubles. "May I take you for a ride in Hyde Park tomorrow?"

"That would be lovely, but—"

He'd known there would be some reason she would enlist to call off.

"—Vi and I have a busy shopping excursion planned."

"I do understand," Harold said. The bow tapped the dock. "We have arrived. I do hope you enjoyed your time at sea."

Ruby stood on unsteady feet. "We were neither besieged by pirates nor taken down by merfolk, so I believe our voyage was most agreeable."

They made their way back to the ballroom much as they had when they'd left, yet, now Ruby clutched Harold's offered arm and he noticed her subtle glances in his direction.

Harold suppressed his smile and hoped they

could possibly turn a new corner. He was shocked to realize he hadn't thought about her suspicious behavior and secretive activities since they'd descended the steps into the garden.

He was optimistic that their breakthrough would last past this evening and into the coming days.

CHAPTER 9

HAROLD HELD THE newly arrived letter—or should he say letters—clutched in his hand. He wanted to flip a table or put his fist through a wall, but that would accomplish nothing but damaging something that wasn't his to destroy. Violent outbursts solved nothing, and only compounded the preexisting issues. Every time his father had scolded, beaten, or berated his children, it had changed nothing. They couldn't live up to his impossible moral standards, and Harold and his brothers certainly never respected the vicar for his aggressive displays. The amount of times the good vicar had thrown his supper plate against a wall had not improved their mother's cooking skills.

Parsons, Brock's valet, had just delivered the morning's post to his room. Today, Harold had received three letters from his father, each demanding his attendance in the country. Yesterday, one letter had arrived; two notes the day before that.

He couldn't help but think his father would have ample time to complete all of his duties—things he claimed he needed Harold's assistance to do—if he spent more time attending to them and less penning threats to his son.

He'd need to ask William if he too received never-ending letters of complaint.

Alas, his father more often than not made zero sense.

The idiocy of the suggestion that the good vicar could not handle the repairs needed was unfathomable. His father had a number of strong, willing parishioners eager to help him, if only he would call on them.

Brock informed him that funds had been allotted to the family church for much-needed renovations now that the Haversham stables were completely remodeled. But there was no rush, as materials had yet to be ordered from the local mill.

No—Harold would not fall prey to his manipulative behavior. He would not run home. He would not bend under his father's thumb. He would not let another dictate his life.

Not yet, at least.

One day he would have to return home and take over the responsibilities his father had relegated to him. He'd do his utmost to continue on in the family vicarage, serving Brock and his growing family, as his father and grandfather had before him. He would not shirk his duties forever.

But today was not that day.

And if the business venture William had proposed was successful, then a new course for his future may very well be possible. It was imperative that they start immediately.

Harold balled the thin papers in his hands as he paced his room.

He needed more time. Before he resigned himself to a life of mundane routine, he needed to live. To experience all the world had to offer. Would it make his future more tolerable? He didn't know. But he did know his father had never traveled further than a few hours' horseback ride from their home in all his life. He'd never sampled the delights of London, the relaxation of Bath, or the thrill of crossing the Scottish border into a foreign country. Harold had barely accomplished the first and knew London held so much more for him than he'd seen thus far.

The vicar had been happy to marry Harold's mother, the daughter of a neighboring farmer, while Harold dreamed of so much more for himself.

Harold stopped his pacing and dropped into the chair situated before the window in his room. The sun shone bright, sitting high in the sky. The sight usually lifted his spirits and filled him with hope for the day, but since his arrival in London he'd felt oddly unfulfilled. His encounters with Ruby were the only thing that made him feel useful, alive. Now, with William's plan, he hoped to again instill a sense of purpose to his daily life.

A knock sounded at his door. Not waiting for his permission to enter, Brock pushed the door wide and strolled into the room.

"Go ahead and walk in like you own the place," Harold muttered, trying to shake his gloomy mood.

"Did you forget I do own the place?"

"And what if I had been indecent?"

"I would have called everyone within shouting distance to come take in the sight," Brock jested. "But they would only get a peek. I like to keep you for myself." He followed the statement with a wink and sat in the chair opposite Harold, stretching out his booted feet and crossing them at his ankles.

They sat in silence, Brock's eyes on him, but Harold refused to shift his gaze from the window.

"You are killing me," Brock finally said. "What has you in such a sour mood?"

Harold held up his hand, the letters still wrapped tightly in his fist.

"Ah. I heard you've been receiving quite a few letters from home. I hoped they were from a lady friend, and not the indomitable Vicar Jakeston," Brock said. "But from your expression and mood recently, they must be from the latter."

Harold grudgingly looked to his friend. "Latest word is that my father's workload has never been weightier, while his strength continues to wane."

Brock was silent a moment. He appeared vexed. "There's no reason your father's burden should be any heavier than it has been in years past. If anything, it should be lighter—I've been quite attentive to his needs. The last I saw him, he had his shirtsleeves rolled and a crew of able-bodied parishioners working alongside him. But I understand if you feel you must retire to the country to attend his demands."

Harold laughed, startling himself at the madness of the sound. "Oh no, my father will not get his clutches on me that easily."

"But if he needs help—"

"He does not. And what's more, you know he does not—you've made your point."

"We could ride there at any time to check on your family," Brock persisted, more serious now. "If you are concerned, we would be back by sundown, assuming all is well."

"You know he will not let me return to London once he has me home. If you think otherwise, you are as foolish as everyone says."

"Who says I am foolish?" Brock asked.

"That's what you take from that?"

"Of course. I care little for your family drama, but if someone speaks ill of me, I am very interested."

Harold knew it was all meant to be jest. Before Brock's disappearance and then after his return last year, he'd been very involved in Harold's life. They shared everything, including their family struggles. There was not another being who knew Harold's struggles as Brock did. There was not another person with whom he could share all he was, all he wanted, and all the demons that held him back.

"You do not have to take over the vicarage." Brock's tone remained uncharacteristically serious. "I can find another vicar to serve my family. The place is fairly obsolete, anyways, for I am rarely about the estate." Since Brock had found Lady Haversham, he'd let his own demons go in favor of love and peace.

Harold didn't know how to respond. He wanted to jump at the chance to wipe his hands of the responsibilities he'd never wanted. He sat a little taller, the weight of expectation lifted from his shoulders, but with that came the daunting question of 'what then?' The vicarage had been a burden, but it had also provided security—the knowledge that some semblance of stability was in his future, just waiting for him to accept his role. Without it, he must forge his own path, find his own way in the world.

And that scared the hell out of him.

He wasn't ready to give up his guaranteed livelihood.

Yet, his meeting with William brought new opportunities to light—a way of life not dominated by his father.

Brock took his silence to mean exactly what it did: Harold wasn't ready to make any decision either way. "You only need say the word, Harold."

"Thank you." He was happy to know his way out remained open, even if he wasn't prepared to take advantage of it just yet.

"Enough of this moping." Brock stood. "The women are shopping for the afternoon, which means we are left to our own devices."

"Oh, really?" Harold asked.

"Yes. Shall we see what kind of trouble we can stir up?"

"What do you have in mind?" Harold laughed, determined to forget his own troubles, at least for one afternoon.

"By trouble, I meant business," Brock said. "I'm meeting with Lord Yorkton about the acquisition of a rather important broodmare and I thought you would like to join me."

"Of course you did." Harold enjoyed accompanying Brock to his many meetings about town. It helped hone his skill at negotiations and kept his mind working. And of course Brock never complained if Harold was able to gain what he wanted at a far better price. "How much do you wish to acquire the animal for?"

"Very astute question, my man. The price is not overly important to me, but the acquisition itself is. You see, the mare is a gift for Lady Haversham."

"Ah, now I see."

Brock nodded. "I suppose you do. I know how very much she misses her horses. While running a foal ranch is impossible with my obligations to Parliament, I'm sure she would enjoy having a mare here in town, possibly breeding her with Sage."

There was only one thing Brock loved more than his stallion, Sage, and that was his wife. Her happiness came before all.

"That's commendable of you. When shall we depart?"

"Lord Yorkton is expecting us shortly."

The name registered with Harold. He'd been in the man's study only nights before to escape the tediousness of the forced social engagement—and there had his first encounter with Ruby. Odd that Brock would have a meeting with one of the men on Ruby's mysterious list. Maybe he should be concerned for Brock's well-being where Ruby's activities were concerned, as well.

"Then let us be off," Harold said. "We wouldn't want to keep the good lord waiting, I hear he has an awful temper." The thought occurred to him that just possibly, he would be afforded a look into the man's study, and could turn up whatever Ruby had been searching for.

RUBY WALKED BESIDE Vi, their arms laden with packages, navigating their way to their waiting carriage. The shops were busy with women selecting the perfect fabric for a walking gown, or kid gloves for an evening out, or men selecting the perfect handkerchief to match their lady love's newest acquisition. Because of the crowd, Vi had instructed her footman to wait by the carriage for their return. Hence their loaded arms and Ruby's sore feet.

"Are you sure you feel up to carrying all those packages?" Ruby asked.

"I am with child—and not far along, I might add—not helpless. The exercise will do me good."

Her dearest friend could shop like no other. Granted, they'd spent most of the morning purchasing shirts, skirts, and shoes for children at Foldger's Foundling House, therefore Ruby's aches and pains could be attributed to good deeds and not the spoiled, selfish antics of the wealthy elite, which pleased her immensely.

"After we drop these off, we must find suitable material for new bedclothes. The children will be quite excited if Sarah and the other maids make new covers for their beds." The excitement in Vi's voice was contagious.

Ruby laughed as she shifted the box she held to her other arm. "Oh, we can make lovely purple ones for the girls and green for the boys. You know how Abby adores purple. I can start on them right away."

"Oh no, you do not, Ruby St. Augustin," Vi scolded. "I will not give you another excuse as to why you cannot accompany me out in the evenings."

Ruby knew her explanations were running thin, but she'd hoped to have a few more evenings free to continue her search. "I swear I do not know what you speak of."

"You're incorrigible!" Vi chuckled. "I bring you to London and you barely leave the townhouse. I had to drag you out this morning kicking and complaining."

The only reason Ruby had accompanied Vi today was because she knew her mother's penchant for sleeping late after an evening out, thus greatly reducing the risk they would run into Lady St. Augustin during their excursion. "How could I possibly pass up the opportunity to spend Lord Haversham's money?" Ruby asked, deflecting the conversation.

"I rarely pass up the opportunity myself," her friend confided in a whisper. "Oh, there is the coachman now. Jacobs, thank you for waiting for us."

He took the packages from both women and stored them in the boot of the carriage.

Vi straightened the front of her pink morning dress and rubbed her gloved hands together. "Well, where to now?" she asked.

Ruby looked up and down the street, hoping to see a tea shop close by. Vi could use a few moments of rest, no matter how much she claimed the opposite. "I fear I do not know the area—" Her words were immediately cut off when she spied her mother and Lady Darlingiver exiting a shop a few doors down from where they stood. The women turned in their direction.

Without a word of warning to Vi, Ruby launched herself in the carriage, sinking to the floor and pulling the door shut to hide herself from view. She had good reason to be in London, true enough, but that didn't mean she intended to inform her mother of her presence.

"Lady Haversham," Ruby's mother called.

"How lovely to see you. Are you out alone?" Ruby could picture Pearl St. Augustin and Lady Darlingiver peering around for Vi's escort. It was highly improper for a woman of the *ton* to venture out without her husband, another member of the *ton*, or her maid.

She loathed putting Vi in this situation, but now was not the time for her mother to find her in town against her specific wishes.

"Ummm, well," Vi stalled, and Ruby knew her friend was racking her brain. "No, I am just awaiting Lord Haversham's return. He insisted on purchasing something special for me—and how could I refuse such a grand gesture?"

"Of course, you cannot," Lady Darlingiver gushed. "Your father and I hope to see you this evening. If I didn't know better, I would think you've been avoiding our company of late."

Ruby had begged Vi not to invite Lady Darlingiver, or her mother over for tea, and had refused an invite to their home as well. It was unfair of her and was obviously causing ill will between Vi and her family.

"Quite the contrary, Lady Darlingiver," Vi continued. "I have been busy preparing Foldger's Foundling House for the winter months—and for my own child's birth. I fear my carriage is filled to the brim with supplies."

Ruby knew both women turned their noses up at the thought of any activity resembling work. A bit of charity fundraising dirtied their hands more than they saw appropriate for the upper class. But the mention of another Haversham had both women cooing in delight.

"Oh, you should call upon Ruby any time you need assistance." It was Pearl speaking now. "I am sure she'd be willing to move to Foldger's

Hall once again to help you or come to you once you retire to Haversham House for the new arrival."

Leave it to her mother to hire her own daughter out for manual labor, Ruby thought.

"Oh, I wrote her just the other day and she volunteered to sew *thirty-two* new bed covers for the children." Vi added extra inflection to the amount of bed covers Ruby would be responsible for making, her punishment for abandoning Vi to the clutches of the two matronly women.

Ruby saw weeks of sore fingers and cramping hands in her future.

"Well, I must be going," Vi said. "Oh, look, there is Brock now."

Ruby peeked over the side of the carriage and out the window, hidden from detection by the drawn shade. The women both looked in the direction Vi pointed and waved, trying to get a glimpse of Vi's handsome husband.

"He is waving me over," Vi continued. "He must have a very special surprise for me. It was lovely seeing you both." She curtseyed to Lady Darlingiver and nodded to Ruby's mother.

"We can accom—"

"There is no need for you to go out of your way. He is right there, not thirty feet away." Vi tried her best to deter the women from following her. "Plus, you are headed in the opposite direction. You both are ever so busy, I'm sure."

"Well, yes, Lady Darlingiver, shall we be on our way?" Pearl asked.

"Very well," the other lady responded. "Your father is so excited about the babe. Do come visit soon."

"Of course, my lady."

Ruby sighed when the women moved down the street, disappearing into the milling crowd.

"Ruby, you get your sissy hide out here right this instant!"

She couldn't tell if her friend was raging mad or on the verge of laughter. Raising her head further, Ruby pulled the shade back and peeked out the window.

Vi stood on the sidewalk, hands on her hips. "How dare you desert me to those two vultures?"

"I know you're angry—"

"Do not presume to know what I am." Vi cut her off, but the tension drained from her body. "It is not that you disappeared per se, it's that you left me with little option but to lie. You know I despise lying."

It was true. Guilt filled Ruby. Ever since her friend had deceived Brock into thinking she was someone else, Vi had a very strict 'no lying' policy. "It was not my intention."

"Oh, come out here now."

Ruby used her perch a few feet above the crowded street to search for her mother, but the women had disappeared. Probably into another shop full of frivolous items they didn't need.

"They're gone, I assure you," Vi encouraged her. The footman stepped forward, opened the door, and set the steps down for Ruby. She eyed him, then the steps, and finally Vi before stepping down. "Let us seek refreshments before I pass out on this very street."

"You said you were feeling quite the thing today and that exercise would do you good," Ruby said in alarm, scrambling to Vi's side.

Vi only chuckled.

After the excitement of the morning, Ruby

reflected that it was time she found a more efficient way to assess her list of potential fathers. The reality of one's dire situation is no clearer than when huddled on the floor of a carriage, hiding from one's own flesh and blood. And sneaking into homes, whether occupied by the owner or not, was risky. She needed to find a way to manage that risk...and quickly.

CHAPTER 10

HAROLD STARED DOWN at the three aces and pair of kings before him. Not the first lucky hand he'd been dealt that evening, and hopefully not the last. He itched to place his cards face-up on the table and display his winning hand, but instead he kept his face passive and his fingers steady.

All Harold needed was a few more solid hands and his purse would increase tenfold in just one evening. The notion of winning the money he needed to fund his brother's venture without dipping into his ever-dwindling savings was too good to pass on. When Brock had invited him to White's for an evening of gambling, Harold had jumped at the chance. He'd always been a superior card player—and all activities that involved some risk, including business ventures. Brock liked to jest that was the true reason for their lasting friendship—that, and the standing invitation to stay at the Haversham townhouse.

The Marquis of Drake, Andrew Penton, held his hand close to his chest. Harold was unsure whether it was to hide his cards from view or because his eyes had deteriorated with age. Regardless, Harold was certain he held the finest hand, just as rumor held he always had the finest woman upon his arm. His reputation as a rakehell of his time was legendary, even to those who'd grown up away from society's gossip rags.

Daring a look to his left, Brock eyed him closely. After playing for many years together — and winning their brothers' allowances as soon as the coins hit their pockets — Brock knew Harold's tells. The smirk on his friend's face told Harold Brock was aware he held the top cards, but he was willing to risk his own coin to see what cards he laid down. Brock pushed a short stack of notes toward the center of the table. They both looked to Drake for the next move. With no hesitation, Drake, too, pushed money into the ever-growing pot, leaving only a few coins and a note or two in front of him.

Then, it was Harold's turn. He pondered his cards, giving Drake the impression that he was apprehensive about whether to add his own coin at the risk of losing it all. For more dramatic effect, he swept his forearm across his forehead as if wiping away moisture caused by the tension of the situation. Keeping his breathing even despite the blood running through his veins faster than a star flying across the night sky, he also pushed his money forward.

At the same moment, Brock sat back in his chair and let out a wallop of excitement. "Well, gentlemen," he said. "I do believe we have a winning pot like none have seen in this club in over a decade."

Harold didn't take his eyes off Drake as he waited for the elderly lord to show his cards.

Hopefully, his losing cards.

For a moment, the blink of an eye, Harold pondered the ramifications if the hand did not go in his favor. It would mean losing half of the coin he'd managed to save. He'd be forced to return to his father's home long before he'd planned.

Harold let out his breath when Drake threw down his cards, a hand similar yet far inferior to his own.

Brock threw in his own cards, facedown, admitting his defeat.

Keeping his excitement at bay, Harold laid down his own hand: a full house. He gathered the mound of notes and coins and pulled them across the table, all the while remaining composed. It was ungentlemanly to boast of one's luck at the card table—not to mention it would scare off other players. And Harold needed other players besides Brock, if he was to increase his capital.

"Lucky break," the marquis muttered. "Haversham, are you responsible for bringing this upstart swindler into our club?"

"Oh, don't be such a poor sport. You know as well as I that if one is willing to chance their money on the flip of a card, one must also be prepared to see it leave in the pocket of another." Brock chuckled. "I lost my coin just as you."

"I do hope the man doesn't lack so many manners that he walks away without giving me the opportunity to relieve him of my funds."

Drake spoke as if Harold wasn't sitting

across the table from him. Men of the *ton* were a peculiar breed. "I assure you, your lordship, that I have no other place to be this evening. I will continue our game until you're ready to depart, or I lose all my funds and must beg more from Lord Haversham."

"It's good you know your place, boy," the marquis said. He pushed his losing cards toward Brock, who gathered them to shuffle and start anew. "It's difficult to find men nowadays who recognize their position in society. Is it not, Haversham?"

"Oh, Mr. Jakeston knows his place very well, indeed," Brock said as he winked in Harold's direction. "I have kept him on a tight rein since we were children."

"See that you continue to do just that," the elderly man huffed. "We cannot have these tuft hunters taking over our country."

Harold wanted to laugh at the old man's dated reference to social climbers. If a person could not trace back their lineage three hundred years, then they were obviously setting their sights too high in the marquis' opinion.

"Shall I deal, gentlemen?"

"Very well." Drake eyed Harold suspiciously, as if he expected cards to fall from his shirtsleeve.

Harold nodded his agreement, as well. As Brock shuffled the cards and dealt, Harold looked about the room. He'd hoped a few more men would join their game and increase his potential winnings, but the club was quiet for this time of the evening.

Picking up the two cards dealt to him thus far, Harold saw he held a mediocre set of cards, at best. A queen of hearts and an eight of clubs.

He looked around the table to judge the first reactions of Drake and Brock before picking up his last three cards. He knew the difficulty of hiding one's natural responses—whether good or bad—at first. True to form, a smirk crossed Drake's face before his expression became passive. He most likely held a pair or a set of suited cards.

A round of betting ensued quickly, increasing the pot to more than Harold had in front of him. He picked up his remaining three cards, hoping they rounded out his hand. When he saw another queen and eight amongst the three, he wanted to raise his fist in triumph. Instead he took in the room again, as if his interest lay everywhere but on their game.

A flash of movement outside the front window caught his attention. The evening was late, and the streets of London were not safe for a lone pedestrian, though likely it was naught but a street urchin trying to get a glimpse of the goings-on inside such an exclusive club. Nothing moved outside the window for so long that he thought he'd imagined it.

Harold returned to the game, pushing in only enough to raise the pot without scaring Drake off.

Again, a movement caught his eye. Focusing on the front once more, he finally found what it was. A face was pressed firm to the glass, searching the room. There was very limited area to see into the club from that vantage point, and heavy drapes made it nearly impossible at times. A man leaving the club pushed the door wide, illuminating the dim walk outside the window and, with it, the person intently looking in.

Harold's cards slid from his grip. He

scrambled to right them before his opponents saw his superior hand. He'd know that dark hair and those green eyes anywhere.

Ruby, so preoccupied with her search of the room, didn't notice Harold staring at her as she focused on each face in the room.

"Bloody hell," Harold exclaimed.

"Is it that bad?" Brock asked.

"Oh, no, it is just I must go—"

Brock turned to see what had caught Harold's attention and the room moved in slow motion. The woman was so distracted that she didn't notice she'd garnered attention from inside the club. If Brock recognized her—which he would—then she'd have much explaining to do. But as much as Harold wanted to know what she was up to, he didn't want that at the expense of Lady Haversham's friendship with Ruby.

"Come now," Drake huffed. "We are in the middle of a hand. Haversham, you vouched for this fellow. I have a mind to have you both expelled from this club."

At Drake's threat, Brock turned back to the game and Harold sighed.

"No, I will gladly finish this hand." Harold pushed all his coin to the center of the table.

Brock threw his cards in, not taking the bait.

Drake, on the other hand, let out a loud chuckle and pushed his own coin in to match Harold's bet.

He doubted the man had a hand better suited than his own, but Harold didn't have the time to find out.

When the marquis laid his cards flat upon the table, Harold did the same, pushing his chair back. His hand far surpassed Drake's, and he wondered if the man only called to see if Harold had the nerve to challenge him.

"Ah, well, I am sad to say I am out of time," Harold said as he stood. "I do thank you both for the rousing game. I must be going now."

He addressed the Marquis of Drake. "To be fair, I'm leaving my winnings with Haversham so you do not feel cheated out of the opportunity to win your money back."

This gave Brock no other option but to remain at the table, freeing Harold to leave without the possibility of his friend tailing him.

He turned to leave, knowing Brock's stare held too many questions—none he would be able to answer at this moment. He only hoped his retreating frame blocked the view of Ruby in the window.

As he stalked toward the entrance, Ruby's gaze finally landed on him. Her eyes widened, and in the next instant she was gone. Pushing the door wide, Harold stepped onto the walk and looked to the left, in the direction she'd fled.

She wasn't on the walk as he'd expected.

A hack moved swiftly down the street.

RUBY SUNK TO the floor of the filthy hack as soon as she jumped in, quite possibly ruining her dress.

"Back to Haversham townhouse, quickly please." She breathed deeply when the hack pulled away from the curb. She inched up onto the seat behind her, but kept her head low. It was possible Harold hadn't seen her escape into this particular carriage. Truly, he might not have recognized her at all in the sparse light.

But the expression on his face as he'd rushed

from the club told her otherwise. She had never seen him as anything but calm and reserved, with that usual carefree manner. Tonight, however, she had seen fire in his eyes, fury even—and something else she didn't recognize.

She dared a look over the seat and behind the carriage. The dust rising in their wake from the carriage wheels made it impossible to see if someone followed.

Relief flooded her. Maybe she hadn't been caught...in the act, at least.

It was time she reassessed her plan, possibly put a bit more thought into her ideas before she actually acted on them. Her goal tonight had been fairly simple: confirm that the Marquis of Drake was safely ensconced at White's, whether gaming or drinking, so that she could return to his home and look around.

It should have taken very little thought. Unfortunately, she'd put far too *much* thought into it, hoping to avoid getting caught as she had a few nights before. Ruby had verified the Drake's carriage was parked in the stable, his livery enjoying a spot of cards themselves with other servants awaiting their masters. Instead of leaving posthaste, getting a peek inside the Drake townhouse, and returning home with none the wiser, she'd had to see the man. Whether it was to verify he was seated at a table and busy for the next few hours or for her own selfish need to set eyes on him, Ruby did not know.

It was much the same with every man she looked into. She dreamed at night of laying eyes on a man and knowing, beyond a doubt, that he was her kin. Her nighttime musing spiraled out of control from there. Many nights she awoke with a smile on her face after the man in her dreams also recognized her for who she was, his long-lost flesh and blood returned to him. He would take her in his arms, hug her, and tell her how long he had searched for her over the years. But the smile faded quickly; her father had known of her existence, and he'd never come for her.

Now, she was flying back to the Haversham townhouse in case Harold and Lord Haversham had indeed caught a glimpse of her. She would wait there for a bit, using the time to regroup. Then, she'd see if time still allowed her to complete her task. If it wasn't tonight, she'd have to wait another few days for Drake to leave his house again. Curse the man for being such a recluse and making it so bloody hard to gain entry to his home. Alex could only provide so much information and access before he too put himself in danger of detection.

Ruby would never forgive herself if he lost his position due to her own carelessness. Alex had shared more than Ruby deserved, seeing as how she couldn't tell him why she needed the information. She could not repay his kindness by leading Harold straight to Drake's residence.

The trip back to the townhouse gave her time to ponder what she'd seen. Drake was a lord like any other. She could still see the quality of his clothes, despite him being seated at a table. Nothing about the man struck her as familiar. He was much younger than his form gave off. His frail, stooped stature added at least ten years to his appearance. She would be at a loss for what her mother saw in the man, *if* Drake was the one she'd been searching for.

She called to the coachman to drive round to

the stables when they drew close to the townhouse. It would be far easier to slip inside through the stables unnoticed than entering the front door for all the household staff to witness—and gossip about.

The hack stopped one house down from the Haversham townhouse, in the alley.

"That'll be six pence, miss." The hand he held out to accept his fare was as grimy as Ruby knew her dress was from her time on the floor.

The suspicious look the driver gave her matched the one she'd given his outstretched hand.

Not wanting to waste any more time, Ruby dropped the money in his palm and crawled down from the conveyance, neither seeking nor wanting his assistance.

"Thank ye."

She nodded before making her way back to the Haversham stable, careful to keep to the shadows. Hiring a hack in London—while not too problematic—was tiresome in the extreme. One never knew if they'd make it safely to their destination or not. Thankfully, her driver this night was versed in the streets of London and delivered her home in one piece.

All that was left was to assure herself that no one within the townhouse knew of her departure and subsequent re-arrival, retrieve her lock picks from her stationery desk, and then she could be on her way again.

One day, she hoped to get things right and have just one evening go as she'd planned. With any luck, she'd find out who her father was, give herself the peace of mind needed to resume her life, and put this unfortunate time behind her.

The house was quiet as she left through the

kitchen door, careful to pull it fully shut so Cook did not suspect someone had used it after she'd retired to bed. It would greatly hamper Ruby's ability to come and go if the door was suddenly locked to her. Picking the lock on a desk may be within her limited ability, but the one on this door would take quite a bit more coaxing, and would likely garner some attention with the noise.

The stable was as abandoned as the house. Lord Haversham and Vi were out for the evening and not expected to return for several hours. Most of the stable hands were either abed or out seeking their own evening entertainment.

The lane behind the townhouse was mere steps away, and her intended destination only a few minutes' hurried walk. Perhaps her evening might just improve after all.

A shadow stepped in front of her and her hopes plummeted deep into the dirt beneath her feet.

"We must stop meeting in such dubious surroundings. I much prefer an evening meal or afternoon tea together. But a nightly stroll is also suitable to my tastes."

CHAPTER 11

"I TRULY DO not know why I let you drag me into this reckless search." Harold squeezed between two pieces of furniture draped in white cloth and paused. "Which way now?"

"Oh, that is rich!" Ruby hissed. "I did not ask for your assistance, nor do I want it. In fact, I would take no offense if you called off now." She'd tried to lead him off by telling him she was only visiting the stables, but he'd called her bluff. That had left her with only two choices: Miss her chance to search the marquis' home while he was out, or take Harold with her. If she was to expedite her plan—which she was committed to doing—then another wasted night was not acceptable.

Harold laughed. "Not a chance. You know my penchant for helping damsels in distress. It seems I'm quite adept at it, too."

She regretted her decision greatly.

"And for the millionth time, I will remind

you that I am not—" Ruby paused to emphasize her next words. "—and never will be, in distress. I am perfectly capable of handling my own life and everything it entails."

She followed Harold through the narrow opening and looked around the dusty, deserted room. According to Alex, this room should house the Marquis of Drake's study, but it appeared to have been abandoned and unused for over twenty years.

Harold ran his hand over a flat surface. The cloth either covered a massive desk or a forgotten pile of rubbish. Ruby prayed it was the former, but judging from the look of the room it very well may cover something useless to her search.

"I should at least be given some explanation of *why* we are here, seeing as I might likely take the brunt of the punishment if we are caught."

"Again, I have a very good reason for being here. While you, on the other hand, tagged along without so much as an invitation to do so." The man was infuriating, as usual, yet looked right at home within the massive room. It was still a mystery to her how he'd managed to beat her back to the house from White's.

By the time he had, however, Ruby had needed to get on with her task for the evening. It was only a three-block walk to the Drake's townhouse. The night was not overly cool. With a light shawl, dark walking dress, and comfortable kid boots, she had set out on her excursion, hoping Harold didn't follow—while at the same time knowing the man was incapable of passing up an opportunity to annoy her.

A part of her was thankful for his company, though. The idea of slipping into the marquis' house had thrilled Ruby at first. She pictured herself stealthily traversing the dark interior to find the room she sought. But as she walked alone down the misty, muddy lane crowded behind townhouses, the first tendrils of anxiety, fear, and doubt had taken hold.

His incessant questions on their walk to Drake's hadn't helped, either. She assured him that yes, she knew she was doing something illegal. Yes, she knew the repercussions could land her in a dank holding cell—which she tried to convince him was the reason he shouldn't accompany her. And finally: No, Vi did not know about her after-hours outings or her sneaking around at *ton* affairs.

She'd dreaded her decision not to confide in Vi or at least leave a note with her whereabouts.

But Ruby knew her friend well. Vi wouldn't ask any questions, insisting instead on accompanying her. Dragging the new Lady Haversham into her convoluted situation was unacceptable, particularly given Vi's current condition. Brock would never forgive Ruby if they were found breaking and entering the home of an extremely influential marquis. Ruby craved answers, but not at the expense of her friend's reputation.

Her own reputation didn't matter as much. She was a nobody. The daughter of an impoverished baronet, or so she'd been led to believe.

"Is this what we came here for?"

The whispered question startled Ruby and she sprang into action. Alex had only guaranteed her two uninterrupted hours when Drake attended his gentlemen's club to play cards. The two hours included the time it took her to find his carriage at the club, enter his house, complete her search, and depart unnoticed—and that didn't even factor in the time she'd wasted returning to the Haversham townhouse. Drake's house staff took his time away for themselves, thus ensuring the home would be unattended. Alex kept watch at the stables after showing her and Harold in through a side door in the garden. He'd been shocked—and a bit leery—to see Harold, but had kept to his word. Misleading him was not something she planned to do often, or at all.

She was still confused as to why either man would assist her. She was in danger, and in turn, putting both of them at risk, too. Alex did have a deep sense of loyalty to Vi—and by association, Ruby—which somewhat convinced Ruby that he only did what Vi would have him do.

"Just allow me to have a look around and we will depart," Ruby said.

"Why were you at White's?"

"I don't have time for your questions." Though she should be focused on Drake and anything he could be hiding, she kept stealing glances in Harold's direction. He looked completely at ease sneaking about the marquis' house.

"One might think you never have time for anyone's questions."

"Do be silent before you alert someone to our presence," she scolded. Ruby was gaining much skill in her ability to avoid the inquiry of others, and tonight would not be an exception. She pulled the cover off an impressive desk. If the gods of luck shone in her favor, the drawers would be unlocked and ready for her perusal.

She let out a huge sigh. Immediately, she

pulled drawers open and began her search. Time was imperative, and she hadn't a second to waste. The first few drawers she opened were empty. This could not be the room Drake spent several hours a day in. Her doubts had been immediate when they entered the room to find it covered in years of dust and smelling of misuse.

The last drawer pulled open with a screech on uneven rails, revealing a treasure trove of items. Ruby bent forward for a better look in the dim light. The only source came from the hallway beyond the door, which cast a light that illuminated about ten feet into the room. They could not chance sparking a candle and alerting a passing servant.

"Eureka!" Harold called from right over her shoulder.

Startled, Ruby jerked upright, prepared to flee when her head hit something solid.

"Ouch!" Harold said.

Ruby spun around to see Harold cupping his chin in pain. She irritably massaged what she felt sure would be a knot atop her head. "I told you to be quiet. Now look at yourself. However do you propose to explain a bruised chin? You are insufferable."

The wounded look on his face had Ruby regretting her harsh words.

"Just stay silent, please," Ruby whispered.

He held both hands up, palms toward her, and took a step back in surrender. "Your wish is my command."

She turned back to the drawer, knowing she'd need to move the objects closer to the light to see them clearly. Scooping them into her hands, Ruby stood and took a step toward the door. She'd managed a single step before her foot caught on the cloth she'd removed. The objects flew from her hands as she careened forward in the darkness. Her hands shot out for something to stop her fall and the inevitable noise it would cause. When her hands came into contact with only air, Ruby's future passed before her very eyes.

Expelled from Lord Haversham's house in disgrace.

Forgotten once more at her family's country estate, left to age alone with no answers to her many questions.

What more did she deserve after harrying off to London on this ill-fated mission?

The seconds passed like minutes as her feet sought purchase but only became further knotted in the excess material.

As she braced herself for impact, solid arms snaked around her waist, stopping her seemingly a mere finger's breadth from hitting the floor. The sudden stop sent the last item, tucked under her arm, skidding across the dusty floor before it smashed into the wall. The sound of shattering glass echoed through the cavernous room and out into the empty hall.

Ruby froze, straining to hear the approach of feet or the voices of servants as they rushed to investigate the commotion.

Harold laughed, his warm breath brushing against her ear. His arms tightened around her middle. "As I said, damsel in distress. Feel free to refer to me as White Knight." With another hearty laugh, he flipped Ruby in his arms so they were face to face, their noses almost touching. If she tilted her head just so, Ruby would have to lean a mere inch toward him and their lips would meet. The room disappeared around her, leaving only them. And she wanted…she had no idea what she wanted. Just that she wanted.

The threat of discovery still high, Ruby breathed deeply, begging her heart to calm. "You can set me upright now."

"Oh, that is not what happens when a fearless knight rescues the damsel, even if it is only from herself." His brows rose in shock, his face serious. "Do I not deserve a thank you? Or, dare I say…possibly a kiss?"

It was only then that Ruby realized her hands—those devious things—clutched his shoulders—broad shoulders…muscular shoulders…shoulders made for rescuing damsels in distress.

"Can I help you both?" A feminine voice echoed through the room, breaking the spell that kept Harold's arms wound tightly around her and kept her own hands firmly grasping him for support.

Harold's eyes still bored into hers, unwilling—or unable—to let go of the moment. But Ruby pushed against him until he set her on her feet, her back to the door. She willed the floor to open and swallow both her and Harold. The strength to turn and face the woman in the doorway eluded her.

His brow raised once again in question.

Why had she let him tag along? Was it not enough that she'd jeopardized herself, but now had pulled Harold into it all?

Ruby's eyes were probably the size of saucers. They'd been caught, and now Harold would receive the brunt of a punishment meant solely for her.

"What are you doing in the Marquis of Drake's study?" the girl prodded.

Harold cleared his voice. "My apolo—"

"Please, allow me," Ruby cut him off before he could incriminate himself. Straightening her shoulders, she turned to the figure outlined in the doorway. "I can explain our presence."

HAROLD COULD NOT wait to hear how Ruby planned to justify their presence in Drake's house. He doubted the truthfulness of her explanation, but he looked forward to her trying. Once the situation got out of hand, he would step in—again. It was becoming a trend he much enjoyed.

The woman—merely a girl, truly—stepped into the room. The dim light from the candles lining the hall made her hair appear as red as flames. Her frame was small, yet willowy. "Do not bother. I can see with my own eyes what is happening here."

Odd that she had an idea of what was going on when he hadn't the faintest clue. Even more peculiar was that he did not care what Ruby's reasons were. Though he was justifiably suspicious of her actions, he still found it difficult to distrust her outright. Something more had to be behind her behavior—and beyond that, Harold found he enjoyed her company. Despite the circumstances, when he was called to return to take over for his father, she would be a distant memory of a better time.

"I am truly sorry," Ruby mumbled. "It is just—"

"If you are looking for a tryst, here is not the place." The girl's hands settled on her hips, the posture oddly familiar.

He bent and whispered to Ruby. "Let me know when you'd like your white knight to take over and rescue you from this unfortunate situation."

"Let me remind you that we would not be in this situation if you hadn't scared the wits out of me," she countered. Though she was the culprit for them being in the position for him to scare her, she didn't think now was the time to accept that burden of responsibility.

"Not a tryst?" The girl paused to look them both up and down. "Mayhaps you are planning on relieving the marquis of his valuables? Nothing more than common thieves. I must admit, I have never heard of a female burglar, but one should not be surprised by the depravity of society."

The girl didn't have the look of a servant, her dress cut from fine cloth and her hair tied high with a matching ribbon. Her speech was cultured and refined. Possibly a relative of Drake's, a niece or cousin. With the man's reputation, Harold found it hard to believe any upstanding member of society would allow their daughter to live under the Marquis of Drake's protection.

Whoever she was, however, Harold could not stand by and allow her to speculate any further. "I assure you we are not common thieves—only people who have lost their way, I fear."

"Lost your way? Into the private study of a marquis?" Her voice conveyed her doubt. "That is highly doubtful and suspicious, do you not think?"

Harold looked to Ruby for insight, but her eyes only held panic. "My lady..." he started, hoping to at least draw the girl's name or some other key to her identity.

A closer look told him she could not be more than sixteen, barely out of school. What mother would be so lackadaisical about their daughter's reputation as to allow her to stay with the marquis, fabled to have fathered half of the youth in London?

The chit could be Drake's own offspring. He hadn't heard that the man actually claimed one as his own.

"We only came to consult with your father on a business matter of great importance," Harold said. "Your servant showed us here to await his arrival."

"He is *not* my father," she seethed the words. "And furthermore, he is not home." She crossed her arms, keeping her distance. Was the girl not fearful of them at all?

"Then we should be going," Ruby said.

She'd found her tongue, but Harold wasn't quite ready to take his leave. The girl was not about to sound the alarm at their presence, or she already would have. "I am sure we can await his arrival."

"Are you crazy?" Ruby asked in a whisper.

"Only as crazy as you for dragging us into this," he replied.

She flashed a pleading look at him. "Please, let us out of here."

"I fear it is too late for us to depart unscathed."

"The marquis never handles business here, nor do the servants use this room," the girl retorted. "Now, I must decide what to do with the pair of you."

"What to do with us?" Ruby sounded breathless beside him.

The girl cocked her head in thought, her finger tapping her pinched lips. "Maybe I will call the magistrate."

Harold had wanted a little adventure, to make a few memories before he was forced to settle down, but taken to the Newgate? He could not imagine explaining this to Brock, let alone his father.

"That will not be necessary," Ruby pleaded. "This was all a misunderstanding. If you'll only give me the opportunity to explain."

Ruby had insisted that Drake was out for the evening and not expected to return until the wee hours of the morning. That had been the only reason Harold had even entertained the idea of letting her follow through with her absurd plan. It was clear that she felt the outcome of her search could affect her greatly, but he wanted to know how—even if that put him in peril. The punishment for stealing from the wealthy and titled was grave, since every man in Parliament was of wealthy and titled birth. They did not take kindly to those who sought to take what they saw as their own.

It was highly doubtful that either of them would be smiling if they were sitting in a jail cell, eating moldy bread and drinking putrid water from the River Thames.

"I believe we started on the wrong foot. Let us introduce ourselves," Harold began his last-ditch effort to save them both.

Ruby stiffened at his side. "No—"

Harold clasped her elbow in comfort. "I do apologize for the confusion. We are here on official business." He executed a slight, awkward bow, keeping his hold on Ruby firm. "You see, my associate is a representative of Foldger's

Foundling House, an orphanage in Hampshire. I wrote the Marquis of Drake to set up a meeting for this evening to discuss a sizable donation."

The girl snorted—actually snorted. He'd never heard a female make that particular sound, but for some reason it fit the young woman. "While that sounds completely believable and—for any other member of the *ton*—a generous cause, you have obviously never made the acquaintance of the marquis. One, he would rather gather his shillings in a bag and toss them in the ocean than donate them. And secondly…" She ticked her reasons off on her fingers. "He is more likely to throw children in after his money than to see it spent on them."

"I beg your pardon?" he stuttered, sure he had misheard her.

"I said, he would rather sink his money and orphaned children along with it than willingly give coin away." A catlike smile overtook her face.

She enjoyed their discomfort. The little minx!

"Now, I would be remiss if I allowed the pair of you to walk out of here without paying for your deception," she continued, her smile growing ever more devious. "So, are either of you gamblers?"

Harold shook his head, and he sensed Ruby doing the same. "I do believe if you think on it a bit, no harm has been done. I can contact the marquis at a later date that works within his busy schedule."

"Lucky for you both, I am." She turned from the dark room and signaled for them to follow her, without giving the impression she'd heard Harold's words. "This way, please. We will need a more hospitable place to discuss our wager."

They followed her, single file, down the dim corridor. Harold tried to situate himself in front of Ruby in a misguided attempt to protect her from the unknown dangers posed by the slight figure in front of them. But true to form, Ruby—head high and shoulders squared—marched as if on her way to the guillotine. He maneuvered himself to her side, determined to face whatever lay ahead unified. A bulk of the responsibility for their situation set firmly on his shoulders, he was fully aware. He was the man, after all, and should have been able to waylay her plan, if not dissuade her completely. No part of their situation was funny, yet he found himself chuckling at the thought of ever dissuading Ruby when she had her mind set on something.

His laugh stopped abruptly when Ruby shot a glare at him, followed by an almost identical glare from their unknown capture. He hadn't the time to ponder the resemblance before they all stopped outside a room off the dark corridor, closer to the main entrance.

As they entered, Harold gazed around the foyer. With no servants in sight—and Brock keeping the marquis occupied at White's—they very well may escape before anymore notice was given to them.

"Sit, please." The girl swung her arm wide, ushering them into the room lit by several candles and a blazing fire, overly warm for the mild weather outside.

Ruby immediately moved to sit on a straight-backed chair, her head lowered as if she were waiting to be scolded by her schoolmarm. Harold opted for an armchair, directly across from Ruby. The chair was comfortable, which he considered fortunate. There was no telling how long the girl planned to string them along, threatening detainment by the magistrate.

The only other available seat facing them was a long, low-slung lounge chair. Not surprisingly, the girl opted to pace the length of the room, her arms clasped tightly behind her as she surveyed her prey.

Yes, Harold felt as if he were a mouse, eyed from above by a falcon waiting to swoop down and sink its talons deep.

"Where were we?" she asked. "Oh, yes! What to do with two unwanted intruders."

The girl was toying with them, that was all. She would get a laugh out of their discomfiture and let them leave eventually.

"Would it be so awful to let us go, just as we came, no one the wiser?" Ruby said. She looked at the girl defiantly, hopefully coming to the same conclusion Harold had.

She snorted again. "But I would be the wiser. How do I know you are both not hiding the good silver under your clothes?"

"You can check us both," Ruby offered.

"Oh, but think of the fun if the magistrate searched you both."

"You must be jesting with us," Harold exclaimed, his patience wearing thin. "This is absurd. We came for a meeting with Drake. He is unable to meet with us, so we will take our leave now." Harold stood and motioned for Ruby to do the same.

"Do not think you will depart as easily as you arrived." The girl stopped pacing and faced them. "I may be forced to spread the news about the pair of you caught in a most compromising position."

"What compromising position?" Ruby

exploded.

"I did find you alone in a dark room with this kind sir's arms wrapped most inappropriately around your midsection, did I not?"

They both stayed silent, not wishing to fuel the girl's fire.

"Sir." She turned to him. "Can you please await your *partner* outside?"

"I would rather not—"

"Thank you, I do appreciate your immediate departure from this house. Your miss and I have much to discuss. Privately, if you please."

The little hellion. He was being dismissed in no uncertain terms, and at the moment there was nothing he could do about it. The risk was too great that she'd sound the alarm and have them both hauled from the house, in shackles, for all to see.

He bowed to Ruby reluctantly. "I will be upon the front steps awaiting your departure."

"I would feel better if he stay—"

"Unfortunately, that is not up to you," the girl said. "If you pride yourself on your ability to wander about without restraints—namely bindings about your wrists and ankles—then you will leave us."

He looked to Ruby. If she asked him to stay, he would. Damn the consequences.

"Good evening, your lordship," a servant's voice drifted into the room.

"Very good, the marquis is returned. Shall I call him to join us?" the girl asked.

"That will not be necessary." Harold gave Ruby a reassuring smile. With Drake returned they would not be able to stop her from announcing their presence, but Harold may be able to distract him long enough for Ruby to remove herself from the house. "I will step out and have a word with him myself."

She shook her head. "Harold?"

He leaned close and whispered, "All will be fine, trust me."

The girl clapped, as if enjoying their discomfort. "Well, that is settled. You may go, *Harold*," she said, and he moved toward the door as she continued to address Ruby. "Now that he is gone we can speak freely."

"What could you possibly have to speak with me about?" Ruby sounded so uncertain that Harold almost turned around.

"But one thing. Namely…" she paused dramatically, "…how I can be made to forget the scene I stumbled upon…"

The girl's words trailed off when he closed the study door behind him.

Ruby was safer in the room with their young captor than she would be coming face to face with Drake.

Pasting a smile upon his face, Harold took the few steps toward Drake and bowed in greeting. "Your lordship." Harold mimicked the servant's greeting.

"Mr. Jakeston?" Drake blustered. "What are you doing here—at this time of night?"

"I came round as soon as I completed my business," Harold said. "It was very inconvenient that I had to depart in such a rush earlier and I wanted to inquire when you will again be at White's. I owe you another game of cards to make up for my rudeness."

As he spoke, Harold noticed the marquis looking over his shoulder to the closed salon door expectantly.

"Ah, very well. It is the least you can do after calling off this evening."

Thankfully, the door remained closed behind him and no female voices drifted out. "As you may know, I reside at Haversham House with Lord Haversham for the time being."

"Yes, Haversham mentioned that this evening. Along with the announcement that Lady Haversham is expecting their first child," Drake said.

"That is very true. Miss Ruby St. Augustin has accompanied her to town to keep a close eye on her." He waited for any sign of recognition at the name.

Harold was rewarded when Drake asked, "I know that name. Is that Sir St. Augustin's eldest daughter?"

"Actually, his only child," Harold said. "Were you acquainted with him?"

"No, never met the man, but I had occasion to run into Mrs. St. Augustin over the years." At the shift in conversation, Drake appeared measurably uneasy. "Well, that is a long ago and better left forgotten time. It is late and I find these old bones tire fast these days. If you don't mind, my butler will show you out." His tone quivered ever so slightly with agitation as he gestured to the door and his butler.

"Good evening, your lordship."

"This way, Mr. Jakeston," Drake's butler attempted to usher him out.

Only when Drake reached the first landing on his way up the stairs did Harold concede and turn to the front door.

The girl hadn't sounded the alarm on them, and she surely wouldn't harm Ruby with Drake home and servants about the house again.

As he paced outside the townhouse, Harold pondered Drake's revelation. He'd learned two very important things this night: Firstly, Drake was acquainted with Ruby's mother, and secondly, he wanted to keep the first hidden. Unfortunately, neither meant anything to him, and he was no closer to discovering Ruby's ulterior reason for her activities, but the connection was clear. Drake was either acquainted with Ruby, or knew of her existence.

CHAPTER 12

RUBY WALKED AS quickly as her gown allowed out the front door of Drake's townhouse and right past Harold. She fairly jumped from the entry porch, down the three steps, and to the sidewalk below. While she didn't chance a look behind her—afraid the girl would change her mind about sounding the alarm—she knew Harold was fast on her heels.

And though she was loathe to admit it, she was grateful knowing he was there waiting for her.

"Stop," he called behind her. "What did you just agree to?"

She halted mid-step, confident they'd moved far enough down the walk, and confronted him. "That is naught of your concern, but I do believe we have evaded the magistrate for the time being."

Harold threw his arms wide in frustration. "Do you seriously believe she would have called the authorities once the marquis arrived home?"

"I don't know, but I'm not willing to wager my reputation on it—or yours," she said. And that was true. The only luck she'd had recently was bad luck—she was not sure she could suffer through any more.

"I'll worry about my own reputation," Harold countered. "Just as you are determined to tear yours to shreds."

"Is that what you think I'm doing?"

"I see no other reason for your reckless behavior." She was sure Harold didn't want to have this confrontation now, on an influential street for all of London to witness. And yet, he persisted. "And, I was—still am—willing to help you in your quest, despite the repercussions to myself, but I need answers. I need you to tell me what all this is about... That I am not on some foolhardy errand with no chance at reward."

"Foolhardly? Reward?" she stuttered. "If you think by *forcing* me to accept your help you will gain some kind of reward—monetary or otherwise—you are mistaken."

"That is not what I meant, and you know it! I want nothing more than to see the girl I grew up with—and the woman I met last season—return. This secretive, paranoid, and witless creature is not you."

Her chin lifted and she squared her shoulders, effectively closing herself off from him. She was so angry, she could barely speak. The nerve of the man! "I refuse to continue this conversation in public like this," she hissed. "You may accompany me, or you may stay behind. Witless creature that I am, it matters naught to me which you choose."

Ruby turned and continued along the walk

and down the side lane leading to the stables from which they'd entered. She had to alert Alex to the horrible turn of events in case someone had seen him aide their entrance. Vi would be extremely disappointed if Alex lost his position on Drake's livery after she'd used her dwindling contacts to secure him the post.

"And just where are you going?" Harold asked.

"To Drake's stable, of course."

"Are you insane?"

"No more insane than you."

"And why would you think *me* insane?" he asked, exasperated. "I'm not the one putting myself in danger night after night on some wild goose chase for God knows what!"

She stopped so suddenly he ran into her, almost knocking them both to the ground. "Wild goose chase? Is that what you think I'm doing? Wasting my time and jeopardizing myself on a flight of fancy?"

"What other explanation have you given me?" he countered.

Every word he spoke was correct, but Ruby knew she couldn't trust anyone with her secret—not even Lord Haversham's closest friend. "I did not invite you to come along. In fact, I distinctly remember asking you to leave me to my own devices on several occasions." She wanted to scream, to throw her hands up in frustration, to storm off and leave him behind.

"You still plan to tell me nothing?" he asked.

Ruby shook her head. To unburden herself would alleviate her strain, yet the consequences would be too great to herself—and her family.

"So, you will allow me to think the worst? Because that is exactly what's going through my mind at the moment. I can help you…if you'll only allow me."

They glared at each other in the dark lane, neither willing to give. She wanted to accept his assistance more than anything, and she knew he wanted to ease her worries. The strength of his arms when he'd held her in Drake's study told her as much. As he hadn't let her fall then, he would not let her fall now.

If only she had the strength to take what he offered her.

"There is naught you can do for me, but stay out of my way." As soon as the words were out, she longed to take them back. His face clouded in pain and confusion. When she spoke again, she gentled her tone. "Please, let me handle my affairs. They do not concern you."

"May I at least escort you home?" he asked.

"I am sure you have other plans for this evening. Alex will walk me the few blocks back to the Haversham townhouse." He wanted to protest, she could see, but Ruby continued before he could. "I will stay safe, I promise."

"No more breaking and entering?"

"Not tonight. My luck has been tested to the limits for one day," she reassured him.

He sighed. "I meant, no more breaking and entering—period."

"You know I cannot guarantee it won't be necessary again." She paused, wanting to soothe his fears, but unwilling to make promises she couldn't keep. "But I will avoid it at all cost."

Harold lived an open life, secure in his position as a country vicar. He knew a fulfillment Ruby never would. He would make a solid husband, provider, and protector one day—but not for someone with a birthright as scandalous as Ruby's. He deserved so much better.

Ruby hoped one day to discover who she truly was and where she belonged. Until then, she was Ruby St. Augustin—daughter of Angus and Pearl St. Augustin. The daughter of a baron.

She was a lie.

Born out of deceit.

Raised under false pretenses.

Cursed to live a lonely, forgotten existence.

CHAPTER 13

THE AFTERNOON WAS warm, with nary the hint of a cooling breeze. Harold cursed the weather as he adjusted his jacket, seeking some form of relief from the heat as sweat pooled at the center of his back. His only boon was the fact that most members of the *ton* chose to stay indoors during these long afternoon dry spells, which meant less of a chance he'd be discovered lurking about the drive of a certain lord and lady.

He'd tried to dissuade himself from his folly of looking into a few of the men on Ruby's list, but he couldn't help his curiosity. All the men were of a certain age and status about town. Some married, some widowed, some already in their grave. There was no rhyme or reason to the list. Unfortunately, he saw it as the only means for answers she was unwilling to give him. That two of the men happened to be acquainted with

Brock had Harold on edge. If she, in the end, was up to something that would hurt Lady Haversham or Brock, Harold knew he'd have to go to his friend with his suspicions. But by that time, he intended to have a few facts—hard proof of what she was, or was not, doing.

So, instead of sparring with Brock at his fencing club, Harold was here, outside some random gentleman's house—practically sitting in the shrubs…waiting. Waiting for what, he hadn't a clue. The last two men he'd looked into had also shed no light on Ruby or her reasons for being in London. They were ordinary men, going about normal lives. Neither were excessively wealthy nor overtly handsome, not that Harold was a fair judge on the attractiveness of other men. They were distinguished, active members of the *ton*, whose long family lineages were rooted in tradition.

All things Harold did not possess: wealth, prestige, or strong lineage.

The main attributes women longed for when choosing a mate.

Did Ruby seek the same? She'd venomously denied her reasoning had naught to do with marriage. He wanted to believe her more than the average selfish, social climbing miss. He did not know her as well as he'd like, but he'd seen good in her; knew she'd been instrumental in helping Lady Haversham start and run Foldger's Foundling House long before its move out of London's Cheapside.

Unexpectedly, a carriage pulled into the drive not far from where he stood in the shadows. He'd been so entrenched in his own thoughts he hadn't heard the approaching wheels.

Harold pushed a bit further into the shrubbery as he heard laughter erupt from the carriage. Before the conveyance had come to a full stop, a footman jumped from his post at the rear of the carriage and set down the steps. The man opened the carriage door and two girls, no more than thirteen and fifteen, alighted, still laughing.

"Larkens," a deep throaty voice called from inside the carriage. "Please deliver my daughters' things to their rooms. My wife and I will retire to the gardens. And have Mrs. Goods bring tea around." With that, the lord of the house stepped from the carriage. Turning, he held out his hand to assist his wife.

The pair made a striking couple, both with hair of the palest gold and creamy skin. Their daughters bounced into the townhouse, replicas of their mother, both of them so slight they barely reached their father's shoulder. All the while, they smiled and laughed at some joke Harold was not fortunate enough to hear.

He continued to eye the couple as they directed the footman and butler as to which packages should be delivered to which room. Harold was baffled as to why Ruby was interested in this man or his family.

There was little else he could do but watch.

After a few more instructions, the couple followed their daughters into the house, closing the door securely behind them.

The carriage also eventually left, moving around the house to the area where Harold assumed the stables were located, leaving him alone once more.

He moved from his place in the shadows and toward the street. The sun was only just past midday, and he had much left to do before he accompanied Brock and Lady Haversham to the playhouse that evening.

Harold walked the few blocks necessary to a busier street in town before hailing a hack to Cheapside. That morning, he'd sent word to William about meeting to discuss the contacts he'd made within the shipping circles of London, thanks to Brock's willingness to include Harold in a few of his business meetings. The men had readily agreed to meet with Harold, independent of Brock. It was important to him that Brock not be included in his business venture with William; if it failed, the blame could lie only on Harold's shoulders.

If William's venture idea had merit, these men would be able to help. Success meant not only a means of supporting himself, but also an opportunity for his brother to recover financially after his employer's death.

The roads were clogged with midday travelers: expensive carriages taking the women of the *ton* to Bond Street for shopping, or pedestrians making their way to and from their places of employment.

As Harold neared the River Thames, the carriages thinned while the walking traffic increased. Vendors hocked their wares on every corner, shouting after people in hopes of earning coin. The sun was beginning its slow decent, and Harold knew he was late. He hoped William still loitered near the abandoned blacksmith shop.

Harold flipped a few coin to the driver when they arrived and jumped to the street in front of the dilapidated building. His older brother immediately stepped around the corner, as if he'd been hiding from view until Harold arrived.

His attire looked roughly the same—worn, oversized breeches and a sturdy shirt that had seen better days, but at least his face and hands appeared scrubbed. As William made his way closer, his feet dragged. Harold suspected the boots he wore were of a size far larger than necessary.

"How do you fair, brother?" Harold asked in greeting.

"Better now that you sent word. I feared you would be unable to make the connections *we* need."

Harold heard the emphasis on 'we' and, surprisingly, liked the idea of working alongside his brother toward a common goal. It had been many years since they'd spent time together. Even then, their age difference made it hard for them to truly connect as anything more than dueling siblings, boys becoming men.

He held himself back from embracing William this time, knowing the relationship they shared would never be on par with his and Brock's close bond. "I had little trouble arranging a meeting for you."

William smiled. "That is good news. When am I to meet them, and where?"

It was exactly the questions Harold had been pondering for some time. His brother could not possibly handle business in his current state of dress, unkempt as he was. But the situation was more easily rectified then he'd thought.

"I have made you an appointment with a tailor and hired a room for you." Harold slipped a card with the tailor's directions and the name of a boarding house from his jacket pocket and held it out to his brother. "They are expecting you."

He shook his head, not taking the offered card. "No, I cannot be in your debt."

Harold laughed. "I figured you would say exactly that, which is why you will pay me back—every cent."

The Jakestons were a stubborn lot who'd never relished being indebted to another. When Harold had journeyed to London with Brock the previous year, he'd not accepted coin from his father or Brock. It was with luck that he'd placed a winning wager at White's and was therefore able to afford new clothes. His brother, he learned, was much the same.

Still hesitant, William took the card and turned it in his fingers, reading. "Thank you."

"Well, we cannot have you meeting thusly." Harold thumped his brother on the back in jest. "We are now serious business partners, and must appear the part if we are to be treated as such."

"Then you have secured the necessary funds?" William's brow shot up in question.

"Did you doubt me?"

"Never," William said.

By 'securing funds,' Harold had simply counted his remaining wager winnings to ascertain he had enough to fund the venture and also keep himself fed.

After discussing the venture in more detail, Harold was all the more convinced the endeavor would be profitable for them both.

With a confident step, Harold left Cheapside.

CHAPTER 14

RUBY HAD NO idea why she'd agreed to accompany Vi and Lord Haversham. The evening was bound to be chock-full of gossip and needless mingling that did nothing to help move her toward her objectives in London. The playhouse was already filled to capacity with London's elite, ensconced in private boxes with spectacular views of not only the stage, but also of surrounding boxes. People gawked at other members of the town through opera glasses.

Those without a private box or the funds to rent one for the evening milled about in the general admission section. They too scanned the crowd above them, searching for familiar faces or possibly an impressive lord treating his mistress to an evening out while his family attended another social function.

Ruby had retreated to the furthest seat from the railing, shrouded in shadows, but still able to view most of the large room. The only social gathering the *ton* enjoyed more than a grand ball was the theater. Many relished the opportunity to gawk at other attendees, whether from their own social class or above. While the poor laborers ogled their fancy clothes and fine posture, many would have been shocked to learn that most men of the *ton* barely read at more than an elementary level, happy to leave business to their man of affairs.

Vi and Lord Haversham sat in front of her, heads tilted together in conversation as they exclaimed over the set for this evening's production. The stage had been transformed into a magical forest, the lights low, and a brilliant moon suspended overhead. In truth, if it had been any other play Ruby would have found an excuse to call off, but try as she might she could not pass up the opportunity to see the production that meant so very much to her own mother. So much so, in fact, that Pearl St. Augustine had a ruby-encrusted letter opener made for her lover with lines from the play etched into the precious metal.

Ruby knew that in the first act—the very first scene even—of *A Midsummer Night's Dream* the words that meant so much to her mother would be uttered.

'The course of true love never did run smooth.' Ruby believed truer words had likely never been spoken. Something as all-consuming as the love her mother had felt for her real father was beyond Ruby, and she had none other than her mother to thank for that. Through her loss, Ruby knew she would be wiser and more discriminating if a gentleman ever came calling for her. Questioning a person's motives should not be discouraged simply because they were a member of the *ton.* She couldn't help but think that if young women were taught to question men's objectives, they would be happier with their lot in life when they did decide upon a husband.

"Excuse me, is this seat taken?"

"Bloody hell!" Ruby mumbled. She hadn't heard the door open behind her, nor Harold enter the box and take the seat next to her in the shadows.

"Of course not, Harold." Vi turned in her seat to face them with a smile of greeting. "We were unsure you would make it this evening."

Ruby cursed her luck. After the previous evening, the last person she wanted to see—besides the little hellion they'd met at Drake's estate—was Harold.

"I would not miss a night at the theater for anything." Harold looked to Ruby then, their eyes meeting as he uttered his next words. "Especially with such exquisite company."

"Now Harold, I did wear my freshly tailored suit, but please, acknowledge the ladies as well," Brock chimed in. "I fear your infatuation with me will have to come to an end shortly, or Lady Haversham may develop a distaste for you."

Harold laughed, covering the sound of his chair as he pulled it closer to Ruby. "I would not want to insult Lady Haversham or Miss Ruby, who, by the way are both looking ravishing this evening."

"Thank you, Harold." A beautiful glow lightened Vi's face.

"Oh no, you do not, Harold," Brock said.

"What?" Harold looked puzzled, his hand resting on his chest in shock.

"Do not be throwing such words about with

my wife present."

"My apologies," Harold said. He leaned toward Ruby and continued. "You do look quite ravishing this evening."

Ruby glared as best she could from the corner of her eye. "Do you not think we have gotten ourselves into enough trouble lately?"

Could he so easily forget the imminent danger of their association if the girl decided to spill their secret to all? Not that there was even a secret to tell, but misconceptions and unfounded perceptions ran rampant around London. Very rarely did one stop to examine the truthfulness of the gossip they spread.

Harold unfolded his theater spectacles and peered around the large room, focusing on several boxes as he scanned. "I do believe we are in no danger of discovery this evening. It seems not a single lord or lady has their eye focused on us. Which I find extremely odd, as we are a striking pair to behold."

"Do stop that!" Ruby said. The man was exasperating, as always. He seemed to enjoy provoking her.

"What?" he asked, affronted.

"What you're doing. You know as well as I do that our place in society—and as a non-scandalous pair—depends on our discretion."

"As a pair...I do delight in the sound of that." He winked.

"You know I meant nothing of the sort. And I would *delight* in you scooting your chair back to its place."

"I do think thou dost protest too much." With a chuckle, he scooted his seat back to its rightful place, which was still closer than Ruby wanted.

Did he not see she only sought to keep their names out of the gossip mill? Neither of them could afford their character being brought into question. Harold because he needed a wife, and Ruby because she was still unprepared for her mother to learn she was in London.

"My protests aren't nearly as vehement as they should be," she countered.

At that point, the gas lights dimmed and the crowd below sighed in wonder. "Shhhhh," Harold hissed.

The English Opera House, used as both a theater and musical hall, was a luxury entertainment that many could not afford, but scraped together enough coin to attend anyways, sometimes at the expense of a meal—or seven.

Ruby was content to lose herself in the performance, the beauty of the costumes, and the dramatic flair of the actors. The words, filled with such emotion and conviction, washed over her. She understood the draw of the theater; it was almost hypnotic. The sensual temperament of the whole affair was much like the real-life affair her mother and father had briefly shared. Their own relationship played out much the same: a cosmic beginning, an overwhelming climax, and a sad, depressing end that neither could have seen coming—just as the audience sighed or shouted in dismay during the play. It was with a light heart she recalled this play did not end as her parents' torrid affair had. Oberon, Titania, Hermia, and Demetrius were fated a much happier resolution.

"Are you unwell?"

Ruby hadn't noticed the sob she'd let out until Harold mumbled the question and she looked up to see both Vi and Lord Haversham turned in their seats toward her.

"Why does everyone always fear I am ill? I am fine," she said to cover her unintended emotional reaction. "The play is lovely, that's all."

Vi and her husband accepted her words and returned their gazes to the performance. Harold kept his attention on her, his hand coming to rest on her knee.

"Truly, I was overwhelmed by the beauty of the spoken word is all."

He didn't move his hand, nor retreat to his side of the box. Thankfully, the low lighting made it impossible for anyone outside their box to see his hand, or how close he leaned toward her. His hand was surprisingly comforting as the play went on, something she would never admit to a soul.

She made no move. Her breath held in anticipation.

He kept his eyes on the stage as his fingers began a gentle, kneading of her thigh. As the first act wore on, his touch became more demanding, dominating, as though under the spell the play had cast. With each increase in pressure, Ruby's breathing also amplified.

Startled, she felt cool air on her leg. Harold's gentle touch had drawn her skirt up her leg and was now bunched at her knee. She sucked in a large gulp of air and held it as his hand moved to touch her knee.

Skin-to-skin contact she'd never felt before.

Beside her, Harold's breathing also sounded labored.

Frantic, Ruby looked to Vi in front of her. The couple was focused on the play before them.

Ruby relaxed into her seat, enjoying Harold's

warm touch, knowing it would not—could not—last…and she may never experience such pleasure again.

IT TOOK ALL Harold's strength to hold himself back. Overwhelming Ruby with his touch would only drive a wedge between them he'd worked hard to remove, or at least dislodge. The walls she surrounded herself with were proving difficult to navigate, but he was determined to either climb them or tear them down, one by one.

Inch by painful inch, he raised her skirt, making sure to block the view from any wandering eyes with his own outstretched legs. Keeping his eyes on the performance, he gathered the material of her silken gown, lifting it higher and higher.

Finally his skin touched hers and he was ablaze, without the means to extinguish his need. If Brock and Lady Haversham were not mere feet away—and all of the *ton* not within sight—he would have her in his arms, pressed against the wall with his hand further lifting her skirt. His body pressed firmly against her trim form, her hands running through his hair. And most importantly, his mouth on her.

The kiss played through his mind, an extension of his thoughts during their last moment alone together. He imagined the taste of her lips, sweet as honeysuckle. The feel of her hands upon him, sure and filled with need. The press of their bodies together in wanton desire.

His only intelligible thought being how he could make exactly *that* happen—where they could find a moment of solitude amongst hundreds of London's elite.

He stroked his hand ever higher on her thigh, gathering the material as he went.

Ruby kept her eyes trained on the stage, but he felt her tremble, her yearning as great as his own.

She was right to deny his assistance. He could not trust he wouldn't take things too far, ask too much of her—more than she was willing to give.

Would she deny him now? Deny herself the pleasure she so needed?

He pulled his hand away and she whimpered, the sound at once erotic and heartbreakingly innocent. Her purity of body— and heart—was one of the things he admired most.

Harold slid his chair closer once more, to better attend her needs. Needs she most likely didn't know she had or how to satisfy.

Lightly, his fingertips moved to her inner thigh, caressing the soft skin, untouched by another man. Her hips rose into his touch so slightly he almost missed it.

"Ruby." His words were little more than a groan, the muttering of a man who'd certainly lost his mind. A man willing to risk discovery by all to hold this woman—a beautiful, intelligent woman.

Suddenly, the lights rose and applause sounded intermission had arrive.

Harold quickly dropped Ruby's dress back into place and adjusted his own pants to hide his arousal.

Lady Haversham and Brock stood as they applauded the end of the act. "Brava!" They both chimed.

"That was exquisitely lovely," Vi exclaimed, turning. "Did you enjoy your first play, Ruby?"

Harold looked to Ruby when she didn't immediately answer. Her eyelids hung low as if she'd fallen asleep—or possibly her blood pumped through her veins in expectation of a release that would not come.

"Ruby?" Vi asked.

Lady Haversham's voice finally penetrated Ruby's daze. "Oh, yes. I am enthralled with the spoken word. So very different from reading them upon a page in a book."

"I agree, Miss Ruby," Harold chimed, hoping to take a bit of the focus off her.

Brock stepped forward with Lady Haversham in tow. "We are going to step out for refreshments. Would you care to join us?"

The question was aimed at them both, but Ruby failed to respond, leaving Harold to pass on the offer. "I believe I will await you both here." It was too soon for him to stand, for it would surely give away where his thoughts had been during the performance.

"And you, Ruby?" Vi asked.

She sat up straighter. "No, thank you. I will stay here and keep Mr. Jakeston company."

"My dear friend would do well with a nursemaid to keep a close eye on him," Brock laughed as he steered Lady Haversham from their box, securely closing the door behind them.

Ruby was on him instantly. "Whatever were you thinking?" she questioned. "If anyone had seen what was happening, then my little blackmailer would be the least of our troubles."

"Clearly I was not thinking at all." He didn't know how to respond to her hostile words. She had unquestionably enjoyed his touch. "And, we are the guests of Brock and Lady Haversham. No one will question our attendance as anything more than what we are—the impoverished, untitled, yet dearest friends of London's newest influential couple."

"Which is exactly why our association will harm you."

"Harm me?" Harold hadn't the faintest idea what she was talking about. Any association with Ruby was the exact opposite of harmful.

"How do you propose meeting an eligible girl if people think you are courting me?"

The notion stopped him dead in his tracks. "Courting you—or anyone, for that matter—is simply not my objective. I have merely been lucky enough to bump into you at a few social functions and happen to be residing under the same roof. People will expect us to share an acquaintance based off those facts." Although, members of the *ton* believing he was courting her did not sit wrong with him.

But for all he knew, she fought their association so venomously because her objectives in town did, in fact, have everything to do with another man. He'd seen her hastily scribbled notes and her list of men. If she was using the list as a prospective catalog of marriageable men, it needed much revising. Most of the men were either married or too old for any young woman's liking.

Ruby stood. "I only think we should keep our distance, that is all," she said, stepping toward the door.

"Where are you going?"

"I find I need a spot of fresh air."

"I thought you were supposed to keep me company. Who will keep me out of trouble if you are gone?"

She eyed him suspiciously. "It seems we get into more trouble while together than apart. Good evening, Mr. Jakeston." With that, she opened the door to their box and departed.

Her firm manner of closing the door signaled he was not welcome to follow. What she failed to realize was that the performance was only half over. When she returned, he would be waiting.

CHAPTER 15

HAROLD WAITED PATIENTLY for Ruby's return, all the while keeping his eyes trained on the crowd below. Many agreed the playgoers standing in the general admission section were the true entertainment for the night. The crowd this evening was overly boisterous, their jovial mood infusing the room with a lighthearted feel that matched the whimsical nature of the play.

He focused in on a familiar figure, staring back at him. He'd know those green eyes anywhere, but he had no idea why Ruby was milling about the general admission section. The crowd was a wholly unpredictable one, calm and laughing one moment, and in the next fighting and cursing.

Alarmed, he tried to locate Brock in the crowd or someone else she could be with, but no one stood close to her.

Harold stood from his chair and moved to the edge of the box, ready to yell down to her.

Before he could say a word, she moved into the crowd. It was then that her outfit registered in his mind—a bright blue dress, topped by familiar, flaming red hair. The girl below was not Ruby at all, but the young woman from Drake's home.

He took his seat again, determined to have a few words with Ruby when she returned.

But return she didn't.

Brock and Lady Haversham entered the box as the lights dimmed and the actors returned to the stage.

"Where is Miss Ruby?" He kept his question quiet, not wanting to appear overly concerned. The woman had a knack for disappearing. "She stepped out a few moments after you."

"Oh, yes, she met us in the reception area," Lady Haversham said as she took her seat. "She spotted her mother in another box and was inclined to finish the play with her. I'm unsure why she would seek her company now, yet I am not inclined to dissuade her from associating with her own mother."

Brock's brow rose at him. "Don't fret. She'll be returned home safely by Vi's father and Lady Darlingiver, never fear."

"I'm unconcerned with her whereabouts," Harold covered. "I only asked because her seat has a more agreeable view. Are you positive she will not be returning?" When Brock shook his head, Harold moved to her seat to continue the ruse.

The rest of the play dragged on. He again searched every box for her—also keeping an eye on the general admission section for the girl. Both were nowhere to be seen.

Neither did he spot a box with Lord

Oberbrook or Lady Darlingiver.

Harold could only imagine the trouble Ruby was getting herself into now, but there was little he could do at the moment. When the play was over, he thanked Brock and Lady Haversham for inviting him, but declined to continue on with them to their next destination, in favor of returning to the townhouse. He hoped to find Ruby safely in her room—although he knew his chances of that were slim.

The butler had the front door open before he'd even jumped down from the hack. After tossing a few coins, the driver ambled off into the evening.

"Good evening, Mr. Jakeston."

"Good evening, Buttons," Harold said. "Has Miss Ruby returned for the evening?"

"Yes. She retired to her room immediately upon arriving home." If he thought Harold's inquiry was odd, he didn't let on. "Would you like me to send word for her to join you downstairs?"

"No, thank you." The servant sent on that mission would most likely return empty handed; it had been easy for Ruby to slip out of the house unnoticed on more than one occasion recently. He didn't want to alert the household if she'd done it again.

He took the stairs two at a time and turned down the hall, glancing over his shoulder to make sure the butler hadn't followed him. When the coast was clear, he continued past his door, down the hall, and turned left—and ran into exactly the person he sought.

"Pardon me—" she started before realizing who she'd run into. "Are you following me?"

"Would you be angry if I were?"

"Of course." She stepped back, her hands on her hips in displeasure. "I cannot seem to extricate myself from your presence no matter how hard I try."

"Why are you avoiding my company?" He didn't want to admit it—and he never would to another person—but her leaving him at the playhouse had bruised his ego. "I understand my conversational skills are a bit rusty—"

"It's not that." She sighed. "I have things to do this evening that did not include Vi or Lord Haversham—or you, for that matter. Now please step aside."

The only person who'd ever succeeded in dismissing him in a more cutting fashion was his own father. "I most certainly will not step aside. You are too daring for your own good, and I fear you have gotten into something that may very well have you seeing the gallows before long." He took in her dark clothes, made all the grimmer with the lack of light in the hall. "The fact that you're dressed like nothing more than a common burglar would seem to confirm my suspicions."

Ruby looked down at her plain, sturdy gray wool dress. Perfect if one needed to blend into the shadows.

Harold's brow rose in question, daring her to deny the reason behind her attire.

"I most certainly am not dressed like a burglar."

"Then may I ask where you are going?"

"No, you may not."

"Mayhap to visit your dear mother again?" He knew she'd used the excuse with Lady Haversham to cry off the night's entertainment for an activity a bit more risky in nature. Her startled look told him he'd guessed correctly. "I thought not."

"You're insufferable. Why can you not leave me to my own devices?"

"Because your own devices could get you caught in another compromising situation—that includes a man not as honorable as I."

"Honorable?" she huffed.

"Yes." His voice rose in volume.

"An honorable man would not insert himself into the business of a lady who does not specifically need nor want it."

"Perhaps what you need is a nursemaid."

Her face flamed red in fury. "A nursemaid? I take it back, you are not insufferable, you are completely and totally senseless."

"I will show you senseless!" Before she could move, Harold grabbed her, wrapping his arms tightly around her. He leaned her back and smashed his lips to hers. She struggled to push him away, but her arms were pinned between them. After several long seconds, he felt the moment when she conceded, her lips parted, allowing his tongue to explore. It only took a moment before her tongue sparred with his, seeking control as she always did.

Without warning, he let her go and stood her upright. "How was that for senseless?" he asked, slightly breathless.

She stared at him, eyes as wide as saucers, gathering her next words.

And Harold knew from the sparks that flew from her glare, those words would cut him to the quick.

"YOU VULGAR, UNBEARABLE man! How dare you take such liberties with me?"

"You didn't seem to mind the liberties I took at the playhouse."

"I'm not some common woman who would take up with a man out of wedlock." The similarities to her mother's actions and her own—at the same playhouse—were not lost on her, but she would not fall into the trap her mother had. No matter how right his hands upon her had felt, or how much she wanted his mouth upon hers again, she was not so easily led astray.

"I never suggested you were any such thing," he said, confused. "It was little more than a touch—a touch that had you all but purring beneath my hand this eve. Your moods change with the hours."

She knew that if he was like other men, he would expect more. A simple touch here or a kiss there was never enough. He would ask more and more of her; before she knew it, she would be madly in love with him and forsake her own ideals to please him. Ruby had read of the way her mother was discarded, ridiculed, for her love. She was not willing to trust any man with the power to destroy her heart.

"Why do you continue to plague me?" she asked, desperate to push him away before it was too late.

"I plague you to keep you safe."

Of course he did. Everything he did was to protect her, but she didn't want that. "You are mistaken if you think any woman will long for your knight in shining armor act. You are little better than the men about the stage tonight. All show with little to no substance." His despondent look told her she'd said exactly the right thing. Precisely what it would take to drive a wedge between them that would prove unfixable. "You don't belong here. You belong in the country with other such small-minded peasant folk."

The hurtful, angry words dripped off her tongue, taking with them a little piece of her. Of all people, Ruby knew how it felt to be wounded by another. To do everything in one's power to make another love you and take notice, only to be speared straight through the heart by evil words or a cold shoulder.

"Is that what you think of me? A simple-minded dullard?" The sorrow in his words almost had her apologizing for every syllable she'd uttered since the day they'd met.

But she knew she had to push on. "The true fools never see it for themselves. I think it best for everyone involved if you go back to your father's home and take over the vicarage, where you clearly belong—and let me find where I belong."

"Is that how you truly feel?" His eyes searched hers.

She wanted to weep, knowing she'd caused the pain in his gaze.

"Yes. I have been trying to tell you for days." She pronounced every word carefully, as if explaining the simplest thing to a child. "Leave me be, stay out of my life, and—for the Lord's sake—hang up your suit of armor before you impale yourself on your own sword."

CHAPTER 16

HAROLD STARED AT amber liquid as he swirled it in his glass. He had no idea what it was, but he was sure it wouldn't burn as much as Ruby's words had. He wanted nothing more than to swallow his drink in one gulp and then continue through the remaining liquor in the crystal decanter sitting next to him.

Maybe he was the weak man both Ruby and his father thought.

The next rational step was drunkard. Titleless, fortuneless, and a drunkard; what more could his father have predicted for him?

Ruby was right in everything she'd said. He should return to the country. Live the life of an impoverished vicar to a wealthy, titled lord and leave her to find a place where she belonged—to find the man who would become her husband. A man who would give her a home, and children, and financial stability, all things Harold could not guarantee her or any woman.

Still, he continued to assess his glass, weighing his options. The sting of the liquid traveling down his throat would be worth the pain if he could forget—if only for the night—all that had happened, all the heated words she'd thrown at him.

Truly, he had no other viable options.

He hadn't a clue what kept him from slipping into oblivion for the night, drowning his emotions in the fire water of the devil. He'd much prefer a night in hell to one reliving each word that had passed her delicate pink lips. The touch of Lucifer could not scorch him anymore than Ruby's insults.

"Bloody hell!" The glass shattered against the hearth.

Before he knew what he was doing, his rage—at himself, at his father, and at her—boiled over. The decanter was the next to fall victim. Shards of glass hit every surface within range. If his blood hadn't been pumping so fast through his veins, producing a humming noise in his head, Harold would have heard the sound of shattering glass echo through the house, and the resulting curses coming from the front entry.

Instead, Harold picked up a vase and turned it in his hands, studying the painted pattern. The piece was in mint condition with nary a scratch or chip. The thin glass would explode, unlike either the thick tumbler or the etched decanter.

He was sure the resulting shower of glass would satisfy his need for release even more effectively than imbibing large quantities of only the Lord knew what.

Neither would resolve his problems, advance his life, or in any way make him proud of his actions come morning.

"If you do not mind, that was a gift from the lovely Lady Haversham." The vase was plucked from his hands and replaced on its stand.

He should feel shame for his outburst, and remorse for destroying Brock's glassware.

But the fact was, he was tired of apologizing for things, of catering to others. Most importantly, he was done allowing others to direct the course of his life.

"What has gotten into you?" Brock asked.

Harold continued to stare at the shattered glass below the hearth. "I do not know what you're referring to."

"I'm not a dullard." Brock stepped around Harold. "You've never been a man prone to violence...of any kind, and, trust me, I know you've been in several situations where I would not have kept my composure so gracefully."

"Maybe I'm tired of keeping my composure and acting as if everything is as I'd wish it to be." His friend could have no idea what all weighed on him. Harold had thought Ruby to be a simple diversion, something to take his mind off his own impending exile to the country. But she was anything but simple. Keeping track of her had turned into a full-time mission, and it was damned hard saving someone from themselves, especially when they didn't realized they needed saving.

"You wished my fine crystal to be broken all over the floor?"

"No."

"Then what?"

Such a simple question should have a simple answer, yet Harold hadn't the words to express what he needed.

Brock sat in one of the armchairs facing the

open hearth. "Advice?"

"Sure." Harold shrugged and sank into the other chair. "It cannot be any worse than what I've been thinking myself."

Harold lowered his face into his hands, hoping his friend would share some life-changing wisdom.

"If you want something, do what needs to be done to attain it."

"And what if what you want does not align with what others demand?"

"Simple."

"How so?" Harold asked.

"Stop caring what others demand of you and live the life that makes you happy. When we sit here in thirty years, I want to be content with the choices I made and have no regrets about what I've accomplished in life."

"It's easy when you are born to a title and estate." He looked his friend square in the face. "For me, a commoner, there is much more to think about."

"What you say is true. I have never been left without fund or a home when I needed them, but this is about much more than coin and shelter. I could live with neither of those things guaranteed as long as I have Viola and the ability to earn a decent living."

It was as if Brock knew exactly what troubled him. "I wish it to be that effortless."

"You know you will always have shelter under my roof, or any estate endowed to me."

"Yes, but living off another's wealth and title is not the life any man seeks."

"I am not saying you will stay in my spare rooms and eat my food forever, but right now you have the opportunity to attain what you desire without the fear of homelessness and an empty stomach. If in the end you decide to move back to Haversham and take over the vicarage, then at least you've explored other opportunities."

His brother's business venture and the potential for success stuck firm in his mind, only to be invaded by thoughts of Ruby—dressed in simple garb and smiling at him as she completed some domestic task.

How could she be what he wanted? It was likely she was up to no good, and in jeopardy of hurting everyone Harold cared for. She had secrets he could only guess at. And she'd made it very clear how she felt about him.

He should focus on one area of his life that was under his control. If he and William were successful in their venture, then other opportunities would be available to him—such as the potential financial security a wife and family would need.

"I will replace the items I broke," Harold mumbled.

"See that you do." Brock smiled.

Harold did not relish hiding things from his best friend, nor from Lady Haversham. The conflict between his loyalty to their friendship and his need to assess and discover Ruby's motives was not an easy one to rectify.

If all went as planned with William, he would have enough funds and access to rare commodities to replace both the crystal he'd broken and the liquor he'd spilled. Now, he only need get the coin to his brother and arrange the necessary transport.

"Well, I see my job is done here," Brock said. "I will leave you to sort your priorities while I retire upstairs to take care of my own."

Harold barely noticed his friend's departure from the room as he thought of the many plans still needing to be arranged—none of which included the alluring and mysterious Miss Ruby St. Augustin.

CHAPTER 17

"MAY I HELP you, Miss?"

It took a moment for Ruby to gather her thoughts as she stood facing a servant in Drake livery. "Yes, I am here to see…"

The butler stared at her severely as she racked her memory for a name.

She'd failed to ascertain the name of the girl she'd been ordered to pick up and take to Gunter's for ices. "Ummm…the lady of the house."

"My lord is not married."

"Pardon my ineptness, but I fear I have forgotten her name."

He cocked an eyebrow at her obvious discomfort before putting her out of her misery. "This way, please." He stood back and allowed her entrance. "Lady Ellington will attend you in the parlor. I assume you know where that is."

Ellington? That was an odd name for a girl.

Perhaps she'd changed her mind regarding

alerting the authorities. It was quite possible Ruby would walk into the room and be apprehended immediately—and once again she'd left the Haversham townhouse without informing anyone of her whereabouts.

"I am familiar with the room, thank you." It was only a short walk to the parlor where Lady Ellington had taken her and Harold after finding them in the dark, abandoned room farther down the hall. It was much more inviting here than the dim, sheet-covered study.

She still wondered how the girl came to live with Drake. Lady Ellington wore the clothes of a lady, spoke the refined speech of a lady, and most definitely carried herself as if above all others...but there was something off. The butler neither showed Ruby to the parlor nor asked if she'd like tea. Highly inappropriate treatment of a guest in a marquis' home.

Maybe Ellington was a paid companion, as Ruby herself had been, or a lady's maid. But a lady's maid to whom? As far as she knew, the marquis had never married, and no close female relative was listed in *Peers of the Realm*.

Ruby had come partly for insight—information about the truthfulness of the gossip surrounding the marquis, his scandalous past, and especially about the man himself. Throughout the course of her search, this was the closest she'd come to having access to the entire home of a lord on her list. If she befriended Ellington, her access may very well increase substantially. Then she would quickly be able to cross the marquis off her list, his dubious past included.

The thought of this rakehell being her father scared the daylights out of her. Would it be worse to have no clue who her father was, or to have a man whose reputation at seduction—not to mention his extraordinary reproduction record—knew no bounds?

His deplorable treatment of her mother would make complete sense if he turned out to be the man she sought. But would her heart survive a biological connection to a man who was truly ruthless in his sexual pursuits?

Ruby took in the room she'd spent a few moments in the night before. Gone was the overpowering heat from a blazing fire; no heavy drapes blocked out the clear, mid-morning sunshine. The room had a sinister air about it before, a backdrop for dark dealings and midnight masquerading. Today, the room was almost pleasant.

Completely at odds with the girl who'd just entered the room. Lady Ellington scowled at Ruby, hands on her hips.

"You are late," she scolded.

Ruby almost laughed at the ridiculousness of Ellington's fury. Her nostrils flared ever so slightly and her face held a red tint. She appeared the mother reprimanding her child for innumerable transgressions.

"Now, calm yourself," Ruby said quietly. "It is barely luncheon and Gunter's does not open until after the noon-day meal. Why are you in such a hurry?"

Ellington looked over her shoulder before pushing the door closed, sealing off the possibility of a passing servant hearing their conversation. "I am not in a hurry. I only expect you to live up to your word."

"My word?" It was Ruby's turn to be angry. "When I give my word I stand by it, but when I am forced into a situation—"

"A situation of your own making."

"Be that as it may, when I give my word I follow through." The girl was smart, if a bit irritating and brash. "At this moment, I am obligated to be here, do not confuse that with *wanting* or *needing* to be here."

The smile from their last meeting returned. "You both wanted and needed to be in my house not long ago, did you not?"

How many times would Ruby be made to apologize for her actions? "Are you ready to leave?" She hoped changing the topic would lighten the dour mood in the room.

"I was ready at the agreed-upon time—it was you who was late."

"Is this how our afternoon will go?" Ruby was unsure she could stand ten minutes, let alone two hours in the girl's presence.

Her eyes narrowed. "Our afternoon will go exactly as I dictate it will go."

Ruby had no siblings and was at a loss as to how to deal with a snide girl barely out of the school room. "Ellington, I only meant—"

"You only meant what?" she cut Ruby off. "And do not call me Ellington. I go by *Lady* Ellie."

"As I was saying, I only meant our afternoon can be full of nasty unpleasantness, or we can make the best out of the situation we *both* created." Ruby emphasized. Yes, Ruby broke into Drake's house, but Ellington had doomed them both to spending time together.

She'd pondered the girl's reasons for making her agree to these bizarre outings on her short walk back to the Haversham townhouse, but nothing had struck her as true. As far as Ruby could tell, the girl was provided for financially, she wore fine clothes, fancy ribbons, and quality shoes. She also appeared provided for personally: she was bathed, her hair shone a bright red, and her teeth seemed in good health.

What could she gain from an ex-paid companion without a shilling to her name? While Ellington didn't know Ruby's dire circumstances, it would become apparent shortly. Ruby's spare coin was in such short supply that she would rather not spend it on frivolous things—including ices. She'd agreed to time with Ellington—Ellie—but she had not agreed to spend her scarce money.

It was time to get this over with. "Shall we go or would you like to bicker a bit longer?"

With a huff Ellie headed out of the room, not pausing for the butler to open the front door. She took the steps in one leap, as Ruby had the night before, her dress not hindering her in the slightest.

Stopping abruptly on the walk she looked from side to side and then turned back to Ruby as she lifted her walking dress, taking the steps slowly.

"Where is your coach?" she asked.

"I do not have a coach."

Ellie's brow drew down in confusion. "How do you expect us to get to Gunter's?"

It was Ruby's turn to laugh, probably the most genuine laugh since her arrival in London. It bubbled deep within her. "I guess we will traverse the streets of London upon foot."

"You cannot be serious." The bewilderment in Ellie's voice almost had her laughing again.

"I most assuredly am serious," Ruby said. "I do not have the luxury of a carriage at my beck and call."

"But the other night, I saw you leave Lord Yorkton's in—"

The girl realized her misstep at the same time Ruby did. "You knew who I was?" Ruby knew her expression mirrored Ellie's bewildered one from just a moment before. "You little rascal."

Ellington held her tongue.

"You knew all along who I was. Why did you accuse us of being thieves?" Question after question ran through her mind, but the sidewalk outside the marquis' residence was not the place. They were already drawing curious stares from members of the *ton* walking by on their way to Hyde Park or shopping on Bond Street.

If she hadn't been caught inside Drake's townhouse, Ruby would guess Ellington had somehow targeted her.

"I merely suggested the possibility—I did not accuse, per se."

So many things about the girl made her appear so much older, wiser, than her physical appearance suggested. For the first time, Ruby looked at her—truly looked. She took in what she imagined the world saw when they looked at Ellie. She was well cared for, but also had a worldly way about her, as if she'd seen much and lived through double that in her short life. Her emerald eyes, much the same shade as Ruby's, held a depth and knowledge uncommon in one so young. "How old are you?"

Her question threw the girl off and for once Ellie lacked a witty retort. "Old enough."

"And how old is 'old enough'?" Ruby asked. "Say age fourteen, which many believe is 'old enough' to leave the school room. Or age sixteen, which many believe is 'old enough' to attend your first ball. Or possibly eighteen, which is the preferred age for marriage. There are many, many stages of 'old enough' for a young woman. Let us begin our walk. I do not have all day, but there is plenty of time for you to answer my question, and perhaps time enough for you to ask a few of your own."

Ellington walked down the street toward Gunter's, leaving Ruby behind. "I have no need to answer your questions…and certainly no interest in learning anything about you," she called over her shoulder. "Do not dawdle."

Ruby sighed and started in step after her. If Ellie insisted on walking five steps ahead of her the whole way, at least it would give her time to think, something that was seriously lacking in her life of late. Every time she turned around either Vi or Harold was close, ready to engage her in conversation or needless banter.

The view of Ellie was also interesting. She walked with a confident swagger, her step sure and her head high. The self-assurance bred only into a person born to privilege. A sureness of step that Ruby envied.

This girl knew her place in life.

Ellie was assured of her future role in society.

She wished she knew more about the girl—and why she'd targeted Ruby. Which, Ruby had no doubt Ellie had done. Presented with the right situation, the girl had coerced Ruby into agreeing to a few outings. It could be she was lonely, or in need of a suitable chaperone. If so, there were any number of matronly woman who'd have taken on the responsibility of introducing her to society, if only the marquis would have called upon them.

Sadly, Ruby sat precariously on the very edge of polite society, the illegitimate daughter of an impoverished baron and his unfaithful wife. The truth had become so embedded in her daily life that she wondered if others read her secrets, knew her mother's deceit. The confidence evident in Ellie would never be Ruby's.

As they neared the West End, the street traffic became heavy and Ruby sped her pace to keep an eye on Ellie. The girl walked the streets like she'd been raised running amuck. She occasionally nodded to passing ladies and gentlemen, obviously acquainted with London's elite.

Suddenly, Ellie's hand darted out and returned just as quickly.

Ruby blinked. Had she seen what she thought she'd seen?

Keeping a closer eye on the girl, she watched Ellie's hand again flick out as a man in an expensive jacket walked past her in the opposite direction. Her fingers clutched a dark object upon their return and slipped it into a pocket hidden within Ellie's skirt.

Ruby knew a thing or two about hidden pockets and their use. She hid her lock-picking tools in a pouch concealed within the folds of her evening gown.

Her eyes must have deceived her. Whatever could a young lady of the *ton* be doing stealing? As she continued to watch, torn between alerting strangers to the theft or taking Ellie over her knee for a good spanking, the girl lifted a rather large—and expensive-looking—pocket watch.

When Ruby gasped, Ellie looked over her shoulder and slowed her pace to match Ruby's more ladylike speed.

"What are you doing?" Ruby hissed.

Ellie laughed, attracting the attention of two young men walking toward them. The gentlemen smiled and winked at Ellie and continued on their way.

"Shhhh," she leaned and whispered in Ruby's ear. "If I'm caught I will tell all who will listen that you are my lookout. You would not want that, would you?"

Wonderful. "Just stop that!" Now, she would be implicated in yet another crime.

"Not a chance."

"Do you want us to get arrested?"

"Of course not. I spent one night in the lockup, and it is not for me." Ellie gave Ruby a look of disgust and skipped a few feet ahead.

There was little she could do as she watched Ellie pick pocket after pocket as they walked…and they had another three blocks to go before they reached Gunter's.

At least Ruby would not feel badly insisting Ellie pay for their ices. The thought made her want to laugh and cry at the same time. She was an honest person. She'd never stolen from or lied to another person—except since her return to London. But the situation was only temporary, and the reason for her forced deception was a valid one.

Every decision she'd made since finding her mother's journal had led her to the place she was at this very moment.

And where she was, was about to get even worse.

The tall, finely dressed gentleman walking straight toward Ruby was patting his jacket and pants pockets in alarm. He quickly reached into the inside pocket of his jacket but came back empty handed. Disbelief clouded his face and he stopped in his tracks.

Ruby increased her pace and grabbed the billfold Ellie was about to slip into her hidden pouch.

Turning, she called, "Sir!"

The man's head rose and he turned toward Ruby.

"I think you dropped this."

Relief flooded his face even as Ellie gasped behind her.

"Many thanks," he said. He continued on his way, leaving Ellie staring daggers at Ruby.

"That was a plump one." Ellie's irritation was obvious.

But Ruby's displeasure was greater. "Do you realize you put yourself in jeopardy every time you steal something? What if he was a man prone to anger and violent outburst, what then?"

"I can take care of myself—always have and always will."

Ruby's fury evaporated. She didn't know Ellington; who she was or what she'd been through. She could not cast the first stone, lest that stone be returned in her direction. Instead of scolding her once more, Ruby threaded her arm through Ellie's and continued down the street. "Well, I am here now and it would be remiss of me not to save you from yourself." If she kept the girl's hands occupied it was less likely she would get them into trouble.

Their acquaintance spanned less than two days, but Ruby had an overwhelming urge to help the girl, guide her, possibly influence her to be a better person. She recognized the lost and lonely look in Ellie's eyes. The years of hurt that shone through her tough exterior.

"You won't be around for long—your kind never is."

"My kind?" How Ruby wished to question her. Maybe they had more in common than either of them knew. The solitary life was not easy, and most definitely not one she'd wish upon anyone, especially one as young as Ellie. At least Ruby had had her father until she was fifteen.

Ellie kicked a pebble on the street as they walked. "Sure, you know. Grand ladies who pretend to care, all because they want something from me. But who cares, you all are ugly anyway." Without another word or any justification, Ellie pulled out of her grasp and bounded into Gunter's.

Ruby had to remind herself that she'd agreed to three afternoons with the girl—no more. Ellie's past, and most certainly her future, did not involve Ruby. She had her own problems to fret over without the added issues of a young pickpocket.

With a deep, cleansing breath, Ruby followed the girl into the ice shop.

True to form, Ellie insisted on Ruby fronting the coin for their treats. Then, they moved to the small tables on the walk outside the shop to sit.

The ice tasted heavenly, though Ruby ate quickly, not leaving much opportunity to enjoy the rare goodness of the delicacy. The girl also ate in silence, much to Ruby's delight. She'd been at a loss as to how she might approach any subject beyond the weather. Added to that, her argument with Harold still weighed heavily upon her.

While she most certainly regretted her

horrible words, she was not sorry for their effect. He'd allowed her to leave and hadn't followed. In his absence, she had been able to cross another man off her list within a few short minutes of questioning one of the gentleman's upstairs maids. The impossibly well-endowed Earl of Ivertime was told at a very young age that he was incapable of bearing children, eliminating the likelihood that her mother would have found him desirable and worthy of her end objective. Ruby had read every heartbreaking word of her mother's struggle to conceive; every failed year tore at her parent's relationship until her mother had sought out someone to give her what she truly wanted.

"What shall we do next?" Ellie asked.

Looking to the girl, Ruby noticed she'd finished her ice and sat slouched in her seat, staring expectantly at her.

"I hadn't anticipated much else for our afternoon."

The girl huffed and crossed her arms. "You must be jesting with me. If you think to keep your midnight activities from the gossips, then I would put a little more effort into our outings."

"You are still assuming there is something to tell the gossips," Ruby mused. "I am sure your activities would be just as noteworthy if they were known."

"My activities?" Ellie sat up straight. "As far as the *ton* knows, I do not exist."

The comment drew Ruby's attention, not to the words themselves, but the emotion behind them. What person relished living in nonexistence?

"What is he doing here?" Ellie asked suddenly. "I thought I made myself perfectly clear that he was not to be told the terms of our agreement."

Her comment and the fact that the girl stared intently over Ruby's shoulder was alarming. Turning, Ruby saw Harold speaking with a man across the street. Carriages and pedestrians obscured her view, but his tall, confident frame was unmistakable. Maybe her scolding hadn't discouraged his involvement in her everyday affairs after all.

"I have half a mind to continue on to the *Gazette* office three blocks over and share some tasty information about a scandalous tryst between two of London's newcomers."

Ruby turned back to the smug girl. Where the chit gained her information, she had no clue. Not many people had noticed Ruby, let alone knew she was new to the London social circle.

"I most certainly did not betray our agreement, if that is what you insist on calling it." Ruby was angry, although she was uncertain who most deserved her wrath, Ellington or Harold. "And do not think you have the upper hand in this agreement. I am here because I chose to be here, not because of your master blackmailing skills." They both knew her words to be a farce, but Ruby would not bow to the girl evermore. "I am unsure of his business in this part of town, we're hardly acquainted."

As they watched, Harold drew an envelope from his pocket and handed it to the man beside him. At first the man looked like any modest gentleman you'd see walking the streets of London, but upon closer inspection his hair was unkempt and longer than society deemed appropriate, although not in the rebel-about-town way. And the man wore the most enormous boots. His feet could not possibly be large enough to need the size. The man opened the envelope and pulled a stack of notes out, fanning them before his face.

"Hey you!" Ellie shouted, her outburst startling Ruby from her observations.

"What are you doing?"

"What am I doing?" the girl retorted. "What are *they* doing is a much better question."

Ruby looked back to the men, who'd trained their own eyes on them. As they watched, the man she did not know—though he seemed oddly familiar—slipped the envelope into his own jacket and began to amble down the street, his oversized boots never quite leaving the sidewalk.

"Oh, he is coming this way," Ellie exclaimed. "And he does not look happy."

CHAPTER 18

HAROLD HAD WONDERED how the last twenty-four hours could possibly get any worse, but thankfully the answer presented itself in the form of Ruby, seated across the street—watching him hand money to his brother—while in the company of their little blackmailer.

He hadn't a clue what the girl was up to, but it was important enough that Ruby had acquiesced, sending Harold from the room. He wondered if it had to do with her own secret.

The woman was almost too ignorant to be true. Or possibly he was the ignorant one, and they sat across the busy street laughing at his expense. He did not know, but he was set on finding out. Her plan, whatever it may be, was about to come to light and if it so much as came close to jeopardizing Lord and Lady Haversham's reputation, he would out her and make sure she was sent packing back to her family's country home.

Crossing the street, he barely heard the angry shouts of men on horseback and coachmen. He could think of one thing and one thing only: outing the woman for the liar she was. She'd done nothing but scheme and lie since she'd arrived in London. The illogical part of him truly believed she would come to trust him, to confide in him. Why that mattered so much to him he didn't know, but he kept searching the woman in front of him for the person he remembered her to be. Unfortunately, he may very well have to concede that that woman was gone, never to return.

"Good day," he said in greeting as he bowed. He didn't bother to stop the girl as she slipped away unnoticed by Ruby.

"Mr. Jakeston," she muttered. "What a pleasure to see you. But then again, I expect you to be lurking close at all times."

He didn't understand the venom in her words.

She was the one who'd insulted his very manhood.

She was the one caught having an afternoon ice with the girl who held both their reputations in her hands.

She was the one withholding a secret that could potentially destroy his best friend's wife.

And she scolded him?

"Firstly, I do not lurk. Secondly, I would like nothing more than to be out of your way, but I find it is impossible to evade your nefarious outings."

"Please tell Mr. Jakeston—" Ruby stared at the empty seat beside her, abandoned by her co-conspirator moments before. "What..."

"Alone with no explanations once more, I

see." When she stayed silent, he continued. "Every time I tell myself to keep my distance from you—to forget your presence—I find you in the most suspicious of situations. I am left with no other option but to discover your purpose."

"How dare you." She stood, stepping close and staring him straight in the eyes. "You challenge my person, yet you hold secret meetings about town, exchanging money for heaven knows what."

Harold had been aware that she'd had a clear view of his meeting with William, and he had to admit it probably looked as suspicious as her own actions. But that was not what he was here to discuss, and he knew his actions were pure of heart—though he couldn't say the same of her. "Do not change the subject."

"I will do whatever I please." Her voice rose with her words. "Now, if you will kindly excuse me, I have an evening to prepare for."

She pushed past him and started toward the Haversham townhouse—the same direction Harold would be headed, regardless of the circumstances. He fell into step beside her, matching her shorter stride.

"What are you doing?"

"Accompanying you home."

"I think you have done quite enough for me lately." She increased her pace.

"Oh, but I would never leave a lady unescorted on the streets of London, regardless of the sword I may have protruding from my back."

"You know I did not mean—"

"Do not bother apologizing for your rude and careless comments."

"I had no intention of apologizing. I only

meant I should not have verbalized my thoughts." She eyed him from the corner of her eye. "What were you doing giving that man an envelope of money?"

He knew the change of subject was meant to throw him off guard, but he hadn't grown up with two older siblings and countless others about the estate to be fooled so easily.

"Here's a proposition: I answer your questions if you answer a few of mine."

"So this is a fishing expedition?" she asked. "You think you can strong-arm me into telling you all?"

"It is not the worst idea." Harold wanted to laugh. She was smart as a whip, and knew it. Maybe he didn't stand a chance against her. Giving up his quest for answers may not be the honorable thing to do, but would most certainly save his ego from another good beating.

She sighed. "Just tell me who the man is."

She was as tired of the banter as he was, but could he trust her to give him information in return? He shouldn't be surprised that she hadn't recognized William. Even Harold had to admit he was a shell of the man he'd once been. His wasted frame, even in newly tailored clothes, was seriously lacking.

"I find I do not feel inclined to be forthcoming in my business dealings."

"Maybe I will be so inclined as to ask Lord and Lady Haversham about your business dealings."

"Then I will be forced to speak with Lady Haversham about your evening escapades."

Neither noticed they'd stopped in the middle of the sidewalk, forcing others to navigate around them. They stood face to face, toe to toe, drawing the attention of several people.

"I guess we are at what they call a stalemate," Ruby hissed, hands on her hips.

"My lady, we are anything but stale."

Her eyes widened. "Your manners are sorely inadequate."

The words rolled off him, not even piercing the hard shell he'd wrapped his emotions in since their earlier confrontation. "Be that as it may, Miss Ruby, I will be escorting you back to Haversham townhouse. In the future, I will endeavor to stay out of your way, if you'll agree to extend me the same courtesy."

"It will be my pleasure." She extended her hand.

Grasping it, he tucked it into the crook of his arm, and, as if they hadn't only a moment before been close to shouting at each other on a crowded London street, they turned and began the short walk back to Haversham townhouse.

If she thought she could play coy with him, she had another thing coming. He may not have answers now, but he would get to the bottom of her reason for being in London.

And he would do everything in his power to avoid it adversely affecting Lady Haversham.

AS SHE WALKED, her hand securely tucked into the crook of his arm, she wondered if the draw she felt to him went further than she knew. It was as if the powers to be were pushing them together, compelling them closer. Part of her wanted to accept it, while it was most likely only that Harold was following her and nothing to do with anything else.

"A shilling for your thoughts?" he asked beside her.

She peeked up at him, fearing making full eye contact. She turned into a bumbling idiot every time she looked directly at him. It would not behoove her to speak of too much, yet she deeply regretted her previous harsh words. It didn't matter that she discouraged him at every turn, he still tried.

Their evening on the pond had shown her they could have a conversation without revealing too much and without her treating him poorly. If they were to spend the season living with Vi and Lord Haversham, they needed to be civil. Their hosts were not dull, and would most certainly notice the pair avoiding each other.

"Sometimes, even though we are right next to each other, I feel you are miles away. Why is that?"

"I think the same thing," she confided.

"Do you ever just want to let go and not worry so much?" He stared straight ahead as he talked. "Maybe disappear for a while and start something all your own."

Ruby didn't know if the questions were meant for her or if he was examining his own life out loud, but she wanted to keep him talking. Despite doing everything she could to push him away, she couldn't deny her physical draw to the man. The street became less crowded as they neared the Haversham townhouse, straying farther from the busy section of town.

"That is much easier said than done," she said.

"How so?"

"We have friends and family—responsibilities—that tie us to this place at this time." It would be an overwhelming sense of relief to let everything go; not care who her father was, be away from her mother's dictating hand, and start anew.

Harold patted her hand. "Yes, we do, but what a shame."

"You would leave behind Lord Haversham?"

"Brock and I have a friendship that has never been location dependent. It would endure a period of separation—it has before. You would not leave Lady Haversham, even with the promise of a brighter future, knowing your paths would cross again one day?"

"I do not think anyone's future can be guaranteed," she said. "And how dull would that be, if it were?"

"Oh, nothing with either of us will ever be dull. We could leave now, travel to the country— maybe toward Dover—and settle in a small cottage of our own." The excitement in his voice sent a thrill through her as well.

When had they moved from discussing their separate lives, to imagining a future together? Fighting herself every step of the way, Ruby had to admit the picture he painted sounded heavenly. In Dover, it wouldn't matter that she was a bastard, that her mother had betrayed the man she'd adored, or that anyone could find out about any of it.

"We could raise sheep or learn to farm."

"Oh, you could handle a flock of sheep?" She glanced at him in surprise. "And crops?"

"Of course. We can travel to London a few times a year to hock our wares. Visit with Brock and Lady Haversham, and then return to the children."

"You do not think the children would also like to visit with the Haversham offspring?" Again, they built a life—imaginary as it was—together.

"Ah, very true." He looked down at her then, his eyes filled with mischief. "But I would enjoy time alone with my wife, as well."

Her cheeks warmed at his heated gaze, and she quickly looked away. "Fantasy is fine for children," she said, already regretting the words. "We are adults, with adult responsibilities. Adult problems. Plus, we have arrived home. I'm sorry, Harold, but this is the only house we will share."

"As you wish." He still held her arm firmly as they climbed the steps to the house and the butler swung the door open.

They entered the main foyer and stopped, facing each other. She didn't know what to say, still under the spell of their conversation.

"Mr. Jakeston, Lord Haversham awaits you in his study."

"Thank you." He took her hand and brought it to his lips and whispered, "I do hope your wishes change at some point. Have a wonderful afternoon."

He stood straight, bowed, and headed to the study.

Meanwhile, Ruby was left open-mouthed, imagining a whole new future—if only she could let go of the past.

"Miss?" a servant asked at her side.

"Oh, yes?"

"Lady Haversham requests your attendance in her bedchamber."

"Is everything all right?"

"Yes, I do believe she is being fitted for new gowns."

Ruby pushed the thought of what could be from her mind and focused on the here and now.

CHAPTER 19

HAROLD WATCHED HER across the table, pushing her food from one side of her plate to the other, refusing to make eye contact with him. Perhaps she was preoccupied with her own thoughts. Perhaps, certain thoughts he'd put in her head only hours before.

He took full advantage of the view. This was the first meal they'd all shared together since Ruby and Lady Haversham had arrived in London.

Of course, Lord and Lady Haversham were absorbed in their own conversation, leaving Harold and Ruby to their own devices. He'd tried to start a conversation several times, about the weather or what traveling play group was in town currently, but after a few nods and a word here or there the conversation always went stale. Try as he might, they could not return to their easy conversation from that night on the pond, or during their musings on the way home this very day. Her distance combined with her actions of late made it impossible to trust her, much as he had tried.

Brock laughed explosively, bringing both their attention to the couple.

"What has you in such a jovial mood?" Harold asked, grateful for the distraction.

"Oh, I was just telling Vi what we discovered in the book at White's today."

Harold chuckled, unable to stop himself. He'd admit that it might not be morally acceptable, but he was hardly one to shy from a wager—or cast a stone when others showed the same inclination.

"Lord Grafton truly wagered his entire stables on the outcome of Lord and Lady Sully's name selection for their firstborn?" Vi asked, her hand covering her mouth to muffle her laughter.

"Of course he did!" Brock continued. "The winner stands to gain a tidy sum. Lord Sully loves horses and has actively sought to purchase Lord Grafton's broodmare. Harold, tell them the name!"

"Pompous Buckton." Harold had to admit the name was comical, yet he hoped the child was not cursed with it. "Yes, it is likely that the next Earl of Sully will be christened with the name Pompous."

The whole table erupted, including Ruby. The look upon her face when she laughed was like none he'd even seen. In her eyes he saw joy, love, passion... If only she would allow him to make her laugh more often.

Brock was the first to get himself under control. "Not all the wagers are as entertaining, but occasionally it amuses me to have a look. I did win a tidy sum on one myself." He winked at

Harold.

Truth be told, Harold's pockets had filled about the same time.

"And what wager was that?" Ruby joined the conversation. "Tell me it had to do with something worthwhile."

"Oh, yes. In fact it was directly related to the most worthwhile person currently in my life." He looked to his wife, taking her hand and bringing it to his lips.

"You stop it right now, Brock." Lady Haversham pulled her hand back. "We have guests."

Looking affronted, Brock asked, "Guests?" He looked around dramatically. "Where?"

"You know exactly who I am talking about."

No matter how often Harold found himself in his dear friends' company, he never tired of their easy banter. He longed one day to have something similar, if not as grand.

"These two? If the pair are guests, they have most positively overstayed their welcome," Brock continued to joke.

Laughter again floated through the room.

"And what was this wager that left us out of debtor prison about?" Vi inquired.

"It involved the most stubborn and headstrong woman I've had the good fortune to meet."

"Truly?" Ruby joined the conversation again.

"For certain. Someone, who will remain nameless, thought it funny to place a wager after this woman and a very handsome, intelligent man found himself in the middle of a ballroom, causing a scandal."

"And what exactly was the wager?"

"Oh, that said couple—although it is

imperative that you know these two were in no way a couple at that point—would marry within the year." Brock addressed his answer to Ruby, but kept Vi in his peripheral sight.

"That poor woman!" Harold said in exasperation.

"Oh, no...she is an extremely lucky woman," Brock countered.

"Says a most handsome, intelligent man?" Vi asked.

"Of course!"

"More like a man more stubborn and headstrong than said woman," Harold felt compelled to say. His friend had tried to deny his attraction to his wife for so long he'd almost ruined what they currently had.

"What other types of wagers do men make at White's?" Ruby asked. "I mean, other than children's names and potential matches within London's elite?"

Her interest sparked Harold's attention. While Brock and Vi continued to laugh and make jokes, Ruby's demeanor had become serious, and she listened intently.

Brock speared a piece of meat, brought it to his mouth and chewed as he searched for a particularly juicy bit of gossip found in the book. "Well, men wager about horse races, business endeavors, and the like." Harold knew he intentionally kept the subject matter tame, not willing to speak of the more scandalous items bet upon by men.

"Come now," Ruby prodded him. "There must be more interesting goings-on than that."

Harold wondered what information she sought with her inquisitiveness. "You are correct, Miss Ruby." Harold decided to bait the hook, so to speak, and see if he could glean any idea as to what the woman was up to. "They wager on anything from which singer will receive an encore performance at the opera to what the weather will be in a fortnight."

"Now, Harold. You cannot share all of our dirty secrets or Vi will never let me out of the house again. And then I will miss all the fun."

"There must be more important things than that in the wager book." Ruby leaned her elbows on the table, enthralled.

"Oh my, yes!" Vi said. "I have heard there is a list of London's mistresses and illegitimate children."

"Shame on you, Lady Haversham," Brock scolded. "To discuss such delicate topics in front of ladies is the height of impropriety. We must work on your decorum."

"My decorum?" Her outrage didn't quite match the smile on her face.

"You are a most unruly woman! I think it is best to hire a tutor to train you in the ways of London society," Brock continued, Harold and Ruby all but forgotten.

"Well, it will be a huge undertaking, but I will volunteer," Harold chimed in.

"Like hell you will," Brock's thundering voice filled the room. "I will rein in my own wife, thank you all the same."

Harold laughed, his gaze returning to Ruby, who stared intently at nothing in particular. "Is your supper to your liking?" he asked. "Miss Ruby?"

She returned to the present. "It is very good." She picked up her fork and continued eating.

As Brock and Vi fell back into their

comfortable conversation and Ruby concentrated on her meal, Harold watched. He didn't understand the woman, and try as he might, he couldn't make her trust him enough to explain herself.

He vowed then to keep an eye on her, help her avoid getting herself into another predicament like the night in Drake's house, or the evening not many nights before when she'd stumbled upon him in Lord Yorkton's study. If she wasn't careful, she was likely to be caught by someone other than himself.

CHAPTER 20

"ALL I AM saying is that my stables are far superior to most found within England's borders." Brock racked the billiard balls for a new game after losing dreadfully to Harold.

Harold laughed. "You truly believe that mares raised by your lovely wife will produce the best foal this country has seen in over three decades?"

"It is an unstated, yet undeniable fact."

"And you seek to convince every man in London of this fact?" Harold asked.

His friend went far beyond what was deemed acceptable spousal support. Lady Haversham could do no wrong in Brock's eyes.

"Of course...and I will make a second fortune from it!"

Harold knew Brock's insistence in supporting Lady Haversham's horses had naught to do with the money to be made, and all to do with his soothing her hurt and loss over the closing of her foal ranch, Foldger's Foals, the previous year. While the property was anything but fallow—it now housed Foldger's Foundling House—his wife missed her previous life and purpose.

"I wish I'd had the funds available at the time to purchase a few myself," Harold said. "But then I'd also need the coin for a stable...oh, and an estate on which to house said stable."

"As I have said before, money, or the lack thereof, does not totally change one's life."

It had been hard to think of anything else but this since they'd spoken a few nights before. No, money would not change his life completely, but it would allow him freedom.

Harold stepped forward to take his shot. The pool stick moved smoothly through his fingers and the balls pinged off each other and rebounded off the sides, three landing in pockets.

"Well done," Brock said. "I should have known better than to think I could best you at billiards if we only played one more game."

"I gave you the opportunity to bow out with your dignity still intact, but once again, you let it pass." They'd played billiards for years—and for years, Harold had won almost every game. Much like his skill at cards, he had neither practiced nor studied.

"My lord?" Buttons called from the open doorway. "You have a guest."

Harold leaned his stick against the wall as Alex walked into the room.

"Alex." Brock embraced the young man before pulling back and assessing him from head to toe. "It has been too long, my boy."

Harold avoided eye contact, hoping Alex wouldn't betray Ruby's confidence by announcing their brief meeting at Drake House. The young man had no reason to keep Harold's whereabouts private, but Ruby's were another thing.

"My lord." Alex stepped back far enough to bow to Brock. "It has been overly long."

"Listen to you," Brock exclaimed. "You must be practicing your speech, just as Lady Haversham taught you."

"I will be forever indebted to her."

"Have you come to accept my offer of employment?" Brock asked. "As I said, I will double whatever the marquis currently pays you."

"While that is very generous, my lord, I need to make my own way. One day I will have a family of my own to support and I cannot allow Lady Haversham to care for me."

"You will inform me immediately if you are ever unhappy or treated unjustly?" Brock prodded.

"Of course, though I am very satisfied with my current employer, and I am learning much from his stable master."

"Lady Haversham will be overjoyed to hear this. Let me ring for her to attend us."

"That would be grand, but I fear I haven't much time and I came to speak with Mr. Jakeston, if you don't mind." Alex nodded in Harold's direction.

"Oh, most certainly." Brock looked between them. "I hadn't known the pair of you were acquainted."

"Only through Miss Ruby," Harold volunteered before Alex could say a word.

"Very well, then. Harold, I look forward to a rematch." Brock nodded to Harold and patted

Alex on the back before departing the room, pulling the door shut behind him.

Harold could not imagine what Brock thought they had to discuss, but he was happy for the privacy. He was immediately alert to having not seen Ruby in the last few hours—but truly, how much trouble could she get into since mid-afternoon?

"Is everything all right?" he asked as soon as they were alone.

"I am not certain, Mr. Jakeston."

"Please, call me Harold."

The young man nodded, then continued. "You are a friend to Miss Ruby, correct?"

"I am not sure she would use the term friend," Harold responded warily. "But I do find myself looking out for her, yes."

Alex nodded, seeming to accept his answer. "Miss Ruby came to me not long ago and begged to borrow one of my livery uniforms."

"Whatever for?"

"I am afraid she did not confide her plans to me, but she asked several odd questions."

"Go on."

"She wanted to know if the Marquis of Drake was in attendance at his club this evening."

"And your answer?"

Alex sighed, as if Harold should already know the answer. "I informed her that my master only attends one evening a week and she knows very well what evening that is."

Again, Harold felt like he was missing something.

"Mr. Jakeston—I mean Harold," he said, when Harold looked at him cluelessly. "He was there just a few evenings past, when I snuck the pair of you into his home."

"How did she take that news?"

"She was relieved, I presume."

"Very peculiar," Harold mused.

"My thoughts exactly." The young man's stance was one of confidence. "I worried she was going to request my assistance in getting access to the Drake townhouse again. I was greatly relieved when she only requested my uniform."

She wanted the uniform and was relieved to hear Drake was safely ensconced at home.

Which could only mean one thing…

"Alex, thank you for coming to me." Harold pushed past the young man to the door before turning. "Please, do not speak to Lord or Lady Haversham about this."

"Of course not."

"I appreciate your discretion. I will discover what the woman is up to before she is harmed."

"I understand things are not always what they seem," Alex said. "I hope you find her before she does something unwise."

"I plan to, and expect she will be held accountable for her deeds." With a quick wave, Harold started for the stairs. He hoped to find her still in her rooms, but the dread in the pit of his stomach told him he was too late.

Without knocking, he pushed her door wide. Sure enough, the room stood empty. The roaring fire in the fireplace told him her maid hadn't expected her departure this evening. He cast his gaze about the room, searching for anything that would give him concrete proof of where she was headed. Wasting valuable time searching for her in the wrong places might very well cost Ruby her reputation.

The room held the things Harold judged as

common to all women of the *ton*: brushes, mirrors, writing utensils, and stationery.

One thing stood out.

Nestled on her bedside table, between a candle and her wash bowl, was a bound book. The cover, tattered and worn, practically fell from the pages within when he lifted the tome. He turned it in his hand and opened the front cover to see handwritten words. Not the writing he knew well from the papers he'd read of Ruby's, but the neat, flowing script of another, upon aged yellow pages.

Harold flipped through what he now knew was a journal of sorts, every page filled with words written by the same hand.

The words jumped off the paper, bringing into mind the pages he'd read on Ruby's writing desk not long ago. *Do not judge or condemn me for loving a man who cannot love me in return.*

Confused, he flipped to an earlier entry in hopes of finding a better explanation. Instead, he stumbled on more convoluted statements. *This child, how can I love it as it will only bring me sorrow?*

Harold skimmed a page of writing before he found the end of one lengthy record, where a single name was scribbled: *Pearl.*

His heart dropped at the meaning of that simple name.

Ruby's mother.

Within minutes, he'd scanned enough of the entry to glean at least a basic understanding of what the rest of the journal contained.

Page after page of Pearl's sordid confessions of infidelity, her dim outlook on her future…and that of the child she carried, sired not by her husband, but another man. The pieces fell into place. Ruby's list was made of up men of a mature age. She wasn't looking for a husband; she was not set on a path meant to hurt Brock and Lady Haversham. She only sought the man who sired her.

Harold set the book back, exactly as he'd found it.

She needed him, now more than ever. That she hadn't confided in him was not a shock. In fact, he could hardly blame her.

He left her room and headed to the kitchen, toward the door leading to Brock's stable and the alley beyond.

He could think of only one topic that had drawn her attention recently—and he hoped, for her sake, he was wrong about her destination.

CHAPTER 21

RUBY TOOK IN the crowded, smoke-filled room from beneath the cap pulled low to hide her feminine face. No amount of hair tucking and male attire could disguise her form. She'd never seen herself as overly curvacious, but once she'd donned men's breeches it was apparent to all and sundry.

Alex had been correct when he'd said gaining access to White's would be rather simple. All she'd had to do was nod to the man watching the back door and make her way to a room reserved especially for the livery of London's elite. The drizzle and balmy wind had made it necessary for more coachmen to seek refuge in the club, forsaking the meager space in the stables.

After entering the back door, her fear of discovery subsided. Not a single person acknowledged her presence. She was outfitted in Drake livery of black and red.

"Good evening," she mumbled to another passing servant, deepening her voice.

Vexing as it was to admit it, she wished Harold was with her. As much as she tried to deny it, both to herself and to him, the fact was that she felt better, safer, with Harold by her side—as though nothing truly dreadful could happen when he was near. Pushing the wayward thoughts from her mind, Ruby forced herself to return to her plan for the evening.

It was simple. The goal for tonight was to get a peek at the wager book that was such a huge part of White's history. She was fast running out of potential fathers to investigate and her time in London could be up at any moment if anyone caught wind of her search. This wager book could potentially hold exactly the information she sought.

She'd overheard at supper the night before that the book was kept in an alcove in the main room, which made it better and more profitable for the club. Men could see when a new bet or wager was recorded and could levy their own coin by picking a side or certain odds.

There was bound to be something listed about her mother and father. It was highly unlikely their affair had gone unnoticed within London circles. Maybe a wager was placed that hadn't found its way into the gossip mill. After gaining access to the book, Ruby would peruse the months before her birth to correlate any wager made within the time period of her mother's affair. Possibly an unnamed woman linked to a wealthy lord. Lord Haversham had imparted at supper that often times individuals were identified by initials only. And a set of initials was more information to work with than she currently possessed.

The book must be massive in size to hold so many years of wagers, and most likely the volume holding entries before Ruby's birth had long since been removed and replaced with a newer ledger. Alas, it was a possibility she needed to explore.

The task sounded easy enough until the alcove came in to view—and several men were crowded around it placing wagers and recording new bets.

Ruby knew she would not be able to remain undetected for an extended period of time, and this evening would likely be her only chance to search the book. She itched to touch it, turn the pages and discover something about herself. Hanging back, tucked in the shadows of the room far from the fire, and therefore separate from most of the men in attendance, she watched and bided her time. It would behoove her not to rush. She had all evening to gain access. Vi and Brock had left earlier in the evening for a dinner party. Her friend had begged her to accompany them, but said she understood Ruby's request for a 'few hours of solitude,' claiming the demands of *ton* life were exhausting in the extreme.

"May I help you?"

She'd been so preoccupied glaring at the wager book and the crowd of men around it that she'd failed to notice the man standing next to her in the shadows.

She dropped her head, focusing on the floor at her feet, terrified the man would sound the alarm at a female presence within the establishment. "No, I await my lord." She forced her words to remain deep, irritating her throat.

"And who might that be?" he asked.

Ruby refused to look up at the man, but his boots appeared expensive and his voice oddly familiar. She knew the marquis' livery colors were recognizable by all. "The Marquis of Drake, m'lord."

"Oh," he said. "I had not noticed his attendance this evening."

She should have known she'd be caught—and turned over to the magistrate for impersonating a livery servant and entering a club she was not a member of. Her list of crimes expanded almost daily. "Excuse me." It wasn't too late to take her leave and disregard her foolish plan. "I will await his departure with the other servants."

Fingers tightened around her upper arm when she moved to leave.

"Not so fast, Miss Ruby." She looked to the familiar face of Rodney Swiftenberg, Lord Haversham's cousin and current heir to the Earldom. "Fancy meeting you here," he hissed in her ear.

Dread washed over her.

Their stares held.

Ruby was not willing to give in to defeat, despite Rodney's best attempts at intimidating her. It would not work. She wasn't as easily intimidated as Vi had been the year before when Rodney had thought Vi was seeking out Brock's attention with marriage in mind. Eventually, they had married—but that had never been Vi's motive.

"What do you want?" she asked, deciding it was best to be forward with him. Chances were Ruby wouldn't like his answer or have the means to assure his silence.

A cold draft slammed into Ruby when

someone opened the entrance door to the club, admitting a group of men.

"Rodney! You filthy cheat!" a man from the newly arrived group called.

The next moment passed in a blur. One second she was staring Rodney down; the next she was laid flat on the floor, her cheek flaming in pain, unable to focus on the shouting men surrounding her. She pushed into a sitting position and attempted to scoot up against the closest wall and away from the tightly grouped men. Words flew about her as she tried to make sense of it all.

Her head ached and she almost fell back to the floor, dizzy.

She brought her hand to her throbbing cheek only to have her fingers tangle in her loose hair. Her hat had dislodged in her fall.

Still confused, she looked up at the men surrounding her. One rubbed his knuckles as if soothing them. His words finally made sense. "You coward!"

"Me? The coward?" Rodney shouted back. "I am not the one who tried to punch a man without warning."

"I have given you more warning than you deserve. Thinking you can sneak back into town and not make good on your gaming debts to me. You are lucky the lad stepped in my way and took the punch for you."

Ruby could only sit there, hoping neither looked down, therefore delaying her eventual discovery.

"Sir, I am sorry you took the cuff intended for this scoundrel." Unfortunately, her luck continued much as it had her whole life when the man decided to come to her aid. "Allow me to help you to your feet and I will get you—"

His words cut short when he realized Ruby lay sprawled on the ground, her hair tumbled freely around her shoulders, breeches clinging to her shapely legs, and a hand pressed to her face.

Before she could say anything—or the doorman for the club threw her out—arms pulled her to her feet, jammed her cap back on her head and hauled her toward the back of the club. The quick movement increased her dizziness and she wavered on her feet. If it weren't for the strong arms securely about her waist, she would no doubt be on the floor once again, her world continuing to spin out of control.

"Do not relieve your stomach on me," Harold whispered. "It will be hard enough getting you out of here without anyone recognizing you. It will only draw more attention if your evening meal is covering my shirt."

She might well have done exactly that if it wasn't for Harold, arm behind her back for support, practically dragging her from the room. Her feet sought traction on the highly polished floor, to gain her balance and relieve him of all her weight.

Seconds later, they were through the back entrance and past the stable, where servants waited for their lords, moving further into the bleakness of a service alley.

Harold drew to a stop.

"Are you bleeding? Does your face hurt? What happened?" His questions kept coming and her head swam, trying to formulate answers.

"Slow down, please," she mumbled. Bringing her palm away from her injured cheek, she was happy to see no blood. She would never forgive herself if she'd soiled Alex's livery uniform. "My head hurts something fierce. Did I truly get hit in the face just now?"

"Here, sit down." Harold helped her the few feet to a crate left leaning against the back of a building. "Yes, you did. And took it better than most grown men, I might add."

Ruby laughed. She didn't know if she found his comment funny or the absurdity of her situation had finally caught up to her.

"Whatever were you thinking, going into White's—and with Rodney!" Anger infused his words. "That man is a detestable excuse for a human being."

"I did not go—"

"And in nothing more than skin-tight breeches and a cap?" He paced away from her, the shadows of the night clouding his face. "You truly are a danger to yourself."

"How dare y—"

"How dare I? Do you understand the repercussions if someone recognized you?"

He wouldn't let her get a word in edgewise, so she sat in silence waiting for his fury to ebb.

From down the dark alley came, "They went that way."

They both looked toward the direction of White's and the sound of feet headed their way.

"We need to depart. Can you walk or shall I carry you?"

She couldn't allow him to be punished for her hare-brained idea. Hands planted firmly on the crate on which she sat, she pushed herself up. While the thought of being in his arms was welcome, she said instead, "Let us go." Nausea turned her stomach, but she forced the bile down and remained on her feet.

He slipped his arm behind her back once more and they took off at a slow pace down the street.

HAROLD WANTED TO yell at her, berate her for her horrible choices, and at the same time he wanted nothing more than to draw her into his embrace. To convince himself that—for the most part—she was unharmed.

He wanted to confide in her that he knew what she'd been searching for and that he could help, but he knew that his assistance would not be welcome. She'd gone to great lengths to conceal her secret from him; it would be a delicate matter revealing that he was no longer in the dark.

"How did you find me?" She didn't lift her head, keeping watch on the uneven ground as they walked.

"I'm not a fool, Ruby." While he felt like one for arriving too late to prevent the bruise that was sure to appear by morning. "Your interest in our dinner conversation last evening was extremely apparent."

He glanced at her and she tucked her head into his shoulder.

They continued in silence. Ruby leaned heavily against him and Harold accepted her slight weight, glad for the chance to assist her, even though he'd been moments too late. He'd need to keep a better eye on her and her extracurricular activities. He could never forgive himself if she came to further harm. He'd known something weighed heavily upon her…and he'd disregarded his unease. Never again.

He would not be the weak man his father believed him to be—and the malleable simpleton Rodney and Brock's brothers had always called him in their youth.

If he'd learned anything during his time in London, it was that he would one day be his own man, living by his own means, and at the mercy of none. And furthermore, he did not need the validation of others, only himself.

He hadn't given himself time to recognize the hurt he felt at her acceptance of Rodney's help, while she'd shunned his offers, denied him. Rodney could not offer her anything more than Harold himself could.

That is what injured him to his core: Ruby did not trust him—probably would never trust him enough to confide in him.

They turned down another alley that eventually led them to the main street that passed in front of White's Gentlemen's Club, two blocks down. No one had followed them thus far, and Harold hoped they'd given up their search. He paused in a pool of light coming from a nearby building to better gauge her injuries.

He lifted her chin slightly. "Does it hurt dreadfully?"

"Not overly." She pulled her chin away and his hand fell back to his side. "I am sorry to involve you in this."

"I have wanted nothing more than to help, but you have made it clear that you prefer the assistance of Rodney as opposed to myself." He tried unsuccessfully to keep the hurt from his voice. She'd been through so much this evening—truly since her arrival in London—and the last thing she needed was his fury and questioning over her choice of companions.

"I did not seek—"

"You do not owe me any answers," he cut off her words. "I am only happy you are all right and, aside from a headache tonight and certain bruising by morning, you are unscathed, your reputation intact."

She sighed, her shoulders sagging. "Thanks all to you. But Harold…"

At the hesitation in her words, he asked, "Yes?"

"I truly did not know Rodney would be at White's. It was pure coincidence he was in town at all."

He relaxed, her truthfulness apparent in each word. One matter, at least, had come to a satisfactory resolution. Harold couldn't imagine gracefully stepping aside while Ruby had anything to do with Rodney Swiftenberg.

The patter of feet moving quickly toward them caught Harold's attention. His first response was to shield Ruby, tell her to run before they were found. But the figure came from the opposite direction. As the shadowy form ran under lit gas lamps toward them he saw it was a girl, outfitted in a dress of bright green.

Harold squinted as she drew closer and passed beneath another lamp. The gas light shone off flaming red hair.

"Her—" Harold started at the same time Ruby said, "Ellie."

"The girl has the worst timing," he continued. "Get rid of her quickly, before she draws too much attention."

"Thank the heavens." Ellie skidded to a halt in front of them before Ruby could reply. "I've caught you before you did something truly stupid."

"Before?" Harold asked.

"Yes, Alex—I mean, my stable hand—came to me with news that you borrowed his livery uniform and asked all sorts of pointed questions." The girl paused to catch her breath, doubling over with her arms wrapped around her middle. "He was worried and it did not behoove me for you to do something foolish before your penance is paid."

Ruby rolled her eyes and Harold fought hard not to laugh. "Well, I am sorry to report that you are too late."

"Too late?" She looked from Ruby and back to Harold.

Ruby lifted her chin and turned her face so her swollen, already darkening cheek could be seen in the dim light. "See for yourself."

"Hells bells!" Ellie exclaimed. "Now that's a whopper."

"It feels it, to be certain."

Harold set his hand on her shoulder in comfort. "Try not to speak; it will only increase the pain."

Ellie leaned in close. "She needs to have her cheek looked at. Follow me."

"Oh, no," Harold said. "We are not going back to Drake's townhouse. You most certainly have another scheme set up for us to fall helplessly into."

Ellie narrowed her eyes, and he couldn't help but feel a vague familiarity in the expression. "If you will remember, I was not the one who invited you to snoop about the marquis' house in the dead of night. I did not send out lovely notes asking for your visit."

The girl was right, and Ruby most certainly needed to be seen by a doctor to assess that no bone was broken. The swelling was taking over the side of her face rapidly.

Harold relaxed a bit. "I stand corrected." He did not know a doctor in town, and feared he couldn't afford one even if he did. Until his and William's venture started bringing in coin, he was practically a pauper. "Please, lead the way, and I will help her. She is still a bit dizzy."

"Will the two of you stop talking as if I am not here," Ruby said. "I can walk just fine."

She shook off Harold's arm and sidestepped Ellie, while cupping her injured cheek.

"Which way," she called over her shoulder.

"This way, it is only a few blocks."

A bit of pride infused him as Ruby, ever independent, walked before them with her head held high despite the pain she must feel. In that moment, Harold decided it was best to keep the truth of his discovery to himself. Maybe she would come to trust him enough and tell him, but he would not run the risk of her banishing him for meddling in her room.

Ellie took off past Ruby and down the walk, turning at the first corner. He hurried to catch up with Ruby. "Do you trust her?"

Ruby laughed, then winced in pain. "No more than I can throw her, but her brash attitude is a front, I believe."

They hadn't had much alone time to discuss the girl since they'd escaped Drake's house. "Who is she?"

"We spent that brief afternoon getting ices but I fear I know nothing more than before, besides the fact that she is an accomplished pickpocket."

"You jest!"

"I wish I did." Ruby's steps became more

certain the further they walked. "I saw it firsthand; the little minx is precocious. I believe she did it to shock me."

"I happen to remember another girl, equally as precocious at a much younger age." He tried to keep her attention off her pain. "This girl liked to follow the boys about, playing in the mud, and pilfering Cook's pies."

The look she shot his way told him he'd succeeded.

"Oh yes, that gangly girl who was always getting in the way and causing trouble."

He couldn't help but smile. "I do not remember her getting in the way—but I fear it was those troublesome boys who always led her astray." He would not wish his childhood on another, or seek to relive the taunting and maltreatment he'd endured at the hands of his father, although he'd think twice about going back to that time for a few moments' time with an unguarded Ruby.

"Hey, you two love birds," Ellie called over her shoulder. "It's the next building. Keep quiet and allow me to speak for us."

CHAPTER 22

RUBY TOOK A step away from Harold, putting space between them. The distance gave her a chance to think. Her head still pained her, but that very well might be the least of her problems at the moment. She wanted to lean against him, have him take the weight from her shoulders, yet didn't know how to ask.

Ellie paused in front of them and turned to what looked like a boarding house, with a sign out front that read Craven House. "As I said, keep quiet and let me handle things."

The house, nicer than most you'd find in Mayfair, was better kept than any boarding house she'd seen. "What is this place?" Ruby asked.

"Are you sure there is a doctor here?" Harold asked skeptically.

Ellie walked along the side of the building and toward the back. "Of sorts. I never said she needed to see a doctor, only get medical attention."

"Pox on me for not being more specific with my words." Harold closed the distance Ruby had put between them as they followed Ellie to the door. "We can turn around now."

Ruby climbed two steps to a back door, unsure. "We could."

Ellie turned to them before she knocked. "I am not forcing help upon you. I know someone who is versed in this sort of thing. She will take a look, poke around a bit, and we will be on our way."

It all sounded simple enough, and she did need to know how bad it was without the risk of involving Brock and Vi.

"Are you both agreeable?" Ellie asked.

When they both nodded, Ellie rapped on the door.

Someone on the other side knocked back.

Ruby and Harold exchanged a look. Hers definitely questioning their decision to trust Ellie; his seeking to reassure her that he would keep her safe.

Ruby knew he would—not because they'd known each other for so long, but because that was the type of man he was.

"The blue crow flies south," Ellie said, just loud enough for her voice to be heard through the solid door as she stepped back.

Ruby took in the building while they waited, for what she wasn't sure. The yard was well-kept, with a solid stable house in back. The exterior of the building appeared freshly painted and maintained. It was an awfully large home to house a clinic and she did not think even a man of medicine could afford to keep his family so well-housed.

When the door was pulled wide, Ruby looked over Ellie's shoulder into a room shrouded in a dim, golden glow. Whoever had allowed them entry must have stood behind the open door, hidden from view. The room was warm in contrast to the cool breeze outside. As Ruby's eyes adjusted she, noticed the walls and furniture were all varying shades of gold. A length of gossamer gold fabric adorned every flat surface, including a large canopy bed that dominated the room.

Harold's hold on her elbow tightened. Looking to him, he nodded in the direction they'd entered.

An elegantly dressed woman now stood in front of the closed door. Her blonde hair was swept up in an elaborate coiffeur that must have taken a maid hours to complete. Pearls hung delicately from her neck, ears, and wrist. A red silk gown, its plunging neckline barely acceptable by the most lenient of London standards, clung to her petite form and swept out behind her.

"Ellington, I did not expect you this evening," the woman said in a cultured tone, before looking to Ruby and Harold, her brow raised in question. "And who are your companions?" The way she said the word 'companions' made Ruby feel like naught but a dirty street urchin Ellie had collected on her way here.

Ellie lowered her head, as if she'd been scolded. "I know. It is only my friend," Ellie squeezed out the word, sounding embarrassed to call Ruby her friend, "was hurt and needed someone to look at her face. I could think of no one else to ask."

The woman, a full head shorter than Ruby, turned to her. "I am Marce Davenport and welcome to my—" she paused, searching for the right word, "—home. Come this way, and I will have a look. Ellington, please let Jude and Sam know I have company and then attend us in the front salon."

If the woman wondered why Ruby was dressed in men's breeches, shirt, and cap she said nothing.

"Of course," Ellie responded with a touch of reverence.

Who was this woman, and what kind of home was this? Ruby had learned long ago not to judge a person by their past—and sometimes not their present.

"Right this way."

Harold had been oddly silent since their arrival. She glanced at him to make sure he was still there. "Well, our evening cannot go any more awry then it already has," she whispered.

"Do not be foolish," Ms. Davenport said. "Things can always get worse, but I would thank you to save that until after you leave my home."

With that, she walked out of the room, her hips swaying to an unheard beat, leaving Ruby and Harold little choice but to follow. The rest of the first floor was much the same, each room they passed decorated in a different color, yet the furniture and layout were identical. Finally they arrived at the salon, the only room drastically different from the rest. This area more closely resembled a pub than a salon. Four card tables sat about the room, only lacking players. A long table sat against one wall, filled with decanters of every size, holding liquids of varying shades. A small table with two chairs were the only acceptable seating.

"You have a lovely home, Ms. Davenport."

"Call me Marce. Thank you, all my gentlemen agree." She smiled at them both. "Please, have a seat, and I will see how badly you are injured."

"Gentlemen?" Harold asked.

"My clients," she answered confidently, acknowledging Harold for the first time. From her smile, Ruby could tell that the woman liked what she saw. "Can I pour you a drink, Lord…"

"Not lord. Just Mr. Jakeston. And I would enjoy a spot of sherry, if it is not too much trouble."

At his reply, Marce's smile faded and she focused her attention back on Ruby. "You will find everything you seek in the next room. I do not keep sherry in here." She pointed to the door, bringing a candle close to Ruby's swollen cheek. She turned Ruby's face this way and that.

Pain shot down her cheek and into her neck.

"If you think this hurts now, wait until the morning." She made a tsking sound. "Who hit you? Your lover over there?" She tilted her head in the direction Harold had departed.

Shocked, Ruby pulled from the woman grasp. "He is not my—" she gulped down air to get the word out, "—lover!"

"Ironic that what you took from my comment is that I insinuated he was your lover." She laughed, taking her chin once more. "I do not judge if he is. Or if he's the one responsible for your bruise. I see it all the time. One day you won't stand for it any longer."

"Harold is not my lover, and he would never hurt me." She winced in discomfort again when Marce probed at her cheek.

"Abuse rarely comes from the expected place."

Ruby was relieved when Marce finally sat back. She wanted a warm bath, maybe some ice to soothe the hurt.

"Luckily for you, nothing is broken. Unfortunately, you will have quite the bruise by morning." She stood and moved to the sidebar to pour a drink—Ruby expected for herself, since she hadn't asked her if she wanted one. "I suggest ice to reduce the swelling. The bruising will last about a week. I have some cream that should cover it rather effectively. Drink this."

Ruby looked at the clear liquid she held out to her. "No, thank you, but—"

"Drink it, fast, you'll be happy you did. The pain will be something fierce soon."

She swirled it in the glass and brought it to her lips, swallowing it in one gulp. It burned as it went down.

"It will warm you up, as well."

Ruby coughed, trying to catch her breath. "May I ask you something?"

Marce eyed her suspiciously. "If you wish."

"How are you acquainted with Ellington?"

"Her mother and I were dear friends. Are you ready to find Mr. Jakeston? I am sure you would like to rest."

"One more question?" she asked tentatively.

"If you must."

"What is this place?"

Marce laughed. "Heaven for some, hell for others."

"I do not understand."

"Do you not wonder why Ellington saw fit to bring you to me?"

"I was not in a place to argue."

"It is very common for men to abuse women—"

"I told you, it was not Harold who hit me."

Marce held her hand up, signaling for silence. "I am uninterested in who hit you. But unfortunately, I see it more often than most. Girls come to me for all sorts of reasons; whether it be financial misfortune, an abusive father or husband, or just wanting to find a place where they're able to belong and be themselves."

Ruby still hadn't the faintest idea who and what Marce was.

"This is a brothel and card house," Marce finally said with a sigh, as though Ruby was too dense to be believed. "I cater to rich, entitled men. The occasional incident occurs in which I must patch up my girls, but that man is never allowed back. Violence, in any form, is not allowed within these walls. I protect what is mine, just as I have tried to protect Ellington since her mother's death."

Ruby didn't know what to say. The woman's words were unexpected to say the least, but made an odd sort of sense now that they were out.

Thankfully, Harold and Ellington returned before further conversation became necessary. Ruby felt sure she would not only nurse her injury tonight, but also ponder all she'd learned about Ellington. And she would try hard, extremely hard, not to dwell on the fact that she'd spent her evening in both a gentlemen's club and a brothel.

"Are you ready?" Harold asked. "Vi and Brock will be returning shortly from their evening out. If we hurry, we should be able to slip back in unnoticed."

Ruby nodded. "Thank you, Marce. I will not forget your kindness."

"You will forget me quickly enough, I am sure." She slipped a small container into Ruby's hand when she made to leave. "But, do not forget this. It will help cover your bruise until it fades. If you need more, send Ellington to fetch it."

Ruby smiled and took Harold's elbow. "My thanks again." When they turned toward the door, Ellington remained. "Are you coming, Ellie? We can walk you home before continuing on our way."

"Nah," she mumbled. "I can make my own way home."

Ruby was torn between staying to make sure Ellie returned home safety, or keeping hold of Harold and allowing him to take care of her. When Marce nodded from the open doorway behind Ellie, Ruby knew the young girl would not come to harm.

Smiling, she looked up at Harold, whose eyes held only concern for her. "Shall we go? I find myself exhausted and in need of a restful night."

"It would be my pleasure."

CHAPTER 23

WITH THE IMMEDIATE danger behind them, Harold couldn't deposit Ruby fast enough. Only one thing dominated his mind: Finding Rodney and beating the pulp out of the bloody scoundrel. How dare he put Ruby in harm's way and then leave her to her own devices? His blood boiled thinking of the consequences for her because Rodney had somehow involved himself.

His boots echoed down the hall and servants ducked into other rooms as he passed. He could only imagine the fury they saw on his face; he was a volcano about to erupt, and no one wanted to be near when it happened.

Only question now was where to find the man. It was late, the card games at White's having wrapped up an hour before. Most of the *ton* would be departing their evening entertainments shortly.

But Harold's luck must be improving, because no more had he ran through possible methods of finding the rascal when a hack pulled along the street a house down from Brock's townhouse and Rodney jumped down, headed toward him.

"Rodney," Harold called. "You son of a bitch!"

Rodney's steps faltered and he looked behind him to the hack, moving down the street in search of its next fare of the night. He turned back to Harold, knowing his chance of escape was nil.

"Lovely evening, is it not?" Rodney asked when he was within hearing distance. "A bit chilly, but comfortable."

"Do not patronize me."

"Whatever are you speaking of?"

"You know exactly what I am speaking of." Harold reached forward, taking the front of the man's coat in his fists, bringing them face to face. "Do not play me for the fool."

Rodney flinched, his hands clamped over Harold's as he attempted to peel his fingers from their hold. "What were you thinking?" Harold continued. "She could have been seriously hurt—or worse yet, discovered."

The scoundrel pushed against Harold. "Unhand me. I have only just arrived in town, and have no idea what you are speaking about."

"The hell you don't." So many emotions flooded Harold. The man was a crook if he'd ever seen one, always with the lies and manipulation. "Nothing has changed since we were children."

"I fear you are correct. You're still riding the coattails of my cousin, living off his wealth and status."

Harold drew his fist back, ready to pummel

the man. Rodney had avoided the fist aimed at him earlier, but there was no escape for him now. Harold had years of pent-up anger to get out, and at the moment all of it was aimed at this very man. As a child, Rodney had ridiculed him, belittled him, and antagonized him unmercifully. Nothing had changed as they'd moved into adulthood. Every occasion they met, the man went out of his way to disparage Harold, frequently embarrassing him in front of others.

He'd never been a fighter, but Harold would crush the man responsible for the bruise on Ruby's face.

"Harold." The frantic female scream broke through his fury. "Harold, let him go."

"Yes, Harold. Do release me this instant." Harold's grip relaxed and Rodney chuckled. "Now run along like a good little boy and hide."

Harold released Rodney's coat and pushed him away, not trusting he wouldn't still put his fist through the man's face—something he knew he must avoid doing in the presence of Lady Haversham.

"Be gone," he called after Rodney. "Be advised this is not over."

"What is going on here?" Brock asked. The pair stood outside their carriage, having arrived home from their evening activities. "Where did Rodney come from? I was unaware he was in town."

Harold took a moment to calm himself before responding. He breathed in and out several times to settle his racing heart. He knew Rodney was not particularly welcome at the Haversham townhouse when Brock and Lady Haversham were in residence—not since he'd tried to blackmail Brock's wife before they were married.

Regaining his composure, Harold searched for an explanation for Brock, which would also soothe Lady Haversham. The truth was out of the question, for it would call into issue both himself and Ruby.

Lady Haversham stood next to Brock, a look of fright on her face and her hand gently pressed against her swollen abdomen.

He felt accountable for her dismay. After a long evening out she must be fatigued.

"Lady Haversham," he said. "I do apologize for my ungentlemanly behavior."

"If anyone was acting ungentlemanly I have no doubt it is my newest *cousin* by marriage." Lady Haversham smiled, her demeanor changing. "I do thank you for chasing him off."

"You have done everyone involved a favor," Brock cut in. "If you hadn't chased him off, then I most certainly would have. Let us take this inside. I find myself in need of a drink." Brock took Lady Haversham's arm and they moved into the house, Harold trailing behind.

Harold glanced around the foyer, hoping to catch a glimpse of Ruby while at the same time fearing she'd stumble upon them, her bruise on display for all. Thankfully, she did not appear, so he assumed she was safely up the stairs and in her room by now.

"Well, gentlemen, I am afraid I am exhausted and my feet are sorely in need of a good soaking." Lady Haversham kissed Brock on the cheek and gave Harold a quick hug and a smile. "If you will excuse me."

Both men bowed as she left the room.

Once they were ensconced in Brock's study, drinks in hand, his friend asked question after question.

"So, what happened?"

"Rodney arrived the same time as I and things got out of hand."

"Bullshit."

"You doubt that just encountering the man makes my blood boil?"

"Oh, I do not doubt that," Brock said. "But I also know you are not me. It takes more than a look or a few words to set you off."

"Maybe I have changed."

"Highly doubtful. After all these years of Rodney trying to anger you, now is the time you decided to fight back and put him in his place?"

"That's exactly it."

Brock shook his head. "Sorry, my friend. That just does not ring true."

"Well, it is the truth."

"Fine, you can keep your secrets, but know that I am here for you—and Vi is, too. She loves you like a brother. And furthermore, if I even think you are in any type of trouble, I will step in and you will have no other option but to tell me what is going on."

"What? You think you are my father or something?" Harold asked, jokingly.

Brock sobered and turned a serious look on Harold. "Do not compare my love for you to that man's manipulative and vindictive actions—ever." His friend leaned over and tapped Harold's tumbler with his own and then drained the alcohol.

"To best friends and thankless family," Harold saluted and emptied his own glass.

"Another?" Brock asked.

"Most definitely," Harold answered—because getting drunk was far preferable to talking about things he was in no way prepared to discuss, even with his best friend.

CHAPTER 24

"LADY ELLIE, PLEASE." Ruby handed her new calling card, compliments of Vi, to the doorman. "She is expecting me." She plastered a smile on her face, fearing it didn't reach her eyes when her still swollen cheek ached, though she knew the cream was applied heavily enough to cover the bruise.

Someone once told her that a person could fool themselves into feeling something they did not. So, today, with a smile on her face, a lovely walking dress and her newly arrived calling cards in hand, Ruby had left the Haversham townhouse to take Ellington on their second outing. While she dreaded the hours to follow, she would make the best of the situation knowing she only had one outing left in their agreement.

Then, she and Harold would have naught to worry about. The threat of gossip spreading amongst the *ton* would be gone and they could go on as they always had, without the scrutinizing eye of society beating down on them.

It took her a moment to realize the doorman had left her standing on the front steps when he went in search of Ellie. She'd been in the house twice now, once in the dead of night and the other to collect Ellie for their first outing.

Stepping into the foyer, Ruby closed the door behind her and stared. The grandeur of society homes still left her breathless with awe. It was exorbitant how much it took to maintain a property such as this, something Ruby viewed as the height of wastefulness.

The ceiling, complete with grand chandelier, towered three stories above her head. Her neck hurt after only a few seconds of staring at the exquisite crown molding, painted a delicate cream. She traced the walls down to the immaculately polished granite that stretched in every direction and down each hall. The servants it took to keep this house ready to entertain at a moment's notice also must cost the marquis a small fortune: butler, doorman, maids, cook, valets, and a livery of the finest handlers in all of London.

And Ellie had been raised with all of this. At least, that was what Ruby assumed. It explained a lot about her selfishness and entitled attitude. Ellie was used to getting what she wanted, even if what she wanted was in direct opposition to what was best for her. It was clear she'd had little guidance thus far in her life. She appeared well-educated, yet unruly to the extreme.

The girl had yet to share a morsel of information about herself. She was only vocal on one thing: the marquis was not her father—and her mother was dead, according to Marce. Who did she belong to and how had she ended up with him? Maybe she was the daughter of a family friend or another relative. The more time Ruby thought about Ellie, the more unanswered questions she had. She spoke like a lady, but picked pockets like a street urchin; not to mention her association with Marce and Craven House. There were so many details that didn't make sense about the girl.

Which wasn't so different from everything else in Ruby's life at the moment. The questions surrounding her father, her mother, their deception, and her true identity continued to grow. Part of her had actually enjoyed the time she'd spent with Ellie—the pickpocketing not withstanding—because she hadn't thought about her problems for that brief afternoon. Ruby hadn't eyed every man on the street wondering if he was the one. She hadn't been on the lookout for familiar street names, knowing a potential father lived close. It had been one of her most carefree moments since she'd arrived in town.

While musing about her current situation, she'd walked further into the marquis' home, admiring family portraits that lined a long hall. The regality of each painting stunned her. The artist had an uncanny ability to capture the aloof and elite aura given off by members of the highest circles of society. An exclusive group of people that Ruby would never be a part of—and never wished to. There were many social climbers orbiting around the *ton*, always looking to be associated with a lord or lady of high status or seeking a match far above their own station.

A door slammed, as if hitting a wall when thrown open, somewhere in the house. Angry, muffled voices filled the once-quiet house.

Ruby moved back toward the foyer to better hear the commotion and—if she was being honest—closer to an escape if the necessity arose.

"…you insufferable, horrid…"

The words drifted down the main stairs to the foyer, the rest of the statement beyond comprehension.

"I may be insufferable, but at least I am not a spoiled, entitled, selfish child," a male voice boomed. "I should have left you upon my stoop to perish in the cold."

Ellie's high voice followed. "I wish you would have. It would have put us both out of our misery!"

"My misery started long before you, little girl, and would not have ended with your death."

Ruby gasped at the harsh, cruel words being thrown about. The male voice could only belong to Drake.

"The only thing that I will enjoy more than watching you live in misery every day is watching you die…without benefit of a male heir." Ellie's unpleasant laughed filled the foyer and a chill ran down Ruby's spine. "You will die alone, just as you were when I came to you."

"Do not forget, with my death will also come the end of your gilded lifestyle." It was Drake's turn to chuckle. "Gone will be the pretty dresses, the maids, the pin money, and dare I say, everything you've taken from me without so much as a thank you. It is likely you will starve upon the street."

The words were so clear now, as if the two argued only feet from her.

"I have wanted to leave, begged you to let

me go, for years."

"Oh, but I would never allow you that."

"No, instead you sought to keep me locked up here—your personal whipping post. Why?" The question held all the hurt and pain of a life lived on another's terms.

"I owe you nothing. Nor do I justify my actions to anyone."

The chandelier shuddered above her and Ruby stepped closer to the door to avoid injury if it fell, even though she felt herself compelled toward the stairs—to put an end to the verbal abuse on the floor above her. No person deserved the spiteful comments hurled at them, no matter if they were a full grown man or a child.

Loud footsteps echoed.

"Where are you going? I did not dismiss you!"

"I have plans and they do not include standing by while you insult me." Gone was the pain in Ellie's words, her confidence returned.

"I am not done speaking with you."

"Well, I am sorry. Feel free to shout at the empty room. Or maybe I can send in a servant to stand in my place." Her cocky demeanor restored, Ruby wanted to cheer Ellie on for standing up for herself, for flaunting the rules of the *ton*. "Either would give you the same result."

"Are you running off to spend more time with that other bastard?" he asked.

"Don't you speak of her in that manner." Ellington must have paused in the hall, throwing the words back at Drake.

Ruby wondered who Ellie's other friend was. She could only hope the 'other bastard' was a good, solid influence on the girl, yet dread had

232 | *Christina McKnight*

already started to settle upon her.

"I will talk of her in any manner I deem fit. She is nothing, born of a harlot," his words had also lost a bit of force. "Just as you."

"You do not know her. She is a good person."

"As you are a good person?" he questioned. "You think I do not know of your less-than-model activities when you are not here? Does she also seek the thrill of picking pockets for extra coin? Have you taken her to meet that Davenport woman?"

"Stop!"

"Maybe you both will seek employment as trollops. I dare say gentlemen will enjoy your fiery spirit and red hair. Although, she is a bit old for most men's liking. The apple never falls far from the tree. Why do you not bring her up to meet me?"

A bit old? A bastard? The comments bounced through her head, giving her an instant migraine.

"I will never bring her to you." Ellie's voice once again rose. "You do not deserve her and I will not let you hurt her as you have me."

"Ah! So you have not been honest with her? I expected nothing less from you."

"I have told her enough."

"What will she think when she finds out the truth about you? All the sordid details of your past—your less than noble lineage? Do you think she will want anything to do with you then? The bastard child of a harlot is worthless and disposable."

"Just as you disposed of my mother when you learned she carried your child?"

The similarities in the story unfolding on the

floor above and her own were undeniable—and utterly terrifying.

She'd possibly found her father—and a sister in the process.

Ruby wanted to run up the stairs to stop the abuse, but at the same time found herself rooted to the spot, fearing that if she intruded on them, she wouldn't get the answers she sought. No matter the terribleness of the truth, she wanted to hear it all. She needed to hear every word.

And then she would need time to process everything.

She hadn't dreamed finding her father would include more heartache than she'd been through thus far. No, she'd been naive, her thoughts circling around a father, arms open wide, embracing her, showering her with the love she'd so missed since Sir St. Augustin passed.

Instead, she was faced with a possibility worse than any she could have imagined: A rake who used and discarded women like it was sport for a father. And a rebellious, untamable blackmailer for a sister.

Ruby had a soft spot for Ellington, despite her ugly words and sticky fingers. Her behavior made so much more sense now, hearing what Ellie probably dealt with on a daily basis since she'd come to live with the marquis. Could she blame the girl for doing what she had to in order to survive?

The angry voices had stalled above, possibly seeking more words to hurl—worse words. Something to wound the other as much as they themselves were hurting. What more could the pair dredge up?

"I wish I would have disposed of the pair of

you in a more permanent way!"

And with that, the insults moved to a new level—and she knew she had to put an end to it. There was nothing more anyone would gain from their continued assault on each other.

A door slammed above and muffled shouts erupted.

Ruby took the stairs as fast as her dress would allow and turned down the first hallway, colliding with Ellington.

They bounced off each other, both keeping their balance—and stared at each other.

Ellington's face was puffy and red, her eyes glossy with unshed tears.

"Ell—"

Ellington straightened her shoulders, blinking rapidly to rid her eyes of unshed tears. "You are early," she said through tight lips. "Can you never do anything correctly?"

Ruby wanted to take the girl into her arms, give her the affection she so clearly lacked…and needed. "I was waiting downstairs, but I heard yelling." She didn't want Ellie to think she'd been eavesdropping, but also needed her to know she'd heard every cruel, hurtful word.

"I do not know of what you speak." She made to push past Ruby. "And it would behoove you to stop snooping around the homes of others; it is highly rude and suspect."

Could the girl really compartmentalize everything that had just happened and walk out the front door as if nothing out of the ordinary had occurred? "I only came upstairs to help you—"

"You think I need help? Especially your help," Ellie cut her off. "No one can help me. And if you are smart, you'll depart before you fall too far to be saved, as well."

The depth of those words ran deeper than any ocean.

Ruby didn't know what she could do to help Ellington, besides begging Lord Haversham to allow her to move into Haversham townhouse. She was sure with Vi's support he would agree, but that would mean telling her best friend about everything—all the ways she'd misled her. It would also cause discord for Brock if Drake tried to fight Ellington's removal from his household.

A thought struck her, as well. Alex would likely lose his position in the stables, seeing as he'd gained his position through Vi. So many people would be affected, but the alternative—leaving her sister to continued abuse—was not an option.

"Was what he spoke of true?" Ruby asked. "Are we sisters?"

"Does it matter?"

"Of course it does." How could she think it didn't? It had been Ruby's entire goal in coming to London, the reason she'd deceived so many of her friends and had been avoiding her mother. She'd leveraged everything she held dear in hopes of finding her true father—a place to belong, someone to accept her, and then perhaps she could accept herself, feel at home in her own skin.

"You cannot see the resemblance?"

Ruby's hair was the darkest ebony while Ellington's was clearly of the brightest red, but their eyes were the exact same shade of green, though the girl's eyes were hooded and weighed down by a rough life in direct opposition to the front she presented. They both stood tall for women, their bodies slender. While Ellington's skin was covered in freckles, Ruby's was clear perfection, but their skin tones were both fair, easily burned by too much sun.

"You think you are better than me?"

"No—"

"Because you were raised by a baron while I've remained with only a first name—and a boy's name at that—for my whole life?" Ellie accused. "I am, as he says, worthless and disposable."

The words sounded even more detestable coming from Ellie's mouth. "You truly believe that?"

"They are the words I have heard every day of my life, how could I not hold stock in them?" Ruby could tell the words had found purchase in the girl's subconscious.

"The words of a bitter, lonely man mean naught." She stared into Ellington's eyes, hoping to convey the truth—that her words could somehow uproot all the negative.

Ruby sighed. "Just answer my question. Is he our father? Are we sisters?" Why she needed the confirmation she knew was true to her very core, Ruby didn't know. Looking at the girl in front of her, something deep within her recognized Ellie as her sister. Her soul acknowledged and accepted her as her own—her blood.

"Do not delude yourself. We may be related, but we will never be sisters, just as he will never be my father. I would rather live my life deprived of a surname than be affiliated with that evil, vile man upstairs. He may have me caged now, but he will not live forever."

Her sister—a relationship she'd never expected to have with another human being—

had obviously been planning her escape for longer than Ruby could fathom. "If you are my sister, there will be nothing that can stand in my way of claiming you as mine. My blood." She felt the words so fully that tears sprang to her own eyes.

"I have no want to be claimed by you. In fact, I want nothing more than for you to be out of my house, and my life."

What she said could not be true. Ruby understood if their father wanted nothing to do with her—he'd made that clear when he'd sent her mother away. But for Ellington, a girl with nothing to call her own, one would expect her to cling to anyone who wanted her. "You can't mean that."

"Oh, but I do." Ellington chuckled. The sound mimicked her father's. "You see, I may appear the novelty now, a fun plaything for a bit, but eventually you will return to your real life. Perhaps a home in the country, or to a gentleman you fancy. And I will be forgotten, as my mother forgot me. As my father has wished to hide my existence every day."

Ruby should be the one reeling, lost and overwhelmed by all she'd learned in the past hour, but it was Ellie who needed the time to adjust. Ruby was out of her element, her experience with the wounded limited to her work with Vi at Foldger's Foundling House. While those children were wounded physically, Ellie's scars did not show. Her wounds were emotional. So easy to hide and for others to overlook.

How had she not seen the pain in the girl's eyes all this time? It was so apparent now. "Pack your things. You are coming with me to

Haversham townhouse." She spoke impulsively. "We will figure something out. You cannot remain here."

"I am not going with you anywhere." Ellie's voice held a hard edge. "Besides, do you think he will let me go?"

"He clearly does not enjoy you staying in his home."

"I have tried for most of my life to leave, to get away. Unfortunately for me—yet auspiciously for him—one does not see the advantage in losing one's whipping post. While our *father*, as you call him, cannot stand the sight of me, neither will he let me go." Ellie paused, her eyes pleading with Ruby to find her a way out—a means for escape, but the girl's next words drilled home that even if a way out presented itself, her sister would likely not take it. "Do not delude yourself into thinking you are the first to ponder a grand scheme to fix me— deliver me from the clutches of the 'evil overlord.' I do not need your assistance, nor do I want it. You can take your leave and consider your debt to me paid in full."

Ruby knew her mouth fell open in shock, unable to find the words to convince Ellington that she was nothing like their father or Ellington's mother. She would not tire of, or become annoyed by her sister's presence.

Before she could utter any of the words forming in her head, Ellington said, "Good day, please show yourself out." With that, she started down the stairs, leaving Ruby to stare after her.

Shaking herself into action, Ruby followed her down the stairs, where the marquis' doorman stood with the door open, waiting for her to depart. Embarrassed at the possibility of the servant overhearing their entire conversation, Ruby moved toward the open door so as not to bring anymore scandal for the man to share with the other household staff. She was sure that within minutes of her departure, Alex—even tucked safely away in the stables—would hear the whole of her visit with Ellie and know that she was the illegitimate daughter of the Marquis of Drake, a rogue amongst all London rakes.

Ruby had agreed to take the girl for a stroll in Hyde Park, and now she was faced with her family's horrible secrets being laid out before all the *ton* by supper.

Taking the townhouse steps two at a time, she wondered if now was the time to warn her friends.

CHAPTER 25

"ARE YOU SURE this vessel will do?" Harold eyed the clipper his brother, William, had selected for their first trip to France. The quick jaunt across the channel would turn a fast profit for them. They planned to import anything of high demand at the time: tea, brandy, fabric, and spices. If the demand existed for lady's bonnets, then they would deal in women's finery.

"It is sound. Previous owner says it made the trip across the channel over three dozen times with nary a problem." William stood next to him as they took in their newly acquired asset. "The hull is sound, with no signs of leaks or rot."

The clipper had seen better days—as in, every day before the current one. Harold wondered how the ship stayed afloat, but they had little chance if they wanted to start their venture without delay. He only hoped it didn't sink before it returned with the goods. If they needed a better ship, Harold would have no other option but to include another investor in the project—and he and William had both agreed to keep their activities, and the profits, between themselves.

"What is our next step?" William asked.

"I believe it is time we hire a crew and send them out on our maiden voyage." Harold attempted to suppress his growing excitement. Very shortly his life—and his brother's—could change for the better. "Have you confirmed our first shipment?"

"I received word only this morning," William said. "A load of fabrics and spices await our clipper's arrival in Le Havre. We will load and immediately head for Dover."

Harold had been leery about scheduling their first cargo shipment before they'd acquired a ship, but William had been confident that all would work in their favor. "Le Havre, you say?"

"Yes."

"Is that not a risky port?"

"That is why now is the perfect time."

"How so?"

"With the decrease in trade to and from the port due to the war, typhoid outbreak, and heavy winds, the market is there and others are playing it safe."

His brother had done his research, and Harold would not fault him for his initiative. It was exactly the call he would have made himself. "All very true, brother. But we must remember, if this fails—if our ship sinks in a storm or our crew catches the fever—our livelihoods are at stake. We will have nothing."

"I have thought the same, and decided that in order to ensure all goes well, I will journey with our crew on the first trip."

With the conversation reaching an easy flow, they boarded the ship. Without saying a word, they both moved about the boat, checking weld spots and searching for dry rot; anything that could cause loss of either human life or precious cargo while at sea.

The risk William was willing to wager, more than money or reputation—his very life—garnered an even greater amount of respect. "Do you have experience aboard a ship?"

"I've lived near the port for most of my adult life. I have witnessed sails raised and lowered almost as many times as I've seen the sun rise." William patted Harold's back in reassurance. "How hard can it be?"

Harold had heard many stories of men enduring relentless sea sickness while aboard long voyages—even one that ended with the sailor jumping overboard to stop the unyielding illness. But, William was a grown man capable of making his own choices. It was not Harold's responsibility to convince his brother that his decision was unwise. They both had much at stake in this venture.

"I do believe you are right," Harold said instead.

Their inspection completed, they departed the boat. Harold was satisfied that it was sound, at least as far as he knew.

They both stood, side by side, staring at their new vessel for several minutes. Harold was not ready for their meeting to end; it was not often he spent time with family in any capacity other than forced association.

"Have you written father?" Harold asked.

"Whatever for?" William sounded affronted at the very notion. "I escaped him years ago and do not plan to return."

"What about mother?" That was Harold's one regret. He and his brothers avoided their father like the plague, yet, he knew his mother was the one who suffered. With no one around to take the brunt of Vicar Jakeston's scorn and anger, it left her to absorb it all.

William shrugged. "She married the man, I did not."

Harold wanted to weep for the family he'd likely never have...and the neglected one he did. With no idea how to bridge the distance they'd all put between one another, he knew going home would not solve their larger issues.

"She loves us, in her own way." Harold had to try. "Even though father clouds her affection."

"I agree, brother," William said. "When I return, I will visit her. I am sure she'd find delight in exotic fabrics for a few new dresses...and father will scoff at the extravagance. I think it will be a great homecoming for me."

Leave it to William to plan a trip that would anger their father. Harold might just tag along, to see his father's reaction to their new venture and its spoils.

William jumped back on the vessel and it rocked beneath his feet, with a gentle to-and-fro motion. "Things are moving in the right direction for us, Harold. We are men above and beyond what our father ever thought we'd attain, but I have work to do."

"I would like to help."

"And dirty your pretty clothes? I think not." William chuckled. "This thing looks as if it hasn't been scrubbed since that last nail was driven into place."

Harold eyed his brother as he removed his waistcoat and rolled up his sleeves. "You think I am incapable of a little manual labor?"

"Oh, little Harry is all a-fluster now," William teased goodheartedly. "You are welcome to lend a hand, it is only that I did not want to keep you from any important dealings about town."

He sensed his brother was testing him—and Harold would pass. Jumping on to the vessel he asked, "Well, sir, where do you suggest we start?"

CHAPTER 26

RUBY SLAMMED THE door behind her, overwhelmed at all there was to think about, and longing to dwell on nothing. Her tears as she'd fled the marquis' house had surely wiped the cover from her bruised cheek. The trip back to Lord Haversham's home had passed in a blur, thanks to her ceaseless sobbing. To draw as little attention as possible Ruby had lowered her head, making eye contact with no one. A few times she'd bumped into strangers—with a quiet apology she'd continued on, seeking her room and a place to hide.

She wished she could forget all she'd heard, somehow erase it from her memory and go back to a simpler time.

Before she knew of her mother's deceit.

Before she'd lied to her best friend.

Before she'd been blackmailed.

Before she learned of her sister—a pickpocket.

And certainly, before she learned her father was a rake of the highest order. A man so despicable he saw no person as exempt from his cruel words, even his own flesh and blood.

She slipped onto the seat before her dressing table and looked at the face reflected back at her in the mirror. Unrecognizable, the face looking back at her held defeat, devoid of all strength. Robbed of the one thing she'd held dear all these years—her ability to push forward, no matter the situation.

But all she wanted now was to flee everyone and everything, disappear and return to the anonymity that had been her life thus far. If she weren't in London, surrounded by people who only sought to perpetuate false ideals of themselves, then she could focus on what truly mattered.

At this moment, she did not have the faintest idea what that actually was. She'd lost sight of who she was, where she was going, and what her future would hold.

What had she thought to gain by coming to London? She wasn't capable of the task she'd set for herself, nor had she been prepared for the outcome.

She'd made a mess of everything.

She only hoped it wasn't too late to clean up the disaster that had become her life. Dipping the cloth in the bowl of water on her table, she cleansed the cream hiding the bruise on her cheek. The injury had turned black and blue almost immediately, then varying shades of purple, but now tones of green infused her skin, signaling the healing had begun.

As her bruise would fade, so would her troubles if given time.

Ruby knew she was changed. Going back to the country mouse she'd been or hiring herself out as a companion to another lady in town would no longer suit her.

The door behind her slammed open, hitting the wall with such force that the mirror before Ruby shook, threatening to fall from its perch.

"Ruby, you will never guess…" Vi's words stopped when their eyes made contact in the mirror. Her friend's excitement vanished. "What happened to your face?"

Neither of them moved, or said another word. Vi stood frozen, an evening dress draped over her arm as Ruby continued to stare at her friend in the mirror, her hand cradling her injured cheek as if to conceal the evidence.

"I said, what happened to you?"

Ruby didn't know what to say—what needed to be said to reassure Vi she was all right, there was nothing to fret over, and to leave her room without uttering a word to anyone, especially Lord Haversham.

"Do you think I have not noticed your sneaking about?" Vi asked, breaking their eye contact. Relief flooded Ruby as Vi moved to the bed and laid the gown down. "I have given you space—time to work on what has been bothering you, weighing you down. I've been patient, waiting for you to come to me and share—"

"It is not like that, Vi."

"Then tell me what it is like. Why you have been so distant, why you came to London, why you leave the house through the stables only to return hours later by hired hack. Please," Vi threw her arms into the air. "By all means, tell me what I did to cause you to lie to me. To use me for whatever you are after here in town."

Vi was mad, spitting mad, and Ruby knew that she alone was responsible.

"Have I not trusted you these last eight years? Shared my deepest secrets—good and bad—with you, my dearest friend? Everything that is mine is yours."

Ruby's head dropped in shame. "You deserve better than the horrid friend I have been. I will pack my things and depart for the country."

"You would leave, just like that, rather than confide in me? That is by far more hurtful than anything."

"I cannot burden you with my problems. I hoped to be strong enough to solve my own troubles without bringing you and Brock into it. Once you know me, who I actually am, you may not want to be my friend any longer."

"What about what *I* want?"

Ruby didn't know how to respond.

"I want to be the kind of friend to you that you've always been to me," Vi said. "If you will let me."

Ruby turned in her seat, forcing herself to face her friend. She hung her head. "Things could not be any more of a disaster."

"What is such a disaster?"

"My life." The words were simple, but seemed to encompass everything.

"Start from the beginning, perhaps?" Vi suggested.

"I have no idea where that even is."

"Well, you were in great spirits at my wedding, and you seemed happy to be back at home, and close to Brock and me at Haversham House."

"I was," Ruby conceded.

"And you were adamant that you did not want to join me in London."

"That was true."

"But then you arrived the day I was to leave, requesting to accompany me." Vi stared at her, guessing correctly when all the trouble had begun. "What happened?"

Ruby sighed. "It was not what happened, but what I found."

"Go on..."

Ruby wiped a stray tear from her bruised cheek. "I did not want to burden you with all of this and cause undue strain."

"I am with child, not ailing of a heart condition," Vi comforted her. "I am not an invalid, and find myself tired of you and Brock coddling me. Please tell me."

"I was searching for the trunk that held the lovely dresses your father bought me last season. I was in the attic, covered in dust and sneezing all over the place, when I stumbled upon a book."

And then, she told her—she told Vi all about her mother's journal and the damning entries detailing her mother's affair.

Her friend listened without interruption until Ruby had told her the sordid details of her dubious birth. "So, you came to London to confront your mother?" Vi asked.

Ruby shook her head. "No, I came to find my father—to learn who I am."

"But you know who your father is: he is the man who raised you, doted on you. Nothing can take him away from you or change the fact that you belonged to him."

"I wish it were that simple." Ruby sighed, longing for what Vi had always known about herself. "You know who you are and where your family came from. I don't know—or didn't until recently—if I had another family, possibly siblings... A parent who would cherish me."

"But you know now?"

She laughed, unsure what else to do. "I do." So many emotions rushed through her, as they had on her journey home. "My father is alive and I have at least one sister, that I know of."

"That is wonderful! What is his name? Was he happy to see you?"

"I have not met or talked to him, although he is well aware of me." And he hadn't sought her out. She knew at least of bit of the rejection and pain her mother had lived through in the days after learning of her pregnancy. "But I did meet my sister."

"Oh!" Vi exclaimed. "Tell me about her! Is she older, younger, as beautiful as you?"

"She is much younger, and a pickpocket and blackmailer." It was almost too much to believe. If she hadn't seen it firsthand—and been the target of her sister's deceit—she wouldn't believe it herself. "But she is very smart and resourceful, for lack of a better term."

"Oh, dear heaven!"

"Exactly my thought. Her name is Ellington."

"And your face?" Vi asked. "Did you anger someone?"

The conversation, and a chance to be honest with Vi, had distracted her from the throbbing of her cheek. "That was an accident caused by my careless and naive behavior."

"Hitting a woman is never an accident."

"Oh, but this was most certainly an accident—and my fault. You see, I was at

White's—"

"You were where?"

"Let me explain." Ruby turned on the bench, holding up her hand to silence Vi. "After the other night at dinner, I thought if I got a look at the betting book at White's I would be able to find my father. Perhaps locate a wager about a man around that time who was connected to my mother."

At the look of horror on Vi's face, Ruby continued. "I know how ludicrous it sounds now, but with my other plans failing, I truly believed I could get into the club, search the book, and find some sort of information without anyone the wiser."

"And how did you gain entrance to White's?" Vi stuttered.

Ruby didn't want to implicate Alex in her plan. "I borrowed a livery uniform and slipped in the back door."

"The bruise? Were you found out?"

"I was found, but they do not know who I am," Ruby confessed. "Well, except Rodney."

"Rodney?" Vi fumed. "That insufferable cod…"

"Oh, the man who hit me was just as surprised to see him."

"Someone else hit you? Please tell me this is all a farce and you stumbled into a door or some such nonsense."

"I wish I could, but I was punched squarely in the face by a fist intended for Lord Haversham's beloved cousin."

"I am at a loss for words."

Vi stared at her for a long few moments. Ruby nearly laughed aloud at her friend's wide eyes and the absurdity of the entire story, now that she'd revealed just a few of the sordid details.

"That is just as well, because I have so many more for you."

The words poured from her as if she sought to unburden her very soul.

Ruby rambled on about her ill-conceived plan to find her father, her list of potential men, and the homes she'd searched. It was harder to share her failures with Vi than she'd expected, and with those failures came Harold and Ellie's involvement in her escapades.

"You were caught in a compromising situation with Harold?" Vi laughed. "It is impossible to picture Mr. Jakeston in such a position."

"But it is easy for you to see me there?" Ruby asked, wounded.

"Of course not, I only mean—"

"It does not matter. I fear the situation was not as compromising as Lady Ellington would have people believe." She couldn't tell Vi that if Ellie hadn't barged in she would have kissed him, possibly run her fingers though his hair, and definitely stared into his eyes for the remainder of the evening. Or that she'd since daydreamed of a life with him, their children, and the home she would create. "I tripped and Harold caught me."

"Funny that Brock has mentioned nothing of this," Vi mused. "Maybe Harold is as tightlipped as you have been."

"I am sure he has much more important things to occupy his mind and time."

"You think so?"

"Why do you say it like so?"

"It is only that Harold has been very

preoccupied as of late," Vi said. "He barely attends meals or joins us in the evenings."

Ruby didn't want to say it was because he spent most of his time saving her from herself and trying to anticipate her next slipup. "That is odd."

"But this does explain Harold's severe reaction to Rodney the other evening."

"The other evening?" Ruby asked.

"Yes, we arrived home to find Harold, his hands close to ringing Rodney's neck, out front of our townhouse."

That explained Harold's hasty departure after making sure she was safely at home after leaving Ellie at Craven House. Ruby had been exhausted and in such pain that she'd retired to her room immediately upon returning home.

"He is a good man," Ruby said. "He has saved my reputation on more than one occasion."

"Why could you not just ask your mother?" The subject change threw Ruby off guard—most likely what Vi had intended.

Ruby had shared so much of her life with Vi, but she didn't know if she was prepared to tell her dearest friend about this particular struggle. What girl told another that her mother turned away from all contact with her own child? Especially Vi—how could she understand, having no mother herself, and instead raised by a most loving and attentive father? Any mother, no matter her nature, would be better than none at all. What right did Ruby have to complain? The words would sound like those of a petty, spoiled child.

She went with the only explanation that could make sense, and truly, the only thing that mattered to her. "I did not want to risk gossip getting out and ruining the memory of my father—not the one who turned my mother away, but the man who raised me. I could not live with myself if his friends and other society members found out that his wife had cuckolded him. Besides which, she has lied to me my whole life. Why would she suddenly be truthful with me?"

Embarrassed, she turned back to her table. She knew her mother's choices were not her own, but the shame belonged to her due to the circumstances of her birth.

"Who is your father?"

"I cannot...not yet."

"Do you think I will view you differently because of the knowledge you hold? Because of circumstances beyond your control?" Vi set a reassuring hand on her shoulder. "I am the last person who should cast stones."

Once her secret was out, it could never be taken back—and the consequences would be all her doing. If Vi learned of her dubious lineage, she would surely insist on helping Ruby.

She could be Ruby St. Augustin, daughter of a baron, but not the alternative: Ruby, illegitimate daughter of a rake of the first order, wanted by none.

"I will not push you, Ruby. You are my friend and I trust your judgment. When the time is right, you will tell me," Vi said. "And until then, I will continue to be here for you. No matter the need. I only hope you will ask for my assistance."

"And what about when I do tell you, and you do not like what you hear? What then? I cannot bear the thought of complicating your life."

"Then I will continue to be your dearest friend. We will figure everything out together and if you wish to return to Haversham House, that option is yours to make."

Ruby wanted to cry. Sob for the unconditional love her friend offered, yet her own mother was incapable of giving. "Thank you." The words were all she could muster, although she knew Vi deserved so much more.

"It pleases me that Harold has been such a great help to you."

"Yes, though I have not asked for nor encouraged his involvement."

"You like him, do you not?"

The question took Ruby by surprise. She hadn't allowed herself to acknowledge her desires for him; there was no chance of anything more than a fleeting acquaintance between the two. He would likely find a suitable bride and return to the vicarage, while she would eventually retire to her family's country estate and live the remainder of her days helping Vi take care of the children at Foldger's Foundling House or maintaining her family's estate.

Vi sat next to Ruby on her dressing table bench and looked into the mirror—and straight to Ruby's deepest desires, her very being, before speaking. "To know great love, one must also know great pain."

"I am not sure how that can help me," Ruby looked down where Vi clasped her hand.

"I think you do," Vi smiled, though it held sadness. "Life is like a pendulum. As it swings one way, it is guaranteed to swing the other, with just as much force. Right now you are feeling sadness, despair, loneliness, fear...and probably a hundred other emotions you do not know how to handle. But never fear, the other side of your current pendulum swing will hold joy, hope, belonging, and courage. "

Ruby felt the tears resume their path down her makeup-streaked face and forced a smile to her lips. "I truly hope you are right."

"Have you not learned by now that I am always correct?"

CHAPTER 27

HAROLD WALKED THE crowded room. While many of the partygoers flitted about like they hadn't a care, Harold felt the weight of the world upon his shoulders. His brother had sent word that a crew had been obtained and they were now preparing to set sail. He'd received a bill just that morning detailing all the food and commodities needed for their maiden voyage to France.

He attempted to mingle and keep his mind off the work he should be helping with at the docks. No conversation drew his attention for more than a moment or two. He'd twirled a young debutante about the dance floor and retrieved refreshments for a pair of matrons who were so involved in a conversation about the deterioration of the walking paths in Hyde Park that they didn't notice his hasty departure shortly thereafter.

It was startling how many *ton* members he'd

met in his short time in town. It was true that none had sought a deeper acquaintance, but neither had he. Enjoying his time was one thing; creating a life he would eventually have to forsake was another. The notion of a viscount or earl journeying to the vicarage for a visit was comical at best. He knew he'd have chance meetings with acquaintances when they vacationed at Haversham House, but further than that he had no expectation of a continued association.

Harold stopped by a palm on the outskirts of the dance floor and watched the multicolored dresses and headwear blend and swirl about. The movement in the room stirred stagnant air, simulating a breeze through the room. The music from the string quartet seated on the platform next to the garden entrance could barely be heard above the conversation on the floor and the laughter of rowdy men in the card room.

A group of distinguished men spoke in hushed tones to the left of him. He watched as a group of fashionably dressed women pushed their offspring, each outfitted in a different variation of pastels, toward the gentlemen. The fellows hadn't noticed the group converging on them as yet. The young girls looked frightened, with eyes as round as saucers. Their mothers could be described as nothing less than determined.

This cat and mouse game within the *ton*'s elite nobility was one Harold had no wish to ever be a part of. Neither the seeker nor the prey.

He knew the moment the men realized a trap had been set for them because they scattered like mice in all directions, leaving only one gentleman who'd been too slow to make his own escape.

Returning his gaze to the dance floor, he admired Brock as he swung Lady Haversham in wide circles about the floor, seemingly at ease moving amongst the other couples, even with her growing middle. They were both entranced with one another. It was highly rare for the pair to leave each other's arms while in public. Many would disagree with Lady Haversham's decision to journey into the city for the season in her condition, but all of London appeared to enjoy the couple, despite the scandal they had caused last year. Few would suspect the sordid details of their initial meeting, looking at them now.

Lord and Lady Haversham continued their journey across the dance floor and out of Harold's line of sight. He looked over the crowded room in search of some distraction to pass the remaining time until his hosts were ready to retire home. It was rare for them to leave before the final song was played.

A woman, dressed in the purest of ivory silk, made her way into the room from the terrace on the arm of a dashing figure Harold didn't recognize. The glow from the many chandeliers in the room reflected off the single pearl that hung around her slender neck. Her dark hair was gathered tight upon her head, matching teardrop pearls swinging from each delicate ear.

She laughed, and he could swear he heard the musical lilt above the noise of the band and many conversations in the room. He'd heard the sound only a few times, but it had written itself into his memory. Something the man said had her blushing as he maneuvered her toward the line in front of the refreshment table.

Harold should be the one to make her

laugh—to make her blush. Instead, he only incited her fury and harsh words. If she would only give him a chance…

But no, he needed to stay focused on his venture. If she sought out his help, he would do all in his power for her. Truly, until she was ready to confide in him the secret he had already learned, he could only keep watch over her in order to ensure she neither injured herself nor called into question Lord and Lady Haversham's reputations.

Ruby and her escort made their way through the line and accepted drinks from a servant. Harold watched them make their way along the outskirts of the ballroom, much as he had. The gentleman nodded or exchanged greeting with people as they passed, but never lingered longer than necessary. Ruby rarely made eye contact with those they stopped to speak with, only curtsying and nodding when the need arose.

Suddenly, the room felt overly crowded and swelteringly hot. He needed to depart for cooler air, but could not take his eyes from the couple.

Startled, Harold realized he was jealous of the man, envious of his position at Ruby's side.

He should be the one to escort her about the room—and she should hold her head high, not cast her gaze upon the feet of English nobility. She deserved to be the center of attention; her intelligent musings would delight the entire room. Instead, this man ushered her about as if she was a pet upon his arm, only good for others to look at but never address. She was more than a pretty gem to be admired.

Finally, she excused herself and Harold watched as she made her way to the opening between the foyer and the ballroom. She glanced over her shoulder. When she spotted Lady Haversham, occupied on the dance floor, she slipped through the doorway and disappeared from his view.

Did woman never tire of putting herself at risk?

Before he knew what he was doing, he moved along the perimeter of the ballroom toward the door through which she'd just departed. He passed the man who'd escorted her moments before and brushed against him as he passed, with nary a 'begging your pardon.' Harold was satisfied when the man wobbled on unsteady feet at his nudge.

If he didn't hurry, Ruby would slip from the house and he would not know which direction she'd gone—if she indeed planned on leaving the house. The ball they attended was thrown by a newly appointed, yet wealthy baron and baroness. Ruby's list of men all tended to be of a mature age with a long lineage.

As he approached the doorway, he cut across the fringes of the dance floor, in between two slowly moving couples. Only a few odd looks were cast his way, but thankfully the *ton* resumed their watch of more noteworthy attendees.

At last, he left the room and found himself in the sparsely populated entry. His eyes darted around the cavernous room until he spotted her, not far from the main door. She stood in quiet conversation with Alex, her hand pressed tightly to her mouth, her eyes round with shock and her skin drained of all color.

CHAPTER 28

RUBY RAN THROUGH the door, not pausing to knock nor caring if anyone took issue with that.

The entry hall was deserted.

Her labored breathing made it impossible to hear whether anyone was about. Without thinking, she rushed up the main stairs to the second floor, as if a magnet drew her in that direction. A servant walked slowly toward her when she gained the top landing. The young girl's head snapped up at the sound of Ruby's heavy breathing.

"Where is he?" she screamed. The words echoed through the empty corridor, bouncing off the walls.

With eyes opened wide in shock, the girl pointed further down the hall.

Ruby grasped the folds of the pearly white evening dress and ran in the direction the servant had pointed. All she could think was that she was too late. She wouldn't make it in time.

Her opportunity to know her father was gone. The chance to learn more about him, and herself, had been taken from her forever.

And all by a girl she'd come to love…her very own sister.

Emotions flooded her: love, guilt, hate, betrayal, distrust, jealousy, confusion—the feelings just kept assaulting her, threatening to drag her down.

She passed closed door after closed door, not trying a single one. She knew her father did not rest behind any of them. Instead she continued on to the oversized double doors at the end of the hall, one door cracked. A small pool of light escaped, the kind nothing more than a few candles would produce.

Had he lain alone in his last hours? No one there to comfort him in his time of need…?

Or would she find his doctor, his close friends, and his servants gathered to say goodbye?

She prayed she wasn't too late.

When Alex had found her, enjoying a turn about the dance floor at Lord Somerset's ball, she'd instantly felt guilty. While she'd been prancing about in fancy garb, her father had been sick, possibly struggling to stay conscious through enormous amounts of pain.

She laughed…he lay wasting away.

She danced…he writhed in pain.

She dreamed of a better life, and he'd possibly been alone, fearing for his own.

Now, she stood, almost lifeless herself, in front of her father's massive bedroom doors. Scared to proceed, knowing what she found beyond that door would change her forever— emotionally and physically. There was no possibility of her returning to a quiet existence in the country; she knew that now. She was not meant to be forgotten, left unnoticed to a lowly life of nothingness.

No, she deserved more. Craved more.

Yet, she did not know how to accept the Marquis of Drake as anything other than the horrible man he was. Despite all his ugly words and abusive treatment of Ellie, he was their father. Ruby had wanted to meet the man, regardless of his attitude and scorn for her and her mother. He owed her an explanation for his actions, why he'd tossed them aside as if they meant nothing. It was her right.

She raised her hand to her hair, knotted and windblown from her hurried travel across town, patting it into place to gain some semblance of order. One does not meet their father for the very first time very often, she reflected, and should appear proper for the occasion.

She would meet her father. Get the answers she deserved. And move on. If that included the marquis and Ellington in her life, she didn't know. But move on—move forward—she would.

She had no other choice.

Ruby squared her shoulders and smoothed her gown.

Placing her hand flat on the solid wood door, she pushed.

As she expected of a house so grand, the door swung open on well-oiled hinges, revealing an empty room with a bed, shrouded in thick, midnight-blue curtains. The air was stale, the temperature so warm that the smell of sickness surrounded them.

She stepped past the threshold, taking in all that was her father's most private domain. The masculinity of the space was overpowering—just as Ruby suspected he had been in life. He lived life on his own terms, even though he had clearly hurt many in the process. Drake was not afraid to take what he wanted, discarding the broken shell of a woman when he was done... When the allure of the moment no longer held him.

Could she hate him for that? Should she walk away now, forget him as he'd forgotten her all these years?

Part of her knew he did not deserve her—or Ellington, for that matter. Yes, the child—really a girl on the cusp of womanhood—was a terrible pain with no manners, but could Ruby blame her any more than she could her father for everything that had transpired thus far? Ellington had admitted she knew who Ruby was that night she'd found her and Harold, locked tight in a compromising embrace.

So much could have been different, should have been different, had Ellington been honest with her. They could have started a relationship then, instead of putting each other through this. The harsh words they'd exchanged over their short acquaintance could have been avoided. Ruby would have removed Ellington from the circumstances she felt trapped in. No child deserved the life of abuse that Ellie had led.

Ruby hadn't a coin to her name, but she would have made arrangement for her sister.

As her breathing slowed, she heard a light sobbing.

Moving closer to the bed, Ruby removed her gloves when the heat of the room assaulted her. She saw a small figure sitting within the curtains surrounding the massive four-poster bed. Ruby pulled the drape back to reveal the withered frame of her father, lying motionless beneath a heaping mound of blankets.

Next to the marquis, Ellie sat curled in on herself, clutching her father's feeble hand.

"Ellin—" Ruby set her gloves on a small table not far from her sister.

"He is gone," her sister mumbled between sobs.

Anger flared within Ruby, threatening to take over her very being. "Why did you keep this from me?" When Ellie made no move to answer her or even look at her, Ruby's rage grew. "How dare you steal this from me?"

"Steal what?" For the first time since Ruby had met her, Ellington sounded lost, without an ounce of fight left in her.

But Ruby was too hurt and angry to notice. "You stole my chance to know my father, to have a relationship with him." The words reverberated through her, every word true to her core. "To find my place or *who* I actually am."

Ellington finally lifted her tear-streaked face. "He was not worth your time…or your love."

"That was not your choice to make." Ruby knew she screamed the words when Ellie flinched at the harshness of them. "You had no right to decide whether or not I should have a relationship with him, whatever I chose that relationship to be. And now, I will never know. He treated you unfairly and cruelly, but at least he knew you and you him. You took that from me." The tears fell then, hot and fast down her face and on to the expensive gown Vi had loaned her.

Ruby was tired of people making decisions for her, thinking they knew what was in her best interest. First her mother; now Ellington. And in some way, the marquis, too. He could have sought her out after her father had died—or before.

"Maybe I could have changed things—for you and me. I could have changed him, had he just gotten the opportunity to know me. Maybe as a family we could have worked through all his harsh words, shown him we love him regardless of how he treated us…given him a chance to love us."

"He would have hurt you the way he hurt me…and our mothers."

"You cannot know that."

Ellington wiped the tears from her face. "Really? You think after all these years I did not know my father—our father?"

Ruby had no words—only emotions that no amount of words could express.

"He would have broken you as he did me and our mothers before that," her sister sighed, no fight left. "He destroyed everything he touched."

The words were overly wise and insightful for a girl so young. But that did not negate the wrongness of what Ellington had done. "Did you stop to think that your actions could destroy any relationship you and I could have had? Maybe you are no different from our father." It was too late to take the words back. "But I would not know because you saw fit to take that from me!"

Ruby slung the cutting words at Ellie, as the young girl had done to her on numerous occasions. She didn't care about the damage they did. She didn't feel compassion for the injured look her sister turned on her. She didn't—would never—forgive or forget the injustice done unto her by people who should care most for her.

No, she was done caring about and for others. It led to nothing but anguish for herself.

It was time she went after what she wanted. What would make her happy.

And she knew this was not it, surrounded by and at the mercy of deceitful *family*.

Viola and her family had always been there for her, never letting her want for something she needed. And how had she returned their kindness and love? By deceiving them, by sneaking around behind their backs in her search for information. She'd lied to them just as her mother and Ellington had. Was she that different from her *family*?

And Harold. He'd only sought to be her friend, and she'd pushed him away. She'd been unable to trust him when he was one of the few deserving of her trust.

"So, that is it?" Ellie asked.

Ruby was unsure if this was it or just the beginning of something completely different. "I do not know what happens next." Her anger slipped away with the words.

"Just leave us."

Walking away, as her father had done to her and her mother, was not what Ruby had envisioned when she'd been hatching her plan to find her father and possibly a sibling or two. She longed to find her place, who she was and who she wanted to be. But what choice did she have?

If she stayed, Ellington's destructive behavior would eventually bring them both down. The lying, the pickpocketing, the gambling, the fights—Ruby was not equipped to handle this. Things would undoubtedly escalate to more erratic behavior.

But without Ruby, who did Ellington have?

Marce Davenport, the Madame at the brothel? Or her equally questionable sisters? Ellington could be damned to a life in the workhouses or be taken to jail for her crimes, no matter how petty they were.

Ruby would be unable to live with herself if that fate came to be, knowing that she could have changed it. While the desire to walk away—to wash her hands of the situation—and be like her father was strong, she knew she was nothing like her father. She did not abandon people. Her mother had deceived her for years, but that did not stop or weaken Ruby's love for her. Viola had been embroiled in scandal when they'd met, but that hadn't stopped Ruby from coming to know and love her, and remaining by her side through the rough times the previous year.

No. The word echoed in her head. She would not, could not, give up on Ellington.

But first, she needed to make amends with Harold. She'd said so many horrid things to him and about him, though all he'd done was try to help her.

Ruby turned to leave.

"I guess I should not have expected anything different from you." The hurt in Ellie's tone was like a dagger to her heart.

"I will return." Ruby didn't face her sister when she said the words, but that did not make them any less true. "I must handle something. I will give you time to grieve."

Ellington laughed, the sound high and forced. "You think I need to grieve?" The bed creaked and her sister climbed off it. "It is more like a time of celebration."

The girl was as much a mystery now as she'd been since they met. She'd sat there with tears streaming down her face, clutching his hand, yet now she claimed the time to celebrate was upon them.

"I understand if you do not wish to see me again."

"I said I *will* be back, Ellie."

And Ruby fled the room, leaving behind her broken sister and a lifeless father beyond redemption—and the kid gloves she'd set upon the side table.

CHAPTER 29

HAROLD DIDN'T WANT to contemplate what had upset Ruby and sent her fleeing from the ballroom. One moment he'd been watching her laugh and converse with a group of young ladies, the next she'd hastily departed the room and taken a note from Alex. Harold hadn't the chance to reach her side before she'd fled. She hadn't retrieved her shawl or called for the Haversham carriage to be brought round.

By the time he'd exited the front door, Ruby had already clambered into a hack and they were off, traversing the dark London streets. How she'd managed her hasty departure so quickly in her evening gown, Harold would never know.

Thankfully, the Haversham carriage sat to the left of the drive with the coachman still nearby. After commanding Brock's driver to 'follow that hack,' they also sped into the night. It only took a block to catch the vehicle, and pursuing it through town proved easy at this time of night. When the hack stopped outside Drake's house, Ruby had jumped down unassisted and rushed into the house, not bothering to knock.

Harold had waited outside for what seemed an eternity—then he waited a bit longer, yet he sensed it was only that the minutes dragged by. Every second was like hours, though it hadn't been more than an hour, at most.

The time alone gave Harold the time to think, dwelling not only on his life but on Ruby's. It was then the pieces began to fall into place: her time spent with Ellie, how familiar the young girl seemed, and Ruby's mad dash tonight.

Ruby had found the man she'd risked so much to discover.

The Marquis of Drake.

As the evening drew on, Harold knew he had to either collect her from the house and go back to their evening's entertainment, return to the party alone, or have the driver drop him at the townhouse and return for Brock and Lady Haversham. None of these options suited him. He would appear the brute if he charged the door and demanded her departure, especially if now was a time she needed privacy. Time to work through—with Drake and Ellie—their family connection. If he returned to the party, he'd likely worry all evening about her safety. And if he returned home, well, he would retrieve a horse from the stables and return to Drake's house and his vigil outside.

Harold calculated the time it would take to arrive back at Brock's house, saddle a horse, and return. No more than thirty minutes at this time of night—and if he didn't waste time with a saddle, he could shave at least five minutes from that estimate. Not having the carriage back to Brock would cast a spotlight on himself that could carry over to Ruby and her whereabouts.

Ruby's secrets were not his to expose—or even question, according to her. It was one thing for him to make sure she was not in harm's way; it was another to bring Lady Haversham into the situation. He had no doubt that when Ruby was ready, she'd confide in her best friend.

With that in mind, Harold jumped down from the Haversham carriage at the townhouse and took the front steps as quickly as possible. With any luck, he'd slip into the stable, select a horse, and be back on his way again within minutes. Buttons swung the door open before Harold could turn the knob.

"Good evening, Mr. Jakeston," the butler said. "Your father awaits you in the front parlor."

Harold stopped, almost tripping over his own feet. "Excuse me?"

He cleared his throat. "Um, Vicar Jakeston has been expecting your attendance in the parlor for a few hours. I told him you were out for the evening, but he insisted on awaiting your return."

"Please, inform him I will attend him momentarily." Ignoring his father's continued correspondence obviously had not deterred the man from his mission, as his letters had become threatening and volatile of late. In recent days he'd received two and three a day, outlining Harold's shortcomings and his penchant for continued disobedience, as if he were still a child in short pants and not the man he was.

Harold needed a drink if he was going to make it through this night. He should be returning to Drake's house to ensure Ruby made it back to the ball or home in one piece. Instead, he made his way to Brock's study and straight to the sidebar that held several decanters of spirits ranging in color from clear to dark amber.

He selected the first one, a clear liquid. It did not matter its contents, because he planned to down the drink and get this meeting over with.

"I wondered what kept you from attending me upon your arrival." His father's impatient voice echoed in the room. "I should have known the sins of city life would be your downfall."

"Father, how lovely to see you." He greeted the man who'd belittled him his entire life; made sure he knew his older brothers made their father proud, while Harold had failed every test given to him. Challenges that Harold hadn't even known he faced, yet his father found him lacking. He'd never said his prayers with enough sincerity, never completed his chores quickly enough, nor spent enough of his resources to benefit his family.

He didn't turn, but brought the tumbler to his mouth, thinking only of extricating himself and returning to watch over Ruby.

"But please, finish your drink. I am sure there is not a thing more important than the spirits in your hand." The words, cold and emotionless, sent a chill down his spine. "Your mother will be so proud to learn her youngest son is a drunkard."

Harold didn't dignify his father's accusation with a response; it was but one more thing the man charged him with that had no grounds in truth. He'd learned almost before he could walk that nothing he could say would make any difference, positive or negative. Instead, he calmed his breathing, turned, and motioned to the chairs situated before the unlit hearth. The night was warm, the room stiflingly hot. The walls seemed to close in on him.

Vicar Jakeston took the seat furthest from Harold, continuing the way they always had. His father would push and in turn, Harold would pull. It was a never-ending war of wits without the need for words because actions spoke so much louder. His countermove, true to form, was to deny the seat next to his father in favor of standing. But he knew better than to think his stance meant he held the upper hand.

"You do not plan to deny it?"

His father always retained the upper hand with his congregation and his family—and that upper hand was more often than not clenched into a tight fist. Demanding what he wanted and how things would progress; if anyone refuted, his father's fist would end all discord.

"What would be the point of that? You have convicted me of wrongdoing. You are the judge and jury, allotted your position and power by the Holy Father above." Harold knew he was being overly hostile, but was at a loss to stop himself. He would not allow his father to come here, into his best friend's house, and disrespect him or his host. "I cannot contend with the power vested in you, Father, by the all-knowing, all seeing Supreme Being. Besides, I find I haven't the time nor the energy to continue this discussion."

"Do not mock my faith." Though whispered, the threat was clear in his father's statement. "Why do you seek to thwart and demolish all I have built for you?"

"Built? For me?" Harold wanted to laugh, but knew it would only further infuriate his father. "What you have done has only been for yourself. Never confuse your interests with my own."

He goaded his father, increasing his ire despite knowing that every word he said would keep him longer from returning to Drake's townhouse. Every moment that passed increased the likelihood Ruby would slip away without him to follow. She could be distraught and in need of him.

His father, calm and collected, sat motionless. "Your interests will be as I dictate them to be." The man had nerve, Harold would give him that. "Your mother and I did everything in our power to raise you and your brothers, giving you all you needed. I handpicked lives for each of you. David is happy with his life as a military man, and William has learned the trade of blacksmithing. Both have married well and will give their families good, solid lives," his father continued. "They are men I am proud to call my sons."

"And me, Father?" Harold couldn't help but ask.

Vicar Jakeston sighed. "I still hold out hope for you and your future. Your mother and I pray every day that you will fall into line… Surprise us both and grow into a man."

Harold had lived his whole life under his father's thumb, unable to be the man he wanted to be, unable to even discover who the man was until recently. He thought briefly of tearing down his father's high regard for William, telling him of his older brother's loss of livelihood and fall into near poverty, but while his father hurled words without a care for others, Harold had more integrity than that. William had kept his circumstances from their father for a reason; it was not up to him to betray that confidence.

"You are so very wrong!"

Harold watched his father's eyes grew wide when he realized another was there to hear his evil, hate-filled words.

RUBY HAD SAT by and done nothing when Drake had hurled spiteful words at Ellie, but she would not sit back now and allow another person she cared about to be degraded and hurt by someone who should love and cherish them.

"And who might you be?"

She almost regretted her intrusion on what was meant to be a very private conversation when Vicar Jakeston turned his fiery eyes upon her. She froze.

"Is this—" He pointed at her, but turned his gaze back to Harold "—what you have chosen over your family and your obligations? A strumpet?"

A strumpet? First her own father calls her a bastard, and now she'd been called a strumpet. "I most certainly am not—"

Vicar Jakeston held up his hand to stop her protest. "It does not, in fact, matter who you are and what *service* you provide for my son. He is no longer in need of you and what you offer." He turned to Harold before continuing. "Ready your things, Harold. We are leaving for the Haversham estate now."

"Father—"

"I said, collect your things." His father's voice rose for the first time.

It wasn't the insult thrown at her that sent

Ruby over the edge, but rather the presence of the father who failed to appreciate the honorable, caring, compassionate man he'd raised. "Vicar Jakeston. You may not remember me, but my family's home sits next to the Haversham estate," Ruby attempted to introduce herself. "My name is Ruby St. Augustin. I am no more a strumpet than your son is a disappointment."

"I appreciate your unexpected and very unwarranted praise of Harold, but it is neither needed nor wanted." Vicar Jakeston stepped toward Ruby, waiting for her to move so he could make his exit. "Harold, I will meet you in the foyer in ten minutes to depart."

"Enough," Ruby said, breaking at last. She held her ground, blocking the door. "I am done with people deciding what is best for me."

Both men looked at her, their confusion at her words evident in their expressions.

"Your son is the only one who has stepped back and allowed me to find myself, to discover who I am, and where I belong. Your son—" Ruby pointed to Harold, but kept her eyes squarely on the vicar, "—is the epitome of honorable. He may not fit into the mold you have created for him, but instead he has poured his own mold." In that moment, she realized she wanted to fit in Harold's mold—or possibly pour a new one to fit them both.

"Ruby, you do not have—"

"Oh, but I do. You have saved me from my own foolish mistakes more than I can count. You stood back and let me make my own errors, only stepping in when I most needed you—and for that, I have continually pushed you away. Proclaiming to all that I do not need you, saying hurtful things to drive you from my life." Her words were no better than Harold's father's. She'd yelled and ranted, told him to return to the country where he belonged, far from her. She owed Harold so much, yet he'd asked so little of her.

"You should be proud to call him son, stand taller knowing he is making a name and legacy for himself, not living off the prestige created by his ancestors before him. Have you even asked him what he seeks in life? If you had, you would know that Harold does not seek to be a vicar—to live a life of service to everyone but himself and his desires. Instead, he has chosen to forge his own path."

"And what path would that be?" his father asked. "To be a drunkard about town, living off the pity of Lord Haversham? How does he propose to support a family?"

Ruby had no answers for him. "I do not know, but one thing I do know is that it is not for you or me to decide or dictate for him." She knew how it felt to have others constantly in charge of her life, making decisions for her, just as her mother had done by letting her believe that the baron was her true father, then leaving her to rot in the country. Just as Ellie had, deciding that the marquis was not worth knowing, taking away Ruby's dream of meeting her true father, whether good or bad.

"Your father should be ashamed of the daughter he raised," the vicar said. "Speaking to your elders as you do is the height of impropriety. You should be relegated to the country, where you cannot disgrace the good Sir St. Augustin's memory further."

"Father," Harold said. Ruby flinched at the edge in his tone. "You will not speak to Miss

Ruby in that manner. I think it is time for you to leave."

"I will speak in any way I see fit to whomever I want, when it is warranted," his father retorted. "I will depart as soon as you are ready." With that, the vicar pushed past Ruby. His sure, heavy footfalls could be heard as he retraced his steps to the foyer, no doubt waiting for Harold to follow.

Before Ruby could stop him, Harold also pushed past her and out the door. She wanted to call after him, tell him that what his father thought and said was not important. He knew who he was and his worth—and so did she, which was all that mattered.

Before she could follow him, he pulled the door shut, closing her in the empty room.

CHAPTER 30

"FATHER!" HAROLD'S STRIDE increased as he followed his father into the foyer. "How dare you speak to Ruby thus."

His father halted a few steps from the front door. "Is it Ruby now? I see you've dispelled with formalities. My earlier assumptions were correct." The vicar crossed his arms before him, unbearably smug. "Do you bed her at night? Like a common harlot?"

"Enough. You will cease treating me like a wayward child."

"I only treat you the way you deserve to be treated."

"The way I deserve to be treated?" Harold said, incredulous. "You do not know the first thing about how to treat a person with anything other than scorn and criticism."

"You cannot possibly believe you deserve any more than that from me."

"I do not care what you think I deserve. The woman behind that door definitely does not deserve your shoddy treatment. She is a guest in Lord Haversham's home, and is to be treated as nothing less than a lady of excellent caliber and unquestionable reputation."

For the first time, Harold stood up to his father, who remained quiet. Neither was aware when the balance of power had shifted, but for once Harold was unconcerned with his father's reaction.

"And furthermore," Harold continued. "I do not owe you anything, especially control over my future."

His father laughed, sobering Harold further. "You are as I always believed you to be."

"And what exactly is that?"

"Weak."

Heat coursed through Harold—red, hot fury threatened to explode. "You can go to hell—and take your unjustified, self-righteous attitude with you. Leave this house and never—and I mean never!—think to insult any woman again, or I will personally deliver you to hell."

"You think to sweep me out the door and never return home?"

"If and when I come it will be my decision, not yours."

"How easily you break your mother's heart."

"She will be the only reason I may have cause to return. Now, you will leave this house and London entirely. If you send another missive, know I will burn it immediately."

His father glared at him, rooted where he stood. "A man is nothing if he does not live up to his responsibilities."

Harold met his father, glare for glare. "And a

man is not a man if he cannot assess where his true responsibilities lie. My responsibilities—and my future—are here, possibly in the very next room."

"You misguided fool!"

"You are the only fool here, *Father*."

A movement from the stairway caught his attention and Harold spied several servants watching from the landing above.

"This meeting is at its end," Harold said. "I will not ask you again to leave, or I will be forced to assist you on your way."

Harold wanted to laugh at the helpless look that crossed his father's face before he turned on his heel and stalked out the front door.

A quiet clapping, which grew louder and louder behind him, accompanied the sound of the slamming door.

"Well done, Mr. Jakeston," Brock's butler chimed with a broad smile on his face. "I doubt that vile man will return—pardon my words."

"I highly doubt it as well, but if he should show his face again, he is to be turned away immediately."

"Yes, sir."

As the butler left the room, Harold focused on the woman awaiting him, hoping she hadn't overheard every distasteful detail.

He stood straighter and walked to the door he'd left moments ago. He and Ruby obviously had much to discuss, the least of which being his own family drama.

Opening the door, she stood staring at him with tears in her eyes. "I am so sorry he said such ugly, untrue words to you," he said, pained by the sorrow on her face.

"You can no more control your father and

what he says than he can control you. You have nothing to apologize for. And I am the one who owes you an apology."

Harold took the few steps to stand closer to her. She tilted her head back ever so slightly to look up into his eyes. "You owe me nothing," he said. "It is I who owe you."

"I cannot fathom what you could possibly owe me. I've treated you as I have treated everyone since my arrival in London, with half-truths and outright lies—I have been unable to trust a soul, when so many were willing to trust me. You put faith in me, not pressuring me for anything I was not ready to give."

"Ruby—" He hesitated. If she knew the true reason he didn't push her for answers—that he already had them—he was uncertain what her reaction might be.

"Please, let me finish. All this time I've searched for a place to belong, without realizing that along the way, I'd found exactly that. And with whom."

With those words, Ruby moved into his embrace. An embrace he hadn't offered—and didn't deserve—but he pulled her close, nonetheless.

He didn't say a word, only held Ruby in his arms. He'd sensed the moment he saw her that something was wrong. Her eyes were red with spent tears, the makeup she'd taken to wearing to cover her healing, greenish bruise washed away. A new weight laid across her shoulders. It was possible their meeting hadn't gone well and Harold was prepared to confront Drake if the man had treated her harshly.

At the moment, he didn't want explanations; he only wanted to hold her...for as long as it might last, before she pushed him away again. Five minutes or five hours, it mattered naught. The feel of her, the smell of her, the way her hair brushed against his cheek. He committed it all to memory, knowing when she walked away that he would have to let her go. When she again told him to go back to the vicarage, he would be ready to do just that. Though, that no longer appeared to be an option for him.

She would carry on here, or wherever she decided to make her home, and he would be forced to do the same. Wherever that might be, he knew it couldn't include her. She'd made that clear many times, but he'd been too stubborn to hear her words, instead focusing on the flame he was sure existed between them.

But life was about more than physical attraction, one's body yearning for another's.

Too soon, she pulled back, her hands flat against his chest.

"I need to be honest with you, Harold." She spoke softly.

He didn't want to hear what she had to say, fearing it meant the end of their friendship. "You owe me no explanation."

She took a step back, looking into his eyes. "Yes, I do. I have brought you into the mess that is my life. It is complicated and convoluted and I couldn't bring myself to tell you more before—for fear of how you would react."

"Nothing you could say would cause me to turn away from you."

"I hope that is true." Her eyes welled again with tears. Suddenly, he remembered a time long ago, almost forgotten. He'd watched from a near field as Ruby's father—Sir St. Augustin—was carried in the back of a carriage to their family burial plot. She'd looked so lost and forlorn that he'd wanted to go to her, tell her everything would be fine. But they'd both been little more than children at the time. Neither knew what the future held, whether it was more grief or joy greater than either ever dreamed of.

She looked the same now—lost.

He took her face between his hands and kissed her gently. Her lips were soft and inviting. He forced himself to take a step back and listen before she changed her mind.

"I have been in London searching…" her voice trailed off. He waited, knowing she had more. Ruby shook her head as if to align her own wayward thoughts. "Angus was not my true father, although I am unsure if he knew that." She paused again, trembling now, staunchly holding back her tears. "I found an old journal of my mother's, detailing her infidelity."

"Ruby, you needn't—"

"Please, let me finish. You deserve the truth. My mother fell in love with a man…and I am the result of her affair."

When she fell silent, he asked, "Did you meet him?" He wanted desperately to know what had happened behind those closed doors as he'd waited outside. Something had clearly upset her.

"No."

"Why ever not? If you need someone to go with you—for support, or whatnot—I am here."

"That will not be necessary. He passed away."

"When?" The pieces suddenly fell into place; Alex had brought word to her at the ball.

"This evening."

"I am sorry."

"Do not be. He is—was—a horrible man, or so my sister claims."

"Ellie?"

"Yes."

"I suspected he was Lady Ellie's father all along." He didn't know which was worse; having a rake who was rumored to have fathered children with several of London's most elite women, or a sister whose actions were considerably less than honorable. "Not to mention the resemblance between the two of you."

"What resemblance?"

Harold was surprised she hadn't seen it before now. "You both have the same green eyes. The color is the same, even if the souls looking out have lived completely different lives."

"Truly?"

Harold saw how much she wanted to believe they shared a resemblance; in her eyes, she thought she'd found her place. But how to convince her that she'd always have a place with him, no matter if it was only friendship or something more? "Yes, and do not get me started on your mannerisms and fair skin tone."

"Despite how damaged she appears, I believe there is more to her than fire and bitterness. I've seen glimpses of that, and hope to see more. If we will only get to know her."

"Ellington is no more a child than you are." Did she not see her sister was a woman, even though she acted the child in some ways? "I look forward to making her acquaintance on these new terms, if you will have that."

She smiled for the first time since she'd entered the room. "I would like that greatly."

With her timid smile turned on him, he

knew if she only employed the right techniques she could steal any man's heart, have them relinquishing all they held dear without a second thought. She didn't need to sail the seven seas or wield a pirate sword to capture his heart.

His father had always maintained the belief that one did not need to travel to London or even the next shire to find one's intended mate. Harold's own mother only grew up a few minutes' walk from the vicarage. And Harold had always thought him daft for never seeking out the wonders of the world—or even on a smaller scale, the wonders of his own country.

At least on this one count, Harold had been a fool.

CHAPTER 31

RUBY WATCHED HIM closely, waiting for him to withdraw from her or to break eye contact. To tell her she was on her own and to forget their friendship, a relationship made impossible by her mother's affair and Ruby's bastard birth.

She waited for the deafening silence that would come as he thought through his means of escape.

She waited for the excuses he would use to explain his reasons for distancing himself from her.

She waited for the loneliness and desolation that would follow his physical and emotional departure.

It was inevitable. Most of all, she would have to keep her own emotions under control. He did not deserve the tears and crying that were sure to follow. He'd been so kind to her, had helped her in ways she could never expect to repay. But she did know she would not repay him with histrionics when he decided to end whatever they had between them. She'd done her best to push him away since the day they'd become reacquainted, and now he could only do what she'd been anticipating all along.

Ruby watched him, waiting for him to remove himself physically from her as she felt he had emotionally done already. His pensive expression did little to soothe her nerves.

The hour grew late, and they had both survived much emotional turmoil this night. She should excuse herself and retire to her room, for what was sure to be a sleepless night spent dwelling on all the impending hardships and life changes to come. But she could not tear herself from the room.

She could not tear herself from him.

"You may go," she said at last, her voice awkward and strained.

"Why ever would I do that?" he said. "If you need to rest, of course, I understand. But I am fine here. Happy to talk, to stay with you, for as long as you'll have me."

The words held a weightier implication than she'd known, she suddenly realized. She thought back to the times they had spent together, the conversations they'd had. The many times he had saved her, both from herself and the dangers that abounded in her quest. Those gestures bespoke a man whose devotion truly knew no bounds.

Harold had offered her a home, with him—not a location, but a heart.

And she hadn't realized it.

Hadn't known enough to recognize that where a person belongs isn't a place. To know that love truly existed, beyond one person using another for their own gain.

And who a person is doesn't hinge on a name or a parent's lineage.

Home is where the people she loved resided—and right now, that place was London. Ellie and Vi—both sisters of her heart—were here. She loved them both and they loved her, in their own ways.

"You must be tired as well," she whispered. "I truly have no right to keep you."

"I can think of not another place I'd rather be at this time or any other."

Harold was here, and she suddenly knew he loved her. He'd proved it time after time, even though she hadn't seen it. He'd blamed it on his penchant for saving damsels in distress, but she knew she was the only damsel he ever sought to save—and at the expense of his own future.

Something in her eyes must have told him as much. He pulled her close and set his lips upon hers. It was everything she wanted, while everything she never could hope to have. His lips pressed against hers, coaxing them apart. Not demanding, but far from gentle. Her arms moved to his shoulders, broad and thick compared to his slender frame. She was startled to realize that her body remembered his, craved his contact.

As she wrapped her arms around his neck, it was her lips that became more insistent and demanding. Suddenly her clothes felt binding, more restrictive than they ever had before. His neckcloth rubbed against her chin as their mouths moved together.

She pulled away. Keeping her eyes on his, she tentatively reached for the intricately tied cravat. Her fingers grasped the heavily starched material and tugged.

Harold let out his breath on a sigh when the cloth loosened.

Gradually, Ruby unwound it from his neck. The last bit fell away with a slight pull. The cloth felt just as he did; sturdy and firm, yet yielding to her.

They both watched the length of material fall to the floor before their eyes met once more.

Her breath hitched, lodged in her lungs, afraid to break the spell of the moment with the simplest sigh.

Harold placed his hands upon her hips and gently caressed, trailing his fingers up the side of her bodice.

She could not take it anymore and her breath left her. She wanted...she needed...she hadn't a clue, but she did know she didn't want him to release her. She would be bereft without his touch.

As if he'd read her thoughts, he lowered his lips to hers once more, and his arms wrapped around her waist. He lifted her ever so slightly and stepped the few paces to the chaise lounge. With reverence and care, he laid her on the soft chaise and brought his body to cover hers. His weight settled on her, less constricting than her clothes had felt moments before.

Their bodies molded together with ease, his leg gently nudging between hers. Her knees shifted to accommodate him. All the while, their lips never separated.

She lifted her hips to meet his as she opened her mouth to allow his tongue to explore. Not to be outdone, she pushed into his mouth, her tongue timidly grazing his teeth before retreating to sample his lips.

HAROLD FAIRLY GROWLED as her tongue swept across his lower lip. He wanted nothing more than to rip her elegant dress from her alluring body. He endeavored to hold back, to move slowly, at a pace she was comfortable with, giving her every opportunity to pull away or draw back.

Yet, Ruby didn't—she only pulled him closer.

Her hips pressed into his, driving him closer to the edge with each small movement. She seemed unaware how close he was to throwing caution to the wind and relieving her of her garments here, in the salon of their host and hostess.

His breeches became tighter as his shaft hardened at the thought. Her gown would slip easily from her shoulders. To prove the point, he brushed his hand against the silky material and it slid easily down her arm to reveal a corset of the same color beneath. He drew back and ran his fingers down the whale bone stitching in front that disappeared into the gathered silk at her waist.

A knock sounded upon the closed door.

As if nothing untoward had been very close to happening, Harold reluctantly pulled Ruby's dress back into place, savoring the feel of the fabric as it settled.

"I will be right there," he called, in hopes of stalling whoever sought to intrude.

For only a moment he feared it was his father, returned with another line of inquiry and argument.

He was relieved when only the butler called back, "Very well, Mr. Jakeston. I will await you in the main hall."

"Are you expecting someone?" Ruby's question came on a breathless sigh.

He sat back, assisting her in sitting as well. She touched her hair to assess the damage they'd done with the tumble on to the chaise.

"You hair is still the height of fashion, nary a tendril out of place," he assured her. "I cannot fathom who could possibly seek my attendance at this time of the evening."

"Well, then the situation must be dire indeed." Ruby stood, smoothing her gown and righting her pearl necklace. "Let us not dillydally."

"Us?" It was the first time she'd ever referred to them as a pair without immediately taking back her words.

"Do you wish me to wait here, then?"

"Of course not." Harold realized he still sat as Ruby moved toward the door. Not to be outdone, he hastily maneuvered past her and pulled the door wide, allowing her to breeze by him and out of the room. "After you, Miss."

His eyes were immediately drawn to the sway of her hips as she preceded him down the hall. Next, visions of her encased in only a corset of the purest cream, a single pearl settled delicately between her breasts as they rose and fell with each breath. He had half a mind to grab her about the waist and return to the sanctuary of the salon, or better yet, he'd carry her right up the main stairs to his suite of rooms, where he could better serve her—whatever she desired.

"Mr. Jakeston." Brock's butler met them as

they entered the foyer. "A Mr. Applewood is here to see you. I am unsure he is acquainted, and I can have him rid of quickly if you wish."

"The name is unfamiliar," Harold said.

The butler's apologetic air and nervous glances toward the man standing before the front door made Harold leery.

"It is quite fine, Buttons," Harold assured him before turning to his visitor. "Mr. Applewood, how may I help you?"

The man hurried across the room and extended his hand for Harold to shake. "My lord—"

Harold grasped the man's hand in a firm shake. "No, Mr. Jakeston will do."

"Mr. Jakeston, I apologize for interrupting your evening."

"It's of no concern. What is your need?"

The man was sweating profusely, his collar soaked as if he'd run the whole way to the Haversham townhouse. From the smell of him, he worked at the docks. His clothes were loose fitting and his hair tied back. His age was hard to discern due to the dirt on his face.

"I am the captain of the *Lucky Hand*."

Harold had no clue what the man spoke of, but he was sure it involved his and William's dealing at the docks.

"Your clipper, sir." Applewood looked to Harold for any sign of understanding. "William Jakeston hired me to captain the ship to France."

Leave it to William to select a name for their vessel without consulting him. The name was fitting, however, and he knew why his brother had chosen it. "My apologies, I was not aware we had selected a name as yet. Is there trouble?"

"I am afraid, Mr. Jakeston—the other Mr.

Jakeston—has been injured." Applewood rang his hands.

"How bad is he?" Harold asked, his heart suddenly in his throat. He searched for the butler.

"The dock doctor was called. I left to bring you as soon as he arrived."

"Buttons, have two horses brought round." Harold called, not knowing if the man lingered close.

"Make that three," Ruby called.

He looked at her, startled. "Oh no, the docks are no place for a woman, especially when a man is injured."

"I am going," she said. "There have been many times you have inserted yourself in my dealings. It's time I did the same."

"Are you sure?" Harold asked.

"Of course. I was not even aware your brother was in town."

"Sir, the horses are being readied and will be brought round momentarily," Buttons called. "Shall I send for Lord Haversham's family doctor as well?"

"No, I am sure the dock doctor is versed in all manners of port injuries." Next he turned to Applewood. "Please, tell me what happened while we wait."

He looked at Ruby, then back to Harold.

"She has a solid stomach. I assure you she can handle all the details."

"Yes, please, Mr. Applewood, tell us how bad things are."

"Very well." The man paused as if to gather his thoughts. "We were loading the vessel, preparing to set sail on the morning tide. The hoist was lifting a crate aboard the ship when the rope broke. It landed, pinning Mr. Jakeston—the other Mr. Jakeston—"

"We know which Mr. Jakeston," Ruby assured him.

"Very true," Applewood conceded. "The crate pinned Mr. Jakeston beneath it. We were quick to push it off him, but his leg and hip were damaged."

"Oh, dear!" Ruby gasped.

Harold pulled her hand into his in reassurance. "Let us wait out front. The horses should be ready soon."

A million thoughts ran through his head as they went outside to await their horses. He debated for a moment flagging down a hackney, but knew they would be stalled in town as the *ton* traversed the streets on their way home from their evening entertainments. He could run the miles to the docks, leaving Applewood and Ruby to follow on horse, but he'd be too winded to be of much help once he arrived.

Finally, three horses from Brock's impressive stables were brought round, two steeds and a mare he supposed was Ruby's personal horse.

"You are not dressed to ride." He hadn't even thought of Ruby, still dressed in her evening gown.

With a flip of her hand, Ruby held her foot out for a step-up. "It is only a dress, and can be replaced...a brother cannot. Please, help me up and we can be on our way."

He lifted her up onto her mare and she gained her seat quickly. She'd spent years helping Lady Haversham at her foal ranch, and he knew she was more adept with horses than most men.

"Please, lead the way, Mr. Applewood,"

Harold said when they were all comfortably in their saddles. "Ruby, stay close."

"I am perfectly capable of navigating the streets of London, thank you very much."

"I meant no offense, Miss Ruby." He despised the formality in his voice after their private moment only minutes before. "There are many things that can spook a horse after dark."

Ruby nodded at him and pulled her horse close. "I appreciate your concern, Mr. Jakeston."

It was as if they were only briefly acquainted, rather than intimately aware of one another. From his higher position on his horse he had a breathtaking view of her slender neck and kissable shoulders. His hands would far rather hold her than the reins of his horse.

"I was unaware of your current association with your brother," Ruby stated. "I had been led to believe that you'd lost touch with your brothers years ago." She kept her eyes straight ahead, but he knew she listened intently.

"We had lost touch, but William reached out soon after I arrived in London. I believe you saw us together not long ago."

"I do not recall."

"You were having ices with Lady Ellington, if I remember correctly."

"That was William? I saw you slip money to him."

"Yes. We have a joint venture we've been working on at the docks."

"I had no idea. Why were you so secretive when I asked that day?"

"Your own actions at the time did not inspire me to confide in you." It had been petty—Harold had known it at the time, and it was even more obvious now. He'd kept his dealings private to spite her.

She ducked her head and remained silent.

"We have almost arrived, Mr. Jakeston," Applewood called from ahead of them. "We are down the docks on the left."

Harold needed no directions when they moved into the dock area, for all was quiet but a man's moans of pain. The sound led them quickly to where William lay upon the dirty ground, writhing in agony.

Harold dismounted his horse and jumped into action, calling for an update on his brother's injuries and a full report from the doctor and the men involved in the accident. He learned many men had scattered shortly after the rope had snapped and the crate had been moved off William. Those remaining were the crew of the *Lucky Hand* and its captain, who'd been sent for Harold. The dock medic, really nothing more than a hack with some military injuries training, informed him of the suspected damages to William's leg, back, and hip. Thankfully, he hadn't hit his head overly hard when the crate knocked him to the ground.

"Does anyone have laudanum for his pain?" Ruby called to the crowd around them. "Should I call for Marce Davenport?"

"This is far beyond her expertise, I have no doubt," Harold said, though he admired her ability to keep her head in such circumstances.

As he called for the doctor, she knelt by William and in hushed tones, soothed him. His moaning subsided as she rubbed his shoulder to comfort him.

"Is he able to be transported?" Harold asked the doctor.

"Shhhh," she said quietly to William.

"Harold will find help quickly."

Harold doubted he'd have been as steadfast as Ruby, with the look of William's mangled side and leg.

"Brother," William whispered, "I am sorry."

The words tore at Harold. "I should have been here, helping you, instead of..." He let his words trail off as he pushed the thought of Ruby, held tight in his embrace, from his mind. His brother needed him, now more than ever. "William, let us make it through this and I swear I will be a better partner, more committed." *If* his brother made it through this. He'd do anything— promise everything, to see his brother well and whole.

Harold took his coat and laid it over William. He was helpless; with nothing else he could do, at least he would keep his brother warm.

"Relax," he said quietly. "You will be fine."

The doctor, indistinguishable from the other dock workers, shook his head. "I won't be responsible for carrying him about. We have a ward only a short walk from here. If he be tied to a sturdy plank, he should be fine to be moved there, but no further. Not this night, at least."

Harold would feel much better to have William removed to Haversham House immediately, but he understood the concern. He could have internal injuries not apparent to the eye. Harold hadn't even the chance to leave word with Brock before they'd gone.

A group of men laid a long plank next to William, and Ruby retreated to Harold's side as they picked up the man and slid the board beneath him. At the movement, William's blood-curdling scream made the hair on Harold's arms stand on end.

He was relieved when the doctor stepped forward and uncorked a small glass bottle.

"Hold him still," he called as he lifted William's head and brought the bottle to his lips. "He should sleep soon."

Even with the doctor's words, Harold was not reassured of the man's skill.

"Harold, things will be well." Ruby now held his arm, attempting to soothe his nerves. "We can send word to Lord Haversham's physician as soon as we return home."

"William, stay with me," Harold called to his brother. "Tell me about that time we stole the old Lord Haversham's prized telescope..." He tried to get him to talk, to stay conscious through the pain. He feared if his brother sank into sleep, he wouldn't awaken again.

He'd been the one who allowed William to help at the docks, against his better judgment. His older brother, while versed in city life, had no experience on ships or in a seaport. He was lucky the crate hadn't taken his life immediately.

As the men carried William the short distance to the dock's medical ward, Harold followed, the reins of all three horses in his hand and his other arm draped around Ruby's shoulders. He was unsure if he offered her support after witnessing such a traumatic event or if she gave him the strength to hold his own emotions together.

They waited while William was transferred to a bed. From there, he was given more laudanum to ensure he slept through the remaining hours of the night, or until Harold could send Brock's physician to better gauge his injuries.

The night had grown cold and the breeze off the water felt like ice through Harold's jacket. As they stepped outside and prepared to mount their horses for the return ride to Haversham House, Harold took his overcoat and laid it about Ruby's shoulders, hoping to ward off the cold air. He would not forgive himself if she caught a chill due to exposure.

They rode in silence all the way home, and separated immediately upon their return. Ruby went up the stairs to her room, while Brock bid Harold attend him in his study. Harold had no option but to let her go, their intimate moments shattered and forgotten.

CHAPTER 32

THE MORNING DAWNED clear and warm, which should have brightened Ruby's spirits, but after the emotional turmoil of the day before she couldn't convincingly be her jovial self. She sat half listening to Vi drone on and on about this lady and that lord and their plans for the remainder of the season. Through the idle chatter, Ruby noticed Vi eyeing her expectantly. Her friend craved more information about her newly discovered sister—and her father, though Vi still allowed her space and privacy. They'd known each other long enough for her to know that when Ruby was ready, she would share all.

Her mind wandered to all she'd experienced only hours before. The shock of learning she had a sister, the death of her father, and in the midst of all that, recognizing her feelings for Harold for what they truly were—love. Unconditional, unbridled love.

Then, they'd been shaken by the news of the accident at the docks. They'd stayed with William into the early morning hours.

And during it all, she hadn't the time or the energy to impart the news to Vi. Part of her regretted that she kept so many important things from her best friend, but she knew Vi was also in a delicate condition, and added stress could negatively affect her.

Even after all the hurtful things she'd spewed at Harold only days before, she was certain that he loved her, too. Except for Sir St. Augustin and Vi, no person had loved Ruby without reserve. No one had given her the opportunity to prove her worth.

Harold hadn't needed her to prove anything; he'd known his love for her long before Ruby had opened her eyes to her feelings for him. She still had little faith that their love would go anywhere, brave any storm—mainly meaning, their parents agreeing to a pairing between the families. Harold had never even mentioned any such thing happening.

"Ruby?" Vi asked. "Are you unwell? Has something happened?"

Everything and nothing at all had happened. Ruby hoped to understand and accept how drastically her life had changed, and how much change was still to come, before attempting to explain it to another—even her nearest and dearest friend.

So, instead of opening her wounds and laying everything before Vi, she said, "I am only tired."

"Have you not been sleeping well? You retired before we arrived home last evening." She knew Vi cared about her deeply and was concerned, especially after noticing the bruise on her face. "I came to your room, but it appeared you were already asleep."

"I think I am not used to all the activities of town life." In truth, she hadn't been asleep at all when Vi came to check on her, but had merely pretended. She'd spent hours crying, debating, and discarding her plans for the future. Eventually she'd realized that if she couldn't handle the here and now—meaning helping Ellie through losing their father, exploring her growing feelings for Harold, and somehow confronting her mother—then any planning for the future was needless and a waste of her energy.

"And I am sure it has nothing to do with your search." Vi kept her focus on the ledger she was working on.

Ruby knew her friend better than to think the comment was in any way casual chit chat. Vi was on her own mission and would notice any change, no matter how subtle, in Ruby's demeanor. "No, I have decided to end my search. Possibly retire to the country once more, and hope my mother never learns of any of it." She hoped Vi didn't question her reasons.

A light knock and clearing of a voice distracted both women.

"Lady Haversham," Buttons said. "Miss Ruby has a guest requesting her audience."

"I am not expecting anyone." Muddled, they looked at each other. The hour was far too early for a social call—and not many knew of Ruby's presence in town.

"Did they give you a card?" Vi asked.

"No, your ladyship. The young woman arrived in a carriage. She did not offer a name or

306 | *Christina McKnight*

card, but requested Miss Ruby's," he nodded in her direction as he spoke. "...immediate attention. I did explain the early hour, but she was quite insistent about seeing her. Shall I turn her away?"

The visitor's forthright attitude told Ruby all she needed to know. There was only one person she knew who would insist on having things her way. "No, please, show Lady Ellington in."

Any notion of keeping her situation from Vi—or time to think through everything—was gone.

Ruby set her own writing desk aside and stood, preparing for the onslaught that was her newly discovered sister. Now was as good a time as any for Vi to meet Ellington. A controlled, nonpublic place where Ellington could be herself—which was erratic, self-centered, and completely unpredictable. As the older sister, it fell to her to make sure Ellie was cared for—had a place to live, clothes, schooling, and a proper coming out when the time came. Ruby did not have the means to provide a roof for her own head, let alone for her sister—if Ellie would even accept her assistance. She'd hoped to have the time to enlist Vi's help in the situation.

Due to Drake's reputation there was a good chance more children would come forward to claim what they thought was rightfully theirs.

That excluded both Ruby and Ellie from any part of the estate, but could mean a little security for her sister. If the situation called for her to take full responsibility for her sister, she would. She would find a way to support the both of them, regardless of the sacrifice. Of course, Ellie going back to Ruby's family home was unconceivable under her mother's watchful eye.

"*The* Lady Ellington, the one you mentioned to me only a few days past?" Vi asked. "Shall I ring for tea?"

"Do not bother. It is more likely she will ask for a scotch over ice," Ruby jested. "Ellington—or Ellie, as she goes by—is the daughter of the Marquis of Drake."

"Should I know the marquis?"

Ruby felt badly for her deceit. Well, not truly deceit—but she hadn't been as honest and open as she'd promised Vi she would be if the need arose. "No. He is—was—a marquis. I have told you about my unfortunate friendship with Ellie—or at least it started out as unfortunate." It was the time to tell Vi all, but something held her back. Once she admitted who her true father was, any denial she could have used to maintain the pristine memory of Sir St. Augustin would be gone.

"And…" Vi prompted.

"I do not know what else you want me to say."

"And, since you have previously confided in me that Ellie is your sister, that would make the Marquis of Drake your father, is that correct?"

Ruby nodded.

"Where have I heard that name before?" Vi's pensive expression told Ruby her friend was putting things together. "Wait, is he not the man known about town as a notorious rakehell?"

"Yes." She watched her reaction closely. If Vi decided to turn her away, end their friendship, it was her right. Being linked to the marquis would not improve her rocky status about town. "At least he was known for that in his younger days."

Instead of pulling back, Vi doubled over

laughing. "So, you may very well have any number of siblings *and* be the daughter of a marquis."

"Ah, then you have heard of him."

"Oh yes, my father used to regale me with stories of a man thought to have sired an unknown number of London elite. Do not look so gloomy. Your mother could have chosen much worse."

As Vi's laughter quieted, she heard footsteps approaching down the hall. The butler would be returning with Ellie in tow. "Now, prepare yourself. My sister is a bit of a hellion herself."

"More than you and me?"

Ruby had never seen them as eccentric or hellions, but it would have been an accurate term to describe them up until the previous year.

She hadn't a chance to respond before her sister entered the room. "This man thinks to tell me what to do," Ellie huffed as she pushed past the butler.

"Far more a hellion than us," Ruby whispered to Vi.

"Well, can he tell me what to do, Ruby?" her sister continued. "Because, let us be clear, just because my—our—father passed away does not mean that you or anyone else can tell me what to do."

"I only asked her to wait a moment," Buttons said to Vi. "I did not mean any insult."

"That will be all," Vi said, waving the man off. "It was only a misunderstanding."

When Buttons had gone, Vi turned a sympathetic smile on Ellie and patted the seat next to her. Ruby shrunk back against her chair, waiting for her sister's temper to get the better of her again. To her astonishment, Ellie took the seat offered, crossing her legs at her ankles. If Ruby hadn't already seen her sister in action—ever the con artist—she'd think the girl had been trained in the art of being a lady, and not fluent in running the streets, gambling, and picking pockets.

"You must be Ellington." Vi smiled. "I am Lady Viola Haversham, your sister's dearest friend."

Ellie looked about the room. "Well, you certainly did marry above yourself. This is a right fancy place."

"Elli—" Ruby exclaimed.

"No, that is all right," Vi said, her smile never faltering. "My father is a lord of the realm. Therefore, I married a man within my social circle, not because of our birth status, but because we truly love one another."

Ruby's affection for her friend grew. So many would have rebuffed the girl for her insolence, but Vi was more sensitive than that.

"But you did not come here to discuss my fancy house, did you?"

"No, I came to see Ruby. I have something that belongs to her." Ellie sent a sidelong glance in Ruby's direction and held up a cloth sack she'd been holding. While Ruby would be happy to have her gloves returned, the trip was unnecessary. "Something I should have given her before."

This contrite Ellie was one Ruby hadn't seen before. She'd witnessed smug Ellie, selfish Ellie, conniving Ellie, broken Ellie, enraged Ellie—but never this resigned creature.

Her sister had obviously come for another reason.

Vi looked between the sisters. "I will leave

the two of you to chat." Standing, she closed the ledger she held and set it on the table as she left the room.

"Would you like some tea?" Ruby asked, at a loss for words.

"No." Ellie held out the bag in her hand. "I only came to give this to you."

Ellie tossed the bag into Ruby's lap when she made no move to take it from her. "Go on, it's yours. It won't bite."

She snatched the bag before it tumbled to the floor. "What is it?"

"Something I wanted to return before it was too late." Ellie stood. "I better be going."

"Wait." She didn't know when she would see Ellie again. "We have a lot to talk about."

"I think it best—"

She knew she couldn't let her sister walk out of the house without talking about...well, she didn't know what about, but Ruby had a feeling that if she didn't connect—truly connect—with Ellie now, another chance may not come. "Please, let me speak." She wouldn't give her young sister a chance to dismiss her and disappear.

The girl shrugged. "Suit yourself." But she continued to stand, as if ready to bolt at any moment.

It was hard to find the right place to start—if there even was a right place. How did one apologize for something they didn't do and until recently had no knowledge of? But Ellie did deserve an apology. Perhaps not as it pertained to Ruby, but from Ruby for the way their father treated her.

"I am sorry for your childhood." That was simple enough.

Ellie's eyes snapped up and stared daggers.

Gone was the quiet, humble girl. "Sorry? What exactly are you sorry for?"

"All of it."

"You think you can just say sorry and everything will be better?" her sister asked. "A simple apology does not wipe away the years of abuse. It does not make up for the fact that you lived a life of privilege while I was made to work and earn every meal."

Ruby did not know how to respond. This was the most Ellie had ever opened up to her; perhaps she only needed someone to listen, a warm body to vent to.

"An apology does not make up for living in hiding my whole life. Did you know he never claimed me as his own?"

"No, I did not."

"He had the nerve to tell the servants that I was a gutter rat, left upon his stoop by a lowly harlot dying of consumption."

The evidence of how horrid her father truly was shouldn't surprise her, but Ruby still pulled back in horror, afraid to say a word or move at all for fear she wouldn't hear the rest.

Ellie laughed, the sound of a bitter person years older than the girl who stood before her. "Can you believe it took him a fortnight to realize I was not a boy? He named me Ellington...a bloody male name."

"If I could make things better—"

"No one can make anything better, don't you see? I am who I am, you are who you are. And that is where it should end."

Ruby hoped she'd heard Ellie's words wrong. "Can we not start anew?"

"One can never start anew when the burdens of the past weigh as heavy as mine," Ellie sighed.

"I do know that my horrible past had naught to do with you or your upbringing, but that does not free me from envying you a loving mother and father…and an education…and a chance."

"You can still have that—we can have that together." Ruby did not know how to convince her sister that a better life was possible, a life free of abuse, if they only worked together and depended on each other. "My childhood was not as perfect as you assume."

"Did you have someone hurling insults at you morning, noon, and night?"

"No."

"Did you know who your mother was?"

"Yes."

"Did you have a warm place to sleep?"

"Yes."

"Then how imperfect could your childhood have been?"

"Our father ruined my mother." Ruby could not believe she was standing up for the mother who'd ignored her, left a child unloved for years. "After Drake left her, pregnant and hopelessly in love with him, she was not the same. We have more in common than you could possibly know."

Ellie folded her arms across her chest defensively. "I do not believe you."

"I do not care if you believe me or not," Ruby said, angrily. "Since my father's death—correction, the man who raised me—I have not been hugged, I have not been given a choice in my life, and I most certainly have not felt the love and adoration of a parent. My mother despised me since my very birth, condemning me to be like the father I didn't even know sired me."

Her sister remained quiet, unmoving. Ruby knew she listened to every word.

"But now we have each other. We never need feel unloved or unwanted again, because I want you—and I hope you want me."

"I do not want your pity," she threw back at Ruby.

"That is not what I am offering you."

"—or your charity."

"That is good because I have nothing to give, physically or monetarily."

Ellie eyed her suspiciously.

"All I can offer you is love, understanding, and a place to lay your head... That is, as long as I can find a place for my own." Ruby was making promises she hoped she could keep, knowing that the consequences for breaking them would be losing Ellie for good. "Do you know what happens next?"

"I hadn't really thought about that," Ellie confessed. "I figured I would spend a few days going through his stuff, selling what I could and packing up anything that could be useful to me later."

Drake's solicitor or next of kin wouldn't throw the girl out overnight—at least Ruby hoped no one could be that cruel to a young girl who'd just lost her father. There was the possibility that Drake had provided for Ellie in his will, if his demise came before she was safely wed. Because of English law, there was little chance of the marquis providing anything more than a bit of funds and her personal belongings to his daughter. Technically, everything within the home and all country estates were included in the title, which would transfer to the closest male heir. Ruby had been through the same when Sir St. Augustin had passed. Her mother—and Ruby—lived off a small stipend left for them, and continued their residence at her family home only because the next baron held another title, which allowed him to live on that property.

"And then what?" Ruby knew she was being unfair, pushing Ellie too far. "Where will you go? If Drake never claimed you as his own I highly doubt he provided for you in his will."

"You think I don't have a place to go?" The words sounded harsh, yet Ruby heard the vulnerability in them.

"I haven't the faintest idea if you have a place to go because you have never opened up to me, never confided in me."

"I will go live with Marce at Craven House," Ellie said. "She was my mother's friend."

"You would live at a brothel rather than with me, your sister?" Ruby asked in disbelief.

"If I have to."

"But you do not have to, that's what I am telling you." Exasperation rang in her voice. "Please, think about living with me. We can take care of each other."

"I do not—"

"Do not answer now." Ruby was scared to hear her answer, fearing that changing her sister's mind once she'd made a decision would be impossible. "Just think about coming to live here, with me. If it makes you feel better, stay at Drake House until you are told to leave, but know I will be here, waiting for you."

Her sister had sought her out for a purpose. She was crying for help and Ruby would not disappoint her or turn her away, even though Ellie couldn't at this time verbalize all she needed from her sister. Ruby knew well the pain of being abandoned, recalling the painful days after Sir St. Augustin's death, when her own mother had banished her without explanation.

Ruby could not let her sister's silent plea go unheard.

HAROLD STOOD OUTSIDE the partly open door, stunned into silence. His heart ached for both women in the room—one who'd lost a father who'd never known her, and one who had lost a father she'd never known. And, by the sound of it, was on the verge of losing a sister in the bargain.

He longed to ease both their pain and take away their suffering.

His morning had been consumed with the enormous task of caring for William, and making sure his father had indeed left town. From there, he'd made straight for the jeweler on Bond Street. Harold's place was here, simply because that was where Ruby was. As long as she resided in London, so would he.

Hearing the heart-wrenching discussion on the other side of the door solidified his decision, reinforcing his belief in his actions.

Ruby may not realize now that she needed him, but she did. Both she and Ellie did.

For once in his life he'd stood up and done what needed doing, even though it directly conflicted with his father's demands. But, how to convince Ruby of his convictions? He was left with few options besides flat-out telling her how he felt and what he wanted for their future— basically demanding she marry him. Ruby had been afforded no options in her life thus far, and it would be unfair of him to force his feelings on her, especially if she didn't feel the same.

The chance of her turning away from him after the previous evening together was not something he could risk.

Harold was unsure if the connection they'd shared the night before was true or born out of emotional and physical exhaustion, at least on her part. Alternatively, he'd never been so sure about his feelings and where his heart and future lay.

He only hoped to convince her of the same.

"Mr. Jakeston," the housekeeper said, startling him. "I was just bringing tea to Miss Ruby and her guest. Should I pour a third cup?"

He turned back to the slightly ajar door to find both women staring at him. How he'd never fully grasped the resemblance before, he did not know. Now, he found it hard to see the pair and not instantly pick out their similarities. It went beyond their exact shade of green eyes. At the moment, they both scrutinized him, a look of confusion and irritation evident on their faces, each with one uplifted brow—Ruby's the left, Ellie's the right. Within another year or so Ellie would grow to be as tall as her sister, of that Harold had no doubt.

"Good morning, ladies," he said, stepping into the room. "I do hope I find you both in good health and spirit today." He wanted to tell Ellie how sorry he was to hear about her father, but did not want to betray Ruby's trust if Drake's passing was to be kept between them.

He received identical nods.

The Haversham housekeeper wheeled the tea cart past him and into the room.

"I hope I am not interrupting something."

From the snippet he'd heard from the hallway, he knew he most certainly was interrupting an important conversation. When neither responded, he continued, "I can be on my way if this is an inopportune time."

Ellie spoke first, flipping her hand in his direction. "It matters naught if you are here, or just the two of us. I only came to return something that rightfully belongs to her."

Ruby scrutinized the sack, tied tight with a length of cord.

Her anxiety and trepidation could be felt by all in the room, Harold was sure.

"Will that be all?" the housekeeper asked as she backed from the room.

Ruby looked at the woman, confusion clouding her face. "Oh, I do apologize. Yes, that will be all." She set the sack aside and moved to the tea service. "Mr. Jakeston, how do you take your tea?" she asked, snapping back into her role as hostess in Lady Haversham's absence.

He crossed the room and sat on the sofa which Ellie had recently vacated. "Just a spot of cream, if you please."

As she poured his cup, she asked Ellie the same question.

"I should be going—" Ellie started to protest.

"You shall do nothing of the sort. We have much still to discuss." Ruby poured the second cup of tea and dropped two sugar cubes in before handing it to Ellie when she walked by, taking the seat next to Harold. "Now, where were we?"

Ruby quickly poured herself a spot of tea, adding neither cream nor sugar before sitting back, the sack lying forgotten at her side.

Harold knew he should have fled when he'd

had the chance, leaving the pair to their discussion. Although, he reflected, his presence created a buffer both women seemed happy for, returning the conversation to more socially acceptable topics.

For a bit they discussed the weather and then moved on to the new trend of bright, bold fabrics as opposed to pastels and neutral tones.

Ellie tired of the idle chit chat long before Ruby or Harold did. "I do have many things to arrange. I really should be going." She tried her hand at escape once again.

"Is there anything I can help you with?" Ruby asked.

"Ummm." She refused to make eye contact with either Ruby or Harold. "Well…"

"Ellington, I am here to help you if you will only tell me what troubles you."

The girl shot a furtive look at Harold.

"Mr. Jakeston is fully aware of the situation," Ruby encouraged.

"You told him?" Anger returned quickly to Ellie's tone. "What if he tells someone about Drake's death?"

"Do you not think it is already the talk of the town?" Ruby questioned. "A marquis going to the hereafter, especially lacking a close heir… I assume the vultures are already circling both his townhouse and estates."

"That is the problem."

"What is the problem?" Harold asked without thinking.

The girl looked between Harold and Ruby, her anger gone but replaced with a sheepish expression. "No one knows of his passing."

Both Harold and Ruby spoke at the same time. "What do you mean?" They looked at each other as their words echoed in the room.

"Well, I stayed with him through the night. When I left to dress and come here I instructed the servant—quite severely—that not one person was allowed to enter the marquis' private chambers until I returned."

"Are you senseless?" Ruby asked, standing so suddenly that her tea sloshed over the rim and on to her dress. "You should have called for a doctor immediately. Who is the family physician?"

Ellie shrugged. "No doctor has ever come round. He did not trust any medicine man. Years ago he would visit an apothecary in town and bring home powder he mixed into his bourbon before bed each night. He said it helped with the pain."

"Pain from what exactly?" Harold asked.

Ellie shrugged. "I do not know and cannot say I care."

Suddenly, the conversation moved in an utterly uncomfortable direction for him. Ruby must have felt his unease, for she changed the subject. "And now he is lying in his bed with the possibility of his valet finding him?"

"Do you think me that foolish?" Ellie countered. "I pulled the blankets over his head and drew the heavy drapes about his bed. Not even his valet would chance the wrath of the Marquis of Drake by awaking him."

Ellie's confession didn't put Harold at ease. From the look on Ruby's face and the way she gripped her cup again, her own apprehension was clear. "What are we going to do next?"

"*We*?" her sister asked.

"Yes, *we*. He was my father as much as yours, and I fully intend to stand beside you through this."

CHAPTER 33

RUBY WAS WELL-VERSED in the burial process, having handled her father's—Sir St. Augustin's—funeral when her mother withdrew into herself. Immediately following her meeting with Ellie, she began making a mental list of all that must be done in preparation: notifying the marquis' solicitor, enlisting a funeral furnisher, flowers, arranging transport to his family burial plot… The list went on and on.

She and Ellie should be sharing a time of mourning, finding solace in one another. Instead, Ellie stared at her wide-eyed, and Ruby realized if she didn't take control of the situation, no one else would.

"Do you know who Drake's solicitor was?" Ruby asked the simplest question she could think of. When her sister continued to stare, mouth closed, Ruby tried another question. "Where is the marquis' family home?"

"Yorkshire...I think."

"Have you not been there?" Harold asked.

"Of course not—and neither has he in the last decade. Maybe his valet will know."

Ruby's head pounded as a severe headache started. Massaging her temple, she looked to Harold for assistance.

"I'll retrieve your *Peers of the Realm* guide from your desk. I believe I saw it there not too long ago."

Surveying her private space, he opened a drawer and returned with the book. Ruby now had little doubt that he'd made himself familiar with her personal desk on at least one previous occasion.

"Thank you." She'd wondered for some time if he'd indeed looked through her personal papers before. Now, her suspicions proved true. She set the realization aside as of little consequence for the moment. "Now Ellie, did Drake ever mention any other family? Or possibly a close friend?"

Her sister huffed. "I tried my best to avoid any contact with him."

"No one ever came to visit?" Harold regained his seat next to Ellie.

"He only left the townhouse for his regular evening, once a week at White's. Other than that, he hasn't attended any social functions, holiday parties, or country entertainments since I was very young."

Even though Ellie had lived with the marquis most of her life, she knew him little better than Ruby, who'd never actually made the man's acquaintance. The thought was depressing. If it weren't for Ellie, would anyone have noticed Drake's passing?

"Well, I am positive that Lord Haversham has a trusted funeral furnisher and may also have insight into who handled our father's business transactions."

Ellie straightened. "Why do we need a funeral furnisher?"

"To properly handle his burial, of course."

"We can't shove him into a pine box and ship him to Yorkshire on the next public coach?"

Laughter erupted.

Ruby suppressed a giggle, knowing the time for laughing was not now, and eyed Harold sternly. If he saw the mirth in her upturned lips, he didn't acknowledge it.

"What?" He stopped long enough to ask before chuckling again. "I am sorry, but Lady Ellie only said exactly what we were all thinking."

"Be that as it may, no person—regardless of their demeanor or, for lack of a better term, defect—should be 'shoved in a pine box' and shipped to places unknown to be buried as if they never were."

"I am not a child, and you have no right to lecture me like you are my mother. Furthermore, he was my father." Ellie stood. "I will return and see about locating his solicitor or some papers from his study that may prove helpful. I will contact you shortly."

"I did not mean to offend you," Ruby soothed, "or insinuate you have a lack of attachment to him. I only sought to make clear that I am here for you and will assist in making arrangements." The girl was temperamental, much like Ruby—and, it seemed, the father they shared. "Please, sit and finish your tea."

"You were correct earlier. It was foolish to

leave the marquis in his current state. I should return."

As Ellie moved toward the door, Ruby took in her appearance for the first time. Her hair, while brushed, hung haphazardly about her shoulder in disarray, dark circles beneath her tired eyes. She'd clearly slept in her clothes.

Ruby let her go, sorry for all her sister had lived through, knowing she hadn't learned all Ellie had suffered as a child. If they'd only known of each other sooner, they could have shared a better life—Ellie free of Drake, and Ruby independent of her own mother. Things could have been very different for them both. She would have made sure things were better for them, done all in her power to make sure the deadened look in her sister's eyes had never come to be.

"She is a hellion," Harold said.

"If she wasn't, I fear she would not have made it into her youth," Ruby snapped protectively.

Harold held up his hands in surrender. "You misunderstand my words."

"I am under an immense amount of stress—"

"Truly, you have no need to apologize. It is I who should apologize for my forward behavior by intruding on you and Lady Ellie. You were exhausted last evening when we returned home, and I hoped to finish our discussion."

"Your attendance did not change a thing." Ruby slouched against her seat, her hand brushing the sack at her side. "I fear Ellie is who she is and neither you nor I can change that. I think we only have Drake to blame."

Harold eyed her hand as she caressed the small bag. "Are you going to see what is inside?"

Would he think her a horrible person if she said no? Opening the bag was the last thing she wanted to do at this moment, but blatantly pushing it aside would draw undue attention to her avoidance. Reluctantly, she took hold of the bag. It weighed less than a book, yet not as light as a pair of gloves. She'd sensed from the moment her sister tossed the bag to her that it held more than her forgotten finery. She couldn't imagine it held much, but feared what its contents might be.

The drawstring, tied in a neat bow, slipped from her grasp when her fingers shook.

Harold took the bag from her hands and opened it before she could protest. "Allow me," he said. He dumped the items into his lap and set the sack aside. "A stack of letters, a letter opener, and a note. See, nothing overly shocking or life changing."

Ruby watched him examine each item, unaware how life changing they actually were. The bundle of letters, most still sealed, brought a tear to her eyes. Her mother's heart poured upon deteriorating paper, with ink worth more than blood. She fought not to reach out for them, hold them tight... The writings of the woman who'd birthed her, but about whom she knew so little. One should not learn about a parent through decades-old letters. Would she understand Pearl St. Augustin after reading them? Would her heart soften toward the scorned woman?

"Why in heaven would she give you a letter opener?" Harold asked.

Ruby dared not hope it was the same letter opener her mother spent all her shillings to have commissioned for her lover.

He held the small dagger up, tip pointed in

his palm. "Still sharp, if not a bit worn."

The light that shone in from the window reflected off the inlaid rubies. It was exactly as her mother had described it in her journal— exquisitely handcrafted. Ruby knew if she looked close she'd see the words from *A Midsummer Night's Dream* inscribed on the handle.

Next, Harold lifted the folded note for her to see. "Do you wish for me to read the message?"

She only nodded, afraid the emotions roiling inside her would spill out if she opened her mouth to speak.

Harold unfolded the sheet of paper and cleared his voice, preparing to read.

But nothing came out as he scanned the page and a barrage of emotions crossed his face: astonishment, confusion, fury, grief...and finally pity—for Ruby, she was sure.

Ruby had not set out looking for or wanting pity of any kind. Regardless of her mother and the circumstances surrounding her birth, she'd had a childhood filled with love and all the frilly trinkets any girl could want. It was only when she was older that she'd noticed all was not as it should be with her own mother.

Refolding the letter, Harold looked up at her. "We can save this for another day. Perhaps it is best we start making plans for the marquis' service."

"Oh no, you do not!" If she'd been standing she would have stomped her foot in childish protest. "Either read it or hand it over. I fear if I wait another moment to find out what it says I will likely bust."

Harold looked positively uncomfortable and was probably regretting his choice to eavesdrop on Ruby and Ellie's conversation. "I only think that after the previous twenty-four hours, this letter—" he spread the note before him. "—can wait for another day. But if you insist, I will share it with you."

Ruby reached across him to snatch the paper.

He quickly moved his hand, keeping it just out of her reach. "Ah-ah, allow me."

She sat back, preparing herself.

Harold cleared his voice before he began to read:

"Ruby,

"We have been hurt, unequivocally damaged, by the unfortunate circumstances of our birth. While our father was a cruel man, we are not him and he does not dictate who we choose to be in the future. Mere words cannot express my regret at having taken away your only chance to meet our father. I believe the items enclosed with this note belong rightfully to you."

Ruby wanted to cry. Her sister's note said everything Ruby had never realized she needed to hear from her sister.

Harold continued, *"Signed with fondness, your much prettier sister."*

"Oh, you!" Ruby exclaimed. "She wrote no such thing." She made to snatch the note once again, but landed across his lap when he held the letter over his head and out of her reach.

When she looked up, her face was mere inches from his, her body entirely bent over his lap. Too late, she realized her mistake.

He grabbed her about the waist and sat her down next to him, their legs touching. The heat from his skin could be felt through her skirt.

Their brief moment in the marquis' study and then again in the playhouse swarmed her mind—not to mention the few private moments they'd spent in each other's arms the evening before. She sighed, pushing thoughts of the note aside, replacing it with the feeling of him close. His hand settled on her thigh, kneading through the fabric of her dress until she flamed so hot she wanted nothing more than to rip the material from her own body.

"Harold…" she sighed.

Before she could take another breath, his warm lips were upon hers, demanding yet patient. The light of the room faded, the stress of the moment disappeared with each brush of his mouth against hers, and the future brightened as she sank into his arms. She couldn't remember when, but they'd come to hold her tightly, pressing possessively and securely into her lower back.

His lips moved from hers to trail down her neck, lightly nipping as they went. This was more than a kiss they shared, she realized suddenly. There was a decision he was waiting for—a decision she hadn't even known was hers to make. Whatever it was, whatever their future might be, she knew in that moment that, if it was in her power, she would give Harold all he asked.

CHAPTER 34

RUBY ST. AUGUSTIN STOOD between her sister and Harold, the pair effectively blocking the wind that threatened to rip the hat from her head. Behind her, Lord and Lady Haversham huddled closely against the frigid late morning air, the lord's arms cradling his pregnant wife.

At both sides stood the marquis' household and livery staff, their number nowhere near the amount of hands Ruby suspected it took to care for her father's massive London townhouse. Across from the group, four women stood huddled together close to the house to block the unrelenting wind. Ruby could pick out Marce's blonde curls from beneath her hood. The other women must reside with her at Craven House.

They gathered in the gardens behind the Drake townhouse to say a quick farewell to the father Ruby had never known.

The mood was somber, as one would expect

of such an occasion. The sober atmosphere had little to do with the tragedy of Drake's death, however, and all to do with the uncertainty that every person in attendance faced. The servants worried their employment and livelihood would be stripped when a new relative claimed the title and all endowed to it.

Ruby feared her moments with her sister were coming to an end. Would Ellie disappear into the night; find solace at Craven House with the woman who knew her better than Ruby? The life Ellie would fall into frightened her. She deserved so much more than living in a brothel, surrounded by women of dubious circumstances. While the girl had seen more, experienced more than Ruby had in her short life, she knew Ellie was easily influenced—and that terrified her even further.

Her sister hadn't shed a single tear since Ruby left her the day of their father's passing. It worried her that Ellie was becoming more jaded and hardened to life, and in turn would push the people away who cared for her most. While Ruby was unfamiliar with Craven House and its occupants, she couldn't imagine her sister's life improving if she spent more time on the outskirts of society.

The familiarity of the occasion was not lost on Ruby. While the season was different, her state of mind more mature, and the people surrounding her were more than she could have hoped for, the sadness was the same. This time, however, that sadness was not for her or her own loss, but for Ellie. Her life was to change to a degree that neither of them could predict.

Ruby also mourned for a man who'd never given his daughters a chance to truly know him—to give him the love that every person deserved. He'd led a life of self-destruction, which eventually ended with only a few caring for his departed soul—if anyone present actually cared more than to be witness to his body being lowered into the ground.

She hadn't known Drake, but the man who had raised Ruby had been everything Drake hadn't been: nurturing, supportive, compassionate. The marquis had never had a part in her life, and for that she could be thankful.

Harold released his comforting hold on her elbow and stepped before the small gathering, turning to face everyone. In turn, Ruby moved closer to her sister and wrapped her arm loosely around her waist for support.

"I was asked by the Marquis of Drake's—" Harold cleared his throat before continuing. "—ward, Lady Ellington, to lead this gathering in a short prayer for the deceased."

Ruby marveled at Harold's ease when addressing the crowd. They'd agreed to keep Ellie's true relationship to Drake as vague as possible until they'd ascertained more information about the future. The man had never seen fit to claim his own daughter, even though she'd lived with him nearly since her birth. As far as Ruby's connection to Drake, she was here only as a friend and supporter of Lady Ellington's, and nothing more.

As she stepped closer to Ellie to comfort her, Vi took a step forward and settled her hand on Ruby's shoulder. Ruby had been so worried about Ellie and her well-being that she'd had little time to think about herself. There would be another day for her to delve into her own feelings and sort through them.

Today—this goodbye—was solely for Ellington.

A chance for her to gain closure, to say goodbye—and possibly good riddance—to the man she'd longed to call father, yet was denied and rebuffed time and time again.

Harold's prayer and words of remembrance washed over Ruby. The rise and fall of his voice enchanted her. Despite his ease in the role, she knew the life of a country vicar was not for him—it would be a waste of his life here on earth. He was destined for greater things. His way with people came so naturally, both here and in larger social settings. Given half the chance, he would fascinate the *ton*—make them truly wonder if he did not hold a title and the education of a lord of the realm.

"Let us remember Andrew Penton, the Marquis of Drake, as a man of stature. A man of strong opinion always willing to play a hand of cards with friends," Harold said in closing.

She respected his ability to speak of her father, selecting the right words to honor Drake, without claiming he was a man he wasn't.

"Would anyone like to say a word before we adjourn?" He scanned the small gathering.

Ruby glanced down at Ellie next to her, hoping to encourage her to say a few words, but her eyes were fastened on the ground. Ruby knew pushing her forward would only mean pushing her away.

Looking back at Harold to signal him to move on, she noticed that he stared over her shoulder and into the far reaches of the garden. She turned to see a cloaked woman, her quiet sobs barely reaching Ruby.

Her cloak was fashioned in the latest style, made from heavy, expensive wool. Her head hung slightly as she cried into a small handkerchief, unaware she was being watched by not only Ruby, but Ellie as well.

The wind picked up, flinging the woman's hood off her head to reveal a mane of black hair, startlingly familiar to Ruby.

RUBY STALKED INTO the study—the same room Ellie had brought her and Harold the night Ellie had enacted her blackmail plan.

Her hands shook, she was so enraged. Despite the cold outside, her blood boiled and her skin flushed. If she weren't the proper lady she knew herself to be, she'd likely have uttered every cross word she knew.

"Shut the door," she shouted without turning. She was not one to cause a scene—in fact, she'd seen firsthand the repercussions of causing a scene last season. And she had no intention of causing the stir that Vi and Lord Haversham had. "Sit."

The days of living in the dark, of allowing others to treat her unjustly for fear of making someone unhappy with her were over. If there was one thing she was beginning to learn, it was that life was fleeting and one should not let what they wanted pass them by.

Ruby became uneasy, for Pearl St. Augustin had never been so quiet, so passive. When she turned, her mother sat primly upon the settee while Harold and Ellie stood by the closed door.

"I instructed my mother to follow me, not the pair of you." Some things a person needed to face alone—and it was past time she confronted her mother. Any witness, no matter their association, was unwelcome.

Ruby felt her emotions threatening to overwhelm her already. The last thing she wanted was Harold, or Ellie, to witness her breakdown. She needed to be strong and in control, especially for Ellie. Their level of trust was growing every day; how could her sister depend on Ruby if she saw her falling apart?

When both stayed rooted, neither reaching for the door, she said, "Suit yourselves, but do not say a word."

Harold and Ellie nodded in agreement, and she knew neither would betray the truths spoken within these walls.

"I too would prefer they leave," her mother uttered. "I am uncomfortable with persons not of my family hearing this matter. It is of a private nature."

"Your preferences mean naught to me," Ruby countered harshly. Guilt reared inside her at the severity of her words, yet her mother deserved them—and many more. "Lady Ellington is my family, therefore whatever is said here most certainly involves her. And Harold— Mr. Jakeston—is a trusted friend." The pair smiled at Ruby encouragingly.

She took a calming breath before continuing. "I am at a loss for where to begin, Mother. Your lies and infidelity know no bounds."

Her mother smirked. "It appears the apple does not fall far from the tree. When did you arrive in town?"

Ruby knew that smirk well. "Based on the look on your face, I expect you already know the answer to that." Their conversation would go nowhere if they both skirted the issue at hand. "Enough. Why are you here?"

"My dear, I am in London every season. The real question is, why you are here? The season most assuredly does not suit one of your character."

"*My* character?" Ruby fought to remain focused and not let her mother's wordplay anger her overly. "Why are you *here*, Mother? In the marquis' garden...attending a private moment in his honor?" Her mother and true father were anything but honorable, and she couldn't bring herself to glance at Ellie. After years of abuse—mistreatment Ruby hadn't the stomach to fully explore yet—her sister would also agree their father lacked honor. And integrity. And possibly any sense at all.

For a second, Ruby saw the sorrow in her mother's eyes, but it was replaced quickly with a hard stare. "I am sure you have figured out why I am here—and it is the same reason you are."

"I need to hear you say it—I need to understand how you could betray my father. I heard stories growing up about the great love between Sir St. Augustin and his beloved Pearl—how you eloped to Gretna Green and married without anyone the wiser. How servants caught you in delicate situations over the years, locked in a passionate embrace or simply gazing into one another's eyes. How did that sour?"

When her mother remained silent, Ruby asked the one question that eclipsed all the others. "Why?"

Pearl's smug look disappeared with her reply. "For you, of course."

"For me?" Ruby became more confused with each word her mother uttered, every falsehood and half-truth. "Nothing you have ever done since my birth has been for me."

A sad smile settled on her face. "No, but everything I did before that was for you—to bring you into this world at all."

Ruby wished they were alone, without witnesses to see the tears that threaded their way down her face, to her neck and into the collar of her mourning dress. The implications of her mother's words stabbed deep.

"If I hadn't sought out the marquis, I would have never known the joys of motherhood—and Angus never the fulfillment of fatherhood. A thing he deserved more than any man."

"But..." The right question evaded her. "You loved him. How could you betray him so?"

"Betray him?" her mother asked. "You think I betrayed him by doing exactly as he encouraged me to do? Our love was strong, so strong in fact that I longed to give him everything. And everything he ever wanted was you."

"Me?" She knew she sounded senseless, incapable of a complete thought.

"Oh, yes." Her mother glanced at Harold and Ellie by the door. Both stood motionless and quiet, as if they too waited for the words they knew were coming. "He wanted a child, an heir. Unfortunately, he got an heiress—which he loved just as much as if she'd been born a male... And in the process, I fell in love with another man. Even with all this, I loved Angus greatly. Love him still. But a woman's heart is fickle." Her words were meant for Harold, Ruby had no doubt.

Ruby glanced at Harold, but his eyes were downcast, as if not seeking to intrude on their private conversation while still lending Ruby his support. Her heart swelled. Could she betray a man she loved to give him something he truly wanted, even knowing it could jeopardize all they had together?

The answer was simple: yes.

Would she have gone about giving him all in the same manner her mother had? No.

But she did understand it.

And she grieved for her mother and the loss of her love.

"If any man was deserving of all a woman's love, your father was—Sir St. Augustin was a man above all men. I know I broke his heart, but I also returned it in the form of a child. He loved you with all his heart and treated you as his own, even though his blood did not run through your veins."

"Why did you not try to mend your relationship after my birth?" Ruby asked. "If he loved you before, he could love you again."

Bitter laughter filled the room, and Ruby flinched at its cruel sound. "There were many hurtful words spoken that made the possibility of forgiveness impossible."

"What words?" She searched for anything she could say to Harold to make him abandon her, but thought of naught. With all she'd already said, he had never left her side.

"Before your birth I agreed to leave you with him, as long as he would allow me to live with the marquis. We would both be happy. He would have his child, and I would be with a man who inspired so much passion I was weak at the knees only thinking of him."

But things had gone very wrong. Her mother's journal detailed every heartache, every tear, every day of longing.

"And since your father loved me so, he agreed without a moment's hesitation. Sadly, Drake would not have me—claimed he never loved me and that his heart was consumed with another."

As Ruby stared hard at the woman, waiting for more, needing to hear every word, Harold stepped up and produced a pocket square. It was only then that she noticed the tears streaming from her mother's eyes, mirroring her own. Never in her life had she felt this close and connected to the woman.

"Did you ever think to be honest with me?" Ruby asked. "After my father's death, or once I grew to majority? It is a mother's duty to guide her child, inform her of the perils of life." She'd had no one to fill that role. No one with whom to talk of love and life and the future, except Vi.

Pearl's head dropped as she continued to dab at her face. "I had hoped the need would never come. You were never meant to see London. I'd hoped you would never give your heart to a man. And I never wanted you to experience the loss of a child or a lover. But I find—" she glanced to Harold, "—I am too late."

Were her feelings so clear to others—even a mother who'd spent more time away from her child than with? Ruby herself barely recognized her own emotional state.

"Do not look so puzzled, my dear," her mother chided. "I may have more mistakes in my past than anything, but I am not—and never have been—lacking in sense. You love this man...and I must say, your father would be proud. Both Drake and St. Augustin could not have chosen a more suitable match."

"Mrs. St.—"

Pearl turned to Harold. "Do not try to deny your love for my daughter."

"I would never dream of doing that," Harold said.

"I expect you to never forsake your love for her," her mother continued.

"I am right here—" Ruby started.

"There is not a thing further from my mind," he said seriously.

"And I expect you to show her to the world—not keep her hidden—as I did," her mother said sternly.

"I am in no need of your interference, Mother."

"Nothing would please me more than to parade this woman—" he gestured to Ruby, "—in front of all of London society and claim her as my own."

"Then things are settled. Lady Darlingiver will be quite merry to hear we have yet another wedding to arrange." The first genuine smile Ruby had ever seen spread across her mother's face. "The pair of you will have naught to fret about. We will handle everything. I think the week after next will be perfect. The blossoms are still abloom."

"Wait a moment," Ruby said in disbelief. "I do not need you, Mother, to handle my affairs for me, especially affairs of the heart. And you," she addressed Harold. "I am not a piece of chattel to be bartered over and claimed."

"Well, do you love this man?" Pearl asked.

"I do, but that is naught of your concern," Ruby countered. "Harold and I are perfectly capable—"

"Do you agree to marry him?" her mother

asked.

"I have not been asked properly and will decided that when I am."

"Oh," Ellie muttered from her place by the door.

She'd forgotten her sister's presence and could only imagine the girl's thoughts on Ruby's family drama—a family she was now a part of.

"Ruby?" her sister continued. "I think—"

She looked up from her mother to scold Ellie for getting involved. "Do you seek to give your opinion as well?" Why everyone thought they had a say in her life, she did not understand.

"Open your eyes and see what is right before you, Ruby." Ellie gestured to Ruby's side.

Turning, Ruby found Harold kneeling in front of her, his hand outstretched with a small box perched in his palm. "Miss Ruby St. Augustin—"

"No!" she exclaimed.

"No?" Everyone in the room responded.

"Can you not hear what I have to say before answering in the negative?" Harold asked. "This may well be the only time I am able to kneel before a woman whom I greatly admire and love more than I ever thought possible."

CHAPTER 35

THE TIMING WAS horribly wrong. His knickers a bit tight for his kneeling position. The room overcrowded by two.

But…the woman before him was exactly right, which solved all the wrongs of the moment. She perched on the chaise lounge in her dress of the darkest navy, mourning a father she'd never known. Her posture and poise were that of a woman born into the elite circles of society, and unbeknownst to Ruby, she had been—although her lineage mattered naught to him. He cared only that she was kind, loving, compassionate, and intelligent. There was no doubt that she was all those things—along with opinionated, cunning, strong-willed, and stubborn.

She stared at him for a long silent moment before someone in the room cleared their voice.

It was then Harold realized everyone was

waiting for him to speak. Suddenly, every thought fled his mind. While he hadn't planned to ask for her hand this day, he had started to prepare a speech listing all her amazing qualities and outlining all his attributes—should she need extra convincing—immediately after finding the perfect ring a few days prior.

"Miss Ruby," he started again.

"I believe you can call her plain Ruby," Ellie whispered behind him.

"Oh, certainly. I do believe you are correct, Lady Ellie." He cleared his throat, smiled at Ruby's sister over his shoulder, and attempted to start anew. "Ruby, I do apologize for the untimely moment of this, but..." He stopped flat when he saw tears welling in her eyes.

He'd botched it—possibly his only opportunity.

"I didn't mean to upset you, Ruby. Please, do not cry. We can speak of this another time."

He pulled back his outstretched hand, still clutching the tiny velvet box where the most delicate ruby ring sat nestled inside.

But Ruby reached out for him, stopping Harold before he rose to his feet.

She smiled, the most radiant, heartwarming smile he'd ever seen—and would ever behold again in his lifetime, he was certain. "They are not tears of sadness, though of course this is a sad day. I am crying because I am overwhelmed—"

"I beg of you, we can speak of this at a more appropriate time," Harold cut her off. Now was not the time for her to be making life-changing decisions, and he'd pushed this on her, overwhelming her to the point of tears. "Or never again, if that is your want."

"Harold," Ruby whispered. "Look at me."

He raised his lowered gaze to find her still smiling, the tears having receded.

"I am overwhelmed with joy, fairly brought to my own knees at the immense barrage of emotions I am feeling at the moment. I should not be experiencing such extreme feelings of love and joy on a day for mourning," she continued. "But I am...and it feels abundantly right and good."

"Are you sure?" he couldn't help but ask.

"Do you think I am not aware and in control of my own feelings?"

"I would never seek to offend you in such a manner."

A light tap drew Harold's attention away from the only woman he would happily spend every day of the rest of his earthly existence looking upon. Reluctantly, he turned to Ellie behind him. "Lady Ellington, I believe I am a bit busy at the moment. What can I help you with?"

The girl, always an irritation, leaned closer before speaking. "I think you are neglecting to ask a fairly important question, which by the by, I would turn down due to your common birth."

Ellington's eyes sparkled mischievously.

He knew it would take him time to adjust to the girl's brash manners, but if he ever actually got around to asking Ruby to marry him, she would undoubtedly occupy her sister's frequent attention wherever they decided to live.

"Yes, thank you again, Lady Ellington, ever so much for your redirection of the conversation." Putting the other occupants of the room from his mind, he again addressed Ruby. "I do understand that my lineage is far below the standard of man who should be allowed to ask for your hand in marriage, but I do believe I make you happy. I will work hard from sun up to sun down to provide a stable, prosperous home for you. And if the good Lord is willing and we are blessed with children, I will do all in my power to afford them the best upbringing possible, safe in the bosom of two loving, devoted parents." He paused to take a deep breath before he disgraced himself by fainting where he knelt.

"Still lacking a question," Ellington prodded.

"I am getting there." It would help if Ruby's sister and estranged mother were not breathing down his neck. Thankfully, the latter had kept silent—which was more than he could say for Ellington. He moved slightly to relieve the pressure from his knee digging into the hardwood flooring of the study. Ruby looked on encouragingly. "Ruby St. Augustin, will you do me the great honor of becoming Mrs. Harold Jakeston—my wife."

She stayed silent. For the briefest of moments, the stark possibility that she would turn down his proposal weighed heavy upon him. He loathed the idea of leaving this room without Ruby.

He didn't know when he'd started to envision his future with her, but he now knew he would have none without her.

Harold trembled as he opened the small box, every nerve in his body calling for her consent and approval. He kept his eyes on hers, not wanting to look away for fear he would miss her answer.

He'd perish if she did not reply soon, but he had no other option but to give her time. He'd give her all the time she needed if that meant she would eventually say the words he longed to hear.

RUBY STARED AT the ring Harold held out before her, a simple gold band with an exquisite ruby perched atop it. Thin gold-leaf anchors held the precious stone fast to the band.

The ring perfectly embodied Harold and the life they would share.

Simplicity at its finest.

And she knew that was the life she craved.

A life unburdened by society's expectation. An existence where love meant more than status or coin. An eternity surrounded by what mattered most to her—her family and close friends.

"Of course, I will be honored to become your wife." Truer words had never passed her lips.

She watched as Harold—his hands shaking—removed the ring from its velvet box.

Not another person existed in the room as she held her hand out. The ring glided easily onto her finger, fitting so perfectly that she thought he must have taken her measure while she slept.

"It fits perfectly." He smiled up at her. "Just as we do."

Ruby slid off the chaise and into his arms before her feelings overwhelmed her further. Sinking her head into his shoulder, she wept. She let all the pent-up sorrow and grief of the last few weeks go, giving it all up—and allowed the bliss of the moment to overtake her.

Her tears of sadness turned into tears of happiness, knowing she would always be safe and cherished in Harold's arms. He was a man of worth who would never forget her longings and desires, a man who would give up himself for her.

While her relationship with her mother and sister was far from stable, Ruby knew that with Harold at her side they would mend the bridge to her mother and guide Ellington down the right path to embrace her future.

"I love you with my whole heart," she breathed into his ear as her sobs receded.

"Ruby, I have adored you far longer than you can imagine," he whispered in return. "I have loved you since the first time I saw you gallivanting about the Haversham estate dressed in muddy frocks with braids wrapped tight around your head."

Softly, a door clicked closed behind them.

"I feared they would never depart," Harold said, pulling back to take her lips in a kiss so heartfelt Ruby thought she may well melt before they parted.

EPILOGUE

RUBY HAD SPENT her morning helping Harold ready a guest room at the Haversham townhouse. While she'd hoped it would be Ellington coming to live with her, she was just as happy to welcome William. And to see the lightness in Harold, as if a great weight had been lifted from his shoulders, delighted her most.

With William comfortably ensconced in the blue suite, down the hall from Harold's own room, she ran and collected books for his entertainment while bedridden. The major damage was to his leg and hip, though Lord Haversham's family physician predicted an almost full recovery with time and rest. Despite his reassurances, Ruby did not see how William would ever be able to walk with ease again. His career on the docks—and possibly as a blacksmith—was gone.

She returned to the room to find Harold

perched in the chair next to his brother's sick bed, trying to force the man to drink.

"You know what the doctor said, William," Harold prodded. "If you do not drink water your bones will never heal."

"That doctor was a quack!" William sputtered water on the blanket covering him. "This stuff tastes dreadful. Bring me a glass of scotch. That will have me healed in no time."

Ruby wanted to laugh. The scene was so much like their childhood. The Jakeston brothers were much like Lord Haversham and his brothers, always competing, arguing, and trying to best one another.

"Now you two," Ruby said as she entered the room. "Stop that. What William needs is rest, which he cannot get with you in here fretting about."

She set the books within reach on the table next to William's bed. "I have gathered as many books from the library as I could find that have to do with shipping, sea travel, and ports, so you do not miss your voyage over much."

"Ah, thank you greatly, Miss Ruby." William smiled. His eyes were still full of pain, but his smile was genuine. "I do not know what I'm to do with myself now."

Ruby didn't, either. The man had his future livelihood stripped from him in a matter of seconds, left with bleak prospects to support himself and any family he hoped to have.

"I am sure you will find your new path in life."

"Actually," Harold chimed in. "I have just the thing, if William is agreeable to the idea."

"I find myself in no place to disregard any option for my future."

"Well, I have been thinking these past few days—" Harold started.

"Yes?" Ruby asked.

"Go on," William prodded at the same time.

"How do you enjoy the country life?"

"I have never been opposed to it, I suppose," William said. "I enjoy some time in the fresh air every now and again."

"You have been rather preoccupied the last few days... I am not certain if you are aware, but I've asked Ruby to marry me and she's answered in the affirmative."

William whooped and then grasped his hip, grimacing in pain. "Congratulations are in order, then."

Harold looked to her and she knew her face beamed with happiness.

"Thank you," she mumbled.

"As I was saying," Harold continued. "With our impending marriage—and Ruby's ties here in London—not to mention our business venture, I find I am unable to return to the vicarage anytime soon."

Ruby wondered what he was getting at. She'd suspected they would marry and retire to the country. Women lived where their husbands deemed and she loved Harold, which meant following him to the ends of the earth if that was his plan. While she would dread leaving Ellington in London alone, she'd still planned to try and convince the girl to come with them. If that failed, Vi would be about town to keep an eye on her.

"Just say what you have to say," his brother urged.

"I only thought that you might be interested in taking over the vicarage." Harold looked straight at Ruby when he spoke next. "I fear my life is not meant to be spent as a vicar. Ruby and I will have many responsibilities here in London, with taking care of her sister, Ellington—she is a hellion if I have ever seen one—and of course, the *Lucky Hand* must set sail soon if you and I are to make a profit on the venture."

William's eyebrows drew up in surprise. "You would do that for me?"

"You are the one doing much for me, brother," Harold said. "I would be honored to stay in town and continue what we started...and bringing funds back to you at the vicarage would be a boon our father would not relish."

"As long as you come often and bring your lovely woman with you." William nodded to Ruby.

She could swear she saw the man wipe tears from his cheek.

"Now, you two get going so this old man can rest."

"I would love nothing more than to depart this sick room, brother," Harold joked. "Shall we be on our way?"

Harold held out his arm and Ruby slipped hers into the crook.

For the first time in many years, she felt as if she were exactly where she should be. She was loved, cherished, and knew—beyond a doubt—that Harold would make her happy for as long as they both took breath.

"Miss Ruby, how would you fancy a jaunt to France? I have heard you quite enjoy adventure upon the open seas."

Ruby laughed. There was no doubt that their future would be full of adventures.

AUTHOR'S NOTES

Thank you for reading *Forgotten No More*
(A Lady Forsaken, Book Two).

If you enjoyed *Forgotten No More*,
be sure to write a brief review at any retailer.
I'd love to hear from you!

You can contact me at:
Christina@christinamcknight.com

Or write me at:
P.O. Box 1017
Patterson, CA 95363

www.ChristinaMcKnight.com
Check out my website for giveaways, book
reviews, and information on my upcoming
projects, or connect with me through social
media at:

Twitter: @CMcKnightWriter
Facebook:
www.facebook.com/christinamcknightwriter
Goodreads:
www.goodreads.com/ChristinaMcKnight

Sign up for my newsletter here:
http://hyperurl.co/CMNL

**For more information about
A Lady Forsaken Series, turn the page!**

A LADY FORSAKEN SERIES

This is historical Regency romance at its best. Get lost back in time with the lords and ladies of the "A Lady Forsaken" series and fall in love with the historical romance genre.

Shunned No More
Forgotten No More
Scorned Ever More
Christmas Ever More
Hidden No More

Available in print, e-book, and audiobook

SCORNED EVER MORE
Book 3
Now available

A man willing to sacrifice all...

Andrew Penton, The Marquis of Drake, is a man used to getting all he desires, for nothing in return. But when a mysterious woman catches his eye, he's helpless to do anything but offer her all he is.

A woman determined to take everything...

Lady Lorelei de La Valette, daughter of the French Comte of Epernon, is new to London society and not the lady she appears to be. Her life has been controlled since birth, yet she'll have to decide if her destiny lies with her country or her heart.

A love lost forever...

Check out Andrew and Lorelei's story
in this excerpt from *Shunned Ever More!*

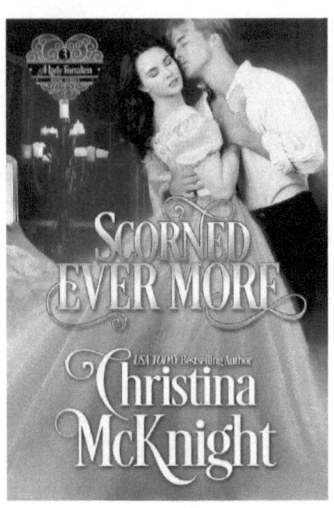

London, England
February 1799

THE MARQUIS OF Drake, Andrew Penton, leaned casually against the wall bordering the gardens. Anyone who stumbled upon him might think his pose nonchalant and tranquil. Yet inside, his discontent festered just below the surface.

There were numerous places he'd rather be, many obligations to which his time would be better devoted. Instead, he flitted around yet another *ton* gathering, acting the self-indulged lord with nothing better to do than discuss the weather with simpering young debutantes, and argue the merits of the war to be waged against their French counterparts.

He'd fled the overcrowded ballroom only moments before when his latest dance partner, pushed upon him by their hostess, had stepped on his booted foot one too many times. That was not the only injustice he'd been dealt during his brief time this evening. Another chit had held him so securely during their promenade about the dance floor that her hands had left sweaty stains on his linen shirt.

He wondered if young women today were properly trained in the art of the quadrille, or if they were sent into the wilds of society wholly unprepared.

And all the time, Andrew's dear friend Benjamin chuckled at his unease.

It had been far simpler when he hadn't tried to be a respectable lord; when he hadn't given a feathering about what others thought of him or his antics about town. The days when he'd only cared about spending his coin and who would warm his bed that night seemed so long ago.

Now, he hid from potential bedmates and begrudgingly paid the new income tax levied against him to help offset the cost of financing British troops fighting in the Napoleonic War. Two shillings per pound was a trifling amount compared to what he'd spent to set up his last mistress in her own London townhouse.

It was past time he returned to the ballroom. The evening would end shortly, and he could return home or to his club for a drink.

Andrew pushed away from the wall, his position hidden from view of the main drive, and started back to the side entrance he'd exited a few moments before. It had been fortuitous that the lord who owned this home had a door leading from his study and onto the drive.

"...we have gone over this several times."

The words floated on the light breeze, meeting Andrew as he stepped inside the study door and the warmth of the house. Pausing, he strained to hear the rest of the conversation, if only to delay his return to the ballroom.

Andrew pushed the doors closed, leaving it open only a crack as footsteps approached on the outside walk. It would not do to be caught eavesdropping.

A trio stopped outside the door, their features obscured by the darkness, though Andrew saw enough to know the group consisted of two females and a well-dressed gentleman.

"See that you follow the instructions given to you." The man took the arm of one of the women and walked on, leaving their third companion behind.

Without the pair blocking his view, Andrew took in the sight of the woman before him. She was gowned in the darkest of blue to match the color of the night sky, her hair piled atop her head, leaving her neck exposed...almost vulnerable.

As he watched, she brought her hands to cover her face, and her shoulders shook ever so slightly as if she sobbed; yet no sound broke the silence of the night.

The urge to step back outside, comfort her when she was clearly upset, was strong—but that was a familiarity he was not comfortable with. If someone happened upon him alone with a young female in the shadows of the front drive, there would be many questions. Questions he was not suited to answer.

Instead, he kept her in view.

The least Andrew could do was ensure that she caught up with her party and entered the ball safely.

After a few moments, her hands fell away from her face and rested at her sides. She squared her shoulders and called, "Do wait for me, *Pere.*" And with quick feet, she hurried to catch up with the pair who'd left her behind.

As speedily as she'd moved toward the front entrance, Andrew closed the study door and made his way back to the ballroom and his place beside Benji on the fringes of the dance floor.

"Where did you run off to?" his friend asked.

"I was hoping our great host had something a bit stronger than sherry stashed in his study."

"Ah, very clever of you." Benji patted him on the back in sport. "And tell me you found an exquisite bourbon or scotch."

Andrew wouldn't share what he'd actually come across or his true reason for escaping the merriment around him. "Alas, it seems our hostess has hidden the good stuff." As he spoke, he kept his gaze trained on the entrance to the ballroom, waiting to see the woman dressed as night descend into the crowd.

"Do not look so despondent," Benji said. "Your side of the wager is nearly fulfilled and you can depart."

"I do not look despondent." Though, if he had to dance with one more simple-minded girl, Andrew was prepared to put himself out of his misery. "Besides, I have already satisfied our wager."

"The devil you have!"

Andrew looked about as members of the *ton* turned their looks upon them. "Do keep your obscenities down."

"Our wager stipulated the first to six dance partners without being approached by their sires after wins ten pounds. You most certainly have not met the number to conclude our wager and take the purse."

Andrew thought back. "There was the cross-eyed chit, the homely creature solidly on the shelf..." He held up his hand, counting the fingers as he went. "...the young girl with the horridly orange dress, oh, and do not forget the sisters who each demanded their turn."

"Ah-ha!" Benji said in triumph. "Only five. It so happens I myself am at five, as well."

It was then that *she* entered the room—and all thoughts of wagers, coin, and his dear friend fled his mind.

"Enough," Andrew commanded his partner to silence. If only every person in the room would do the same so he could behold her in peace.

The glow from the candles lining the walls and hanging from the ceiling showed her beauty for what it truly was: stunning. Exquisitely refined. And utterly dissimilar to any and all women he'd met recently, far surpassing them not only in beauty but poise.

She appeared nothing like he'd expected from her silent sobs and hunched shoulders cloaked in the darkness.

Now she stood tall—exuding a firm confidence that he at once admired and envied. The gems hanging from her neck and ears further enhanced the glow her presence cast on the room. Never would he think her capable of such a vulnerable persona as what he'd seen only moments before from his hidden vantage point in the study doorway.

A quick glance around the room told him that he wasn't the only one enthralled by her sudden appearance, as a few others took in the sight of her.

She spoke to the pair beside her, all serious as they descended the few steps and blended into the crowd. The older couple were likely her guardians, judging from their similar features and complexion—though their outward display of self-assurance aligned, as well.

Would she be as captivating when she spoke as she was by sight alone? He could not help but wonder. On so many occasions, a pretty turn of the lips or a coy glance caught his attention only to be followed by a disappointing one-sided conversation, or worse yet, blank stares without a word uttered.

Andrew kept his eyes firmly on her, urging her to look his way—or better yet, walk in his direction.

His previous need to protect her fled.

The woman radiated poise and composure as she took in the room, as if not a thing in the world could dampen her night, her eyes traveling across the crowd, never lingering too long on any one person or group.

It was then that Andrew realized he wanted her. In his arms—and in his life.

And he would stop at nothing to have her.

LADY LORELEI DE La Valette took in the scene around her. Elegantly gowned women danced with smartly dressed gentlemen, young debutantes hid amongst the palms on the fringes of the dance floor, and servants hurried to and fro with trays overflowing with food and drinks.

She loathed their superior attitudes, yet simultaneously envied them their excessive lifestyle.

After many years of travel, it seemed to her that she should feel no sense of unease when entering a room wherein she knew not a soul, but even to this day, she longed for a familiar face.

"You know how important this night is," her father, the Comte of Epernon, hissed in her ear once again. "These people will compliment your beauty, all while despising your French heritage."

"We have been over and over this, *Pere*." She used the French term and waited for the scolding she knew would follow.

Yet, it came from her mother, which was unexpected. "Lorelei, what have we told you?"

"I am to appear as nothing less than a lady born and raised amongst London's upper crust. I am to blend in with other debutantes and not give reason for anyone to remember me." She only hoped her moment of weakness before entering the ball did not show on her face. The tears had receded before they'd fully started, and she'd hurried to catch up, the night covering her seconds of doubt.

"Very good, my daughter," her father said. Though many would see his words as harmless, Lorelei knew them for what they truly were—a threat. The consequences if she failed would not only impact her, but also her parents.

She was tired of running. If she complied with what was asked of her then it was possible her sires, as well as herself, would come into favor and a new fortune. They were here for a specific task, which could be accomplished in little time, and then they would spirit her off back to France. Her mother's hope was that none would remember her presence.

"Smile, *ma petite,*" her mother whispered as she stepped back and the trio moved farther into the grand ballroom.

Lorelei wanted to ask why they trusted De Pez and Bonaparte—and wanted particularly to know how being in his favor would benefit any of them. Instead, she lifted her chin in defiance and pasted a smile on her face, hoping no one could tell it didn't reach her eyes.

Her entrance into the room had also been carefully staged to maximize her exposure. They'd arrived late—after the receiving line had disappeared—but before the gentlemen had retired to the card room off the main ballroom. Her hair was swept and gathered high upon her head to reveal her slender neck and highlight her dark, exotic coloring. Her eyes, the color of moss, were outlined by a thin line of coal. Her lips held a hint of color, though not enough to start gossip. And her dress, conservative and outdated by French standards, favored a high neckline in the front but plunged in the back to show off her gracefully arched back. The midnight-blue satin clung to her tall frame, smoothly gliding to the floor and pooling about her slippered feet.

A delicate strand of cultured pearls hung around her neck, and teardrops dangled from each ear. They were the preferred stone of the English, and that suited Lorelei.

Taking the final slow step into the crowded ballroom, her parents blended into the background and Lorelei took a champagne flute from a passing servant to steady her shaking hand. Peeking over her shoulder, Lorelei confirmed that the comte and comtesse had indeed given her a bit of space, yet they still kept pace with her. It would not help her to have them shadowing her all eve.

It was known that Benjamin Davis, Lord Chastain, held a fondness for women, and Lorelei had no reservations about preying on that weakness.

Lorelei moved through a part in the crowd quickly, hoping her parents lost sight of her. The group of ladies stepped close, effectively covering her movements, and Lorelei switched directions, traveling parallel to the comte, successfully assuring she had a few moments to herself.

She knew not a soul in the room—nor all of London.

And that terrified her.

For a brief moment, she contemplated whether she'd be able to follow through on the task given to her. The stark reality was, she hadn't a choice.

She tilted her glass to her mouth in hopes it would cover what she was actually doing—searching the crowd.

The British stood on pomp and ceremony, which meant no man would approach her without a proper introduction. The comte had insisted she leave the introductions to him, as he was convinced many lords would flock to his side to discuss the ever-changing governmental systems and the key players in their home country. The political situation in France was strained, particularly in their interactions with England, for the War of the Second Coalition still raged on.

Though who these men and women thought the comte loyal to, she cared naught.

She would not pass on the opportunity to sample life in London society; it was a place she could belong. Amongst the finery, she could find the home she had been lacking, even if only for a short time, though she also understood the dangers of falling in with the wrong people. A group of established wallflowers adorned in every shade of pastel imaginable lined one wall. Lorelei knew to steer clear of the group, or she'd likely end up amongst the palms with them. Nor should she attract the attention of the wealthy, elderly gentlemen currently escorting the most well-to-do debutantes and elite courtesans about the dance floor.

No, she sought the notice of only one man.

She'd studied his portrait thoroughly on their journey to England.

His every feature was imprinted on her mind: the roundness of his cheeks, his fashionable sandy brown hair, and his penetrating stare. She wondered if, when they eventually met, she would feel any tenderness for him, or if he would take a genuine liking to her.

Her research told her he was an avid horseman who craved excitement, but also lavished himself with the finer things in life.

She searched the crowd once more.

Lord Chastain—Benji, as he was commonly referred to by his consorts—stood with another man just outside the room that would hold the evening's card game. He gave off the exact impression she'd expected: an entitled rakehell who stood on the fringe of society by choice.

Both he and his friend stood tall and wore tailored suits that would rival the fashions in Paris. He was as handsome as his miniatures portrayed, but she found her gaze drawn to the man beside Chastain, who appeared equally at ease at the center of the crowd. She noted how other partygoers gave the men a wide berth.

Benji had the reputation of a womanizer and gambler, though there was nothing particularly extraordinary about his appearance to suggest either designation. Lorelei had expected a jovial man, but he laughed only at his companion's remarks and barely acknowledged anyone else who walked past.

However was she to attract his attention if he never took his eyes from his friend, she wondered? Truly, he looked nothing like a man she would ever call 'Benji,' which had always struck her as a child's name.

Her sires thought to accomplish—with all due haste—exactly what they'd journeyed to London for: unlimited access to Benjamin Davis, Lord Chastain, keeper of the plans to the fortified city of Carcassonne, located on a hilltop between the Atlantic and Mediterranean Sea. It had been long held that when Lord Chastain's father had fled France, he'd taken the only set of plans to Carcassonne—which also happened to be a detailed map outlining the best possible way to lay siege to the great trading city.

Lorelei, her glass in hand, moved along the side of the dance floor as the men conversed. While the room was filled with marriage-minded matrons and fortune-seeking fathers, she noted that no one approached the pair, and neither man put their name upon any girl's dance card.

How would her father obtain an

introduction if both men kept so much to themselves?

Lorelei had decided even before their carriage arrived that it would be necessary for her to break free of her mother and father and seek her own introduction. Even then, she sensed her father had again spotted her and was currently staring daggers at her across the crowd as she maneuvered herself farther from him and closer to Chastain.

Though he would be angry with her, she'd gladly accept his wrath later, for he would never cause a scene in public.

Chastain's associate took in the milling crowd. His eyes landed on her briefly, then returned to her for a longer inspection. It felt as if his earnest gaze penetrated to her very soul, uncovered all her secrets, and found her wanting.

She sensed she should turn back and approach Lord Chastain when this man wasn't close, but something drew her attention back to him.

Lorelei smiled.

To her amazement, he smiled back, turned to Chastain and said a few words…then started in her direction.

The crowd moved out of his path as he walked toward her, his eyes never releasing hers.

It was then that she felt her first hint of trepidation. The man was stunningly handsome—not to mention, a friend of Chastain's—and he was coming straight for her, a smile still upon his face.

"I can do this," she mumbled to herself as panic set in. The lady next to her turned a pointed look at her before taking a step away, putting distance between herself and the young lady talking to no one. Lorelei would have done the same had she been in the woman's position.

Before long, the man stood before her. His eyes, while intense, were the softest hazel she'd ever seen.

"Good evening." His voice was a rich, deep baritone. "May I have this dance?"

She hadn't heard music playing, nor the voices of the great number of people surrounding her.

She had only eyes for him.

Shaking her head gently, she snapped from her daze. "Ah, well, it is by chance I have a free space later in the evening."

He smiled. "That is a shame, for I find myself without a proper dance companion at this very moment. Pity."

He made to walk away, but she touched his sleeve ever so lightly, pulling her hand back before anyone saw. "I believe a spot may have opened only just now."

She needed more than a brief moment with this man, though he wasn't the one she'd originally sought.

"Then allow me to ask once more—but only once more," he said. "For I do not find myself in the habit of begging for dance partners. May I have this dance?"

"You may." She smirked. "If it so pleases you, your lordship."

She wanted to giggle at the pompous tone in her own voice. The English were not known for their candor, and a sense of intrigue settled on her at his forthright nature.

He reached toward her, and Lorelei started to retreat before she realized he only sought her dance card, tied loosely at her wrist. He held the card in his large hands and wrote his name upon the first line.

The Marquis of Drake.

The letters were written in a thick, bold script that seemed an embodiment of his masculinity and borderline arrogance.

"Shall we?" he asked, holding his arm out for her to take.

"I would enjoy nothing more, your lordship." Lorelei worked hard to suppress her accent. An import, as many were likely to call her, she did not wish to attract attention for her French blood, as many took offense knowing their countries battled and lives were lost every day. "It is a pleasure to make your acquaintance."

He spun her on to the dance floor, settling one arm around her lower back. "The pleasure is all mine, I assure you."

As they moved to the light strains of music floating through the room, Lorelei caught sight of her father, only a few feet from Chastain. He should be pleased with her progress, aligning herself with someone close to Chastain, opening up the possibility for an introduction.

"May I inquire as to the name of my beautiful dance partner?" the marquis asked.

She returned her attention to him and her breath caught at the sight. Forcing herself to exhale, she answered, "Lady Lorelei de La Valette."

"Ah. While your accent is subtle, your skin tone gives away your French heritage, no?"

"*Oui.*" With her father out of hearing distance, Lorelei let herself fall into her native tongue, fearing naught from the marquis. He did not show himself to be a man entangled in the war between their nations.

"*Charmante.*" His skillful pronunciation had her smiling. He continued to look upon her. "I have not seen you about town. Are you newly arrived?"

"Correct, your lordship."

"Please, call me Drake or Andrew, as my *amis* do."

"That is not proper, your lordship."

He chuckled. "But what do you see as *propre*?" He paused, as if scouring his brain for any other French words hidden there. "A *femme* is most *captivant* when they are themselves, *non*?"

She took her gaze from his, knowing she blushed a deep crimson. No man had called her captivating that she could recall. "You are *juste*, your lordship." She hoped the couples swirling close by did not notice her embarrassment.

"*Je suis toujours juste, mademoiselle.*" He once again paused. "I fear that is the extent of my knowledge of your language."

"Well, you did very well, indeed."

"You have a much more solid grasp of English than I French."

"It is only *juste*, as I have spent many years learning about your country."

Something about him turned her back into the shy schoolgirl she'd been before her parents had changed her whole world. While she was well-traveled and highly educated, Drake gave the impression he'd seen and experienced more than was possible, given his youthful appearance.

"What brings you to my fair city?" he said, lapsing back into English.

"Oh, to escape the dreaded heat of India." It was an effort to keep a straight face, particularly when the marquis willingly continued with the farce.

"Is the land as wild as I have been told?" he asked, appearing equally serious.

It had been a while since she'd enjoyed such an enjoyable exchange. "There are parts still untraveled!" When he only stared, she continued, "—and I will not go on about the inconveniences of outsmarting the monkeys who seek at every turn to rob you of your food."

"From France to India and now England? I dare say, you must be appallingly exhausted after such feats of bravery!"

As they continued round the dance floor, she allowed herself to laugh. "I assure you that it takes more bravery to enter a crowded ballroom than to face down a lion determined to steal my boots and gnaw on the leather."

"Lions? Gnawing on your boots?" he said with bewilderment. "I do agree, I would rather face a whole den of tigers than one marriage-minded matron."

"What always helped me was my ability to scale an elephant and make off before any harm was done." She was enjoying her outlandish tale as much as it appeared he was.

"I must remember to request your counsel when I travel next."

"I would be more than happy to guide your expedition." She paused before continuing. "That is, if I am not indisposed at the time."

"I am sure you will find the time to help a friend. But might I inquire why you'd be indisposed?"

"Well, I may be exploring the colonies at that

time."

"India? The colonies? By heavens, you put most English gentlemen to shame with your geographical exploits."

Lorelei forced herself to stop the banter, recalling the reason that she was here this eve. Their conversation, while amusing, did not suit her main objective. "I fear I am not as well traveled as I appear, though I did have the pleasure of visiting India in my youth, and do plan to sail for the colonies someday."

"As long as 'someday' is not today." He increased his hold on her, bringing her closer to him as they danced. "Back to my original question."

She'd completely forgotten how their conversation of exotic lands had started. "Which is?"

"Why are you in London, Lady Lorelei?"

While he asked one question, Lorelei expected the answer he sought was to another one altogether. "Not to find a husband, if that is what you wish to know."

"My suspicions about you were correct: you are the forthright kind." He looked at her appreciatively, and she relaxed once more. "And I must say, I am very disappointed to hear you are not on the market."

"And why is that?"

"Because I find myself with a lot to offer one such as yourself." When she continued to stare, a smirk on her face, he continued. "You see, I am titled, wealthy, handsome...and dare I say, charming?"

"Oh, you are very charming." Lorelei wanted to laugh but held back, not wanting to offend him. It was not that she feared hurting

Drake's feelings, only how it would appear to others around them. "You will be happy to know, if I were not here on a political errand with my father, I would find you quite suitable."

She should rein in her flirtatiousness with the marquis and focus on an introduction to Chastain, but she was unable to stop herself. It was the first stimulating conversation she'd had since her departure from France. In her mother country, her parents' ever-changing residence was always open to educated men and woman who enjoyed discussing the evolving regime from King to Directory to the man who it appeared would be their next leader, Napoleon Bonaparte. Though the topics might bore another young lady, she found any subject with the potential for debate highly interesting. She'd usually been clever enough to persuade her father's associates to her way of thinking.

During one such conversation, she had even devised a method for solving the horrid stench from the crowded and polluted Paris streets—yet her father called her plans idealistic in nature, no more than the easily dismissed musings of a woman.

No one here in their rented London household spoke to her, and the men who came to see her father avoided her, knowing she was committed to a higher cause and thus not open to their advances. As any woman would, she enjoyed the marquis' undivided attention.

Though they hadn't discussed any subject of great import, his intelligence was clear in his wit.

The music stopped, signaling the end of their dance. "Thank you for restoring my wounded pride. May I request another dance later in the evening?"

"I am sure that would cause gossip of the worst sort, your lordship," she said formally, dropping in a shallow curtsy. "But as I do not much care what society deems proper, I would entertain another turn about the floor with a dance partner as skilled as yourself."

"Until then." He brought her hand to his mouth and pressed his lips to her fingers. After several long seconds, he released it. "May I escort you to your chaperone?"

Looking up, she noticed several sets of eyes on them, some couples stopped in mid-promenade to take them in, though she expected the gawking had more to do with the marquis than herself.

"Oh, that will not be necessary." Lorelei's father was close, she could feel his stare. She needed an introduction to waylay his scolding over straying from their plan. "I find myself parched. Would you be so kind as to escort me to the refreshment table?"

She'd handed her last glass to a passing servant before taking to the dance floor with Drake. Their walk would force them to pass by Lord Chastain, not having moved an inch since she and Drake—Andrew, as she now thought of him after their brief conversation—had taken to the dance floor.

As they walked the perimeter of the room, Andrew peppered her with questions about her trip from France, how she liked his wonderful city, and if she had plans to travel to Bath after the season ended. Lorelei gave him as many noncommittal responses as she could muster in an attempt to give him no useful information about herself or her family, while still hoping to keep his interest. She was pleased to note that their continued conversation had caught Chastain's attention.

The duke, her original intended target, stepped into their path as they drew close. She'd seen the look on his face before from other suitors, and prided herself on her ability to distract men from their own base thoughts upon meeting her for the first time. This night, she'd only planned to gain an audience with him, possibly pique his interest, and hope for him to call upon her soon.

"Drake," Chastain greeted them and turned a slight bow in Lorelei's direction. "My lady."

Lorelei couldn't believe her good fortune. She'd been in the room less than thirty minutes and now stood face-to-face with Chastain. She could only imagine her father's reaction as his child, a mere female, had gained an introduction before him.

Her mind whirled with the possibilities of gaining more ground than they'd planned for this evening, perhaps even a private conversation.

"Lord Chastain, may I introduce Lady Lorelei." Drake's words sounded guarded and not at all happy. "Her family is new to London."

Chastain smiled, a smirk that could only be described as smug. The pair had appeared to be friends earlier, but something about the way they now assessed each other led her to believe otherwise. She hoped that played nicely into her plans, which as yet were limited.

She coyly eyed Chastain from lowered eyelids as she curtsied. "Lord Chastain, I am honored to make your acquaintance."

The marquis moved closer to her side.

Her words gained the response she sought.

"The honor is my own, Lady Lorelei. Drake and I have been friends for more years than either of us can count."

The tension that had shadowed the trio moments before was alleviated, and both men smiled as they chatted about inconsequential topics.

"If you'll excuse us," Drake said as he again settled Lorelei's hand in the crook of his arm. "We were just on our way for refreshments."

"I find myself in need of another glass, as well." Chastain turned toward the table several paces behind him, not to be dismissed. "I shall accompany you."

"That would be delightful, my lord." And exactly what Lorelei had hoped he would say. She needed to find a way to speak privately with him without insulting Drake. While she very much enjoyed the marquis' company—and he was extremely pleasing to the eye—she had other matters on which to focus.

With sherry in hand, they moved toward the terrace doors. She knew the darkened gardens would be a perfect spot for a quiet conversation.

"Lady Lore—"

"Ah, there you are, my daughter."

Her father's voice sounded behind her, and she turned to greet him. His icy stare chilled her faster than the cold winds that moved across the English Channel.

"Father, may I introduce the Marquis of Drake and Lord Chastain, his dear friend." If her father's thought was to steal Chastain away before she had an opportunity to speak with him, he had underestimated how badly she wanted to impress him. "These fine London gentlemen were explaining to me the marvels of England's unpredictable weather patterns. A lady must be prepared for showers every time she leaves her home. How tiresome!"

"Very true, Lorelei." Her father turned to Chastain. "My daughter is very interested in London culture."

Her father, the Comte of Epernon, had never been a man with tact. He was used to getting what he wanted, when he wanted, at no cost of time or money to himself. But London was not France—and his foreign title meant little to the *ton*. Even if her father failed to realize this, Lorelei knew at least that much.

"Father, please!" Regretfully, she slipped her hand from Drake's arm and moved to Chastain. "Now is not the time for dreaded government talks. I believe Lord Chastain was about to escort me to the terrace for a spot of fresh air." She gave her father a pleading look, hoping he'd take the clue and keep Drake occupied.

"Very well, but please bring her back after she cools down a bit." He finally acknowledged the marquis. "Your lordship, I believe they have finally opened the card tables. Would you care to join me?"

Drake gave her one last lingering look before bowing and wishing her a wonderful evening. He'd wanted to stay and dance again, she could sense it, though he was too much the gentlemen to deny Chastain.

She watched her father and the marquis walk side by side to the card room. Though his back faced her now, the memory of Drake's stare lingered. Never had a simple look dug so deeply, making her question the consequences and lasting cost of her mission. There was nothing left to do but allow Chastain to guide her outside and into the cool night air.

Chastain, while every bit as well dressed as Drake, lacked something. From where her hand rested on his forearm, she did not feel the tight, corded muscle of a man who spent hours at his fencing club, and she suspected he did not possess the sculptured legs of a skilled horseman, as she'd been told. His tailor should be commended for the fine cut of his coat, which no doubt covered what he lacked beneath.

It was truly a shame that the marquis was not the man she sought, for after only a few short minutes in his presence, her interest had been significantly piqued.

But her word was her bond—and her allegiance lay not with her own needs and wants, but with what would garner her family approval from the man many said would take control of France. "Shall we, Lord Chastain?"

"Without further ado, my lady."

They walked arm in arm toward the terrace door. All the while, Lorelei refused to glance over her shoulder.

Available in print, audiobook, and e-book now!

ABOUT THE AUTHOR

USA TODAY Bestselling Author Christina McKnight writes emotional and intricate Regency Romance with strong women and maverick heroes.

Her books combine romance and mystery, exploring themes of redemption and forgiveness. When she's not writing, Christina enjoys trying new coffeehouses, visiting wine bars, traveling the world, and watching television.

Email: Christina@ChristinaMcKnight.com
Follow her on Twitter: @CMcKnightWriter
Keep up to date on her releases:
www.christinamcknight.com
Like Christina's FB Author page:
ChristinaMcKnightWriter

A LADY FORGOTTEN BY ALL...

Ruby St. Augustin has to find the truth of her past to know where her future lies. She only has a short time in London to uncover the identity of her real father and the secrets behind her birth. If anyone finds out what she is attempting, she will disgrace everyone she holds dear. What she doesn't expect is to draw the attention of a man who doesn't care about his reputation or her past.

A MAN MESMERIZED BY ONE...

Harold Jakeston is a man without wealth and title. Resigned to a life he detests as a lowly country vicar, Harold has the chance at a few weeks of freedom before he's trapped in a future he wants no part of. When he's drawn into Ruby's mysterious quest, he is enticed at the opportunity to forget the life that awaits him. What he never could have anticipated is falling in love with a woman who ignites his desire to create a new future for himself and for her.

A LOVE NEITHER CAN ABANDON...

FORGOTTEN
NO MORE

www.ChristinaMcKnight.com

ISBN 9780988261747

90000

9 780988 261747